LIVIA DAY

A TRIFLE DEAD

BOOK ONE OF THE CAFE LA FEMME SERIES

*deadlines**

First published in Australia in March 2013
by Deadlines

www.twelfthplanetpress.com

Design and layout by Amanda Rainey
Typeset in Sabon MT Pro

National Library of Australia Cataloguing-in-Publication entry

Author: Day, Livia.

Title: A trifle dead : a cafe la femme novel / by Livia Day ;
            editor, Helen Merrick and managing editor, Terri Sellen.

ISBN: 9780987216298 (pbk.)

Other Authors/Contributors: Merrick, Helen.
                                Sellen, Terri.

Dewey Number: A823.4

For Isabel,

My first editor.

1

You can tell a lot about a person from their coffee order. I play a game with the girls who work in my café—guess the order before the customer opens their mouth. It's fun because half the time you're spot on—the bloke who would rather die than add anything to his long black, the girl who doesn't want to admit how weak she likes her latté, the woman who'll deliberate for twenty minutes as to whether or not she wants a piece of cake (she does), the mocha freak, the decaf junkie.

The rest of the time, you're completely wrong. An old age pensioner requests a soy macchiato, a gang of pink-haired school girls want serious espresso shots, a lawyer in a designer suit stops to chat for half an hour about free trade…The best thing about people is how often they surprise you.

Ever wondered what kind of coffee a murderer drinks? Yeah, me neither.

I tumbled into the kitchen of Café La Femme, arms full of bakery boxes, a vintage mint-green sundress swirling around my knees. Late as usual, but at least I was wearing my favourite sandals.

A gal can cope with anything when her shoes match her bra.

Nin paused in the middle of kneading focaccia dough to stare at me from under her expressive eyebrows. I love her eyebrows. They make Frida Kahlo's look meek. 'They're here again,' she said, and went back to kneading.

My assistant cook doesn't use paragraphs when a sentence will do, so I had to read between the lines. 'They' almost certainly referred to several respected members of the Hobart police force, most of them in uniform, some of them armed. 'Here' meant all the comfortable chairs in the main room of the café, and probably leaning on the counter as well. 'Again' meant that Nin was sick to death of them all asking her where I was, and how I was doing, and I probably owed her a raise.

I couldn't afford to give her a raise, so I piled my boxes of bread rolls, bagels and croissants on the bench and tied on my *Barbarella* apron instead. 'Can I help you with that dough?'

Nin's eyebrows judged me. Hard.

'Okay, okay. I just have to bring in the eggs, and then I'll go front of house. Five minutes.'

I ducked outside and took several breaths of salty spring air before she could object. Five minutes, and I could just about deal with a café full of guns and bicycle clips. Couldn't I? The café courtyard is a gravel square, walled in by sandstone blocks

A TRIFLE DEAD

that were once shaped by convict hands. I keep saying I'll clean it up and put tables out here, but the truth is I don't want to lose my little sanctuary of calm.

Our local egg supplier had left a basket by the back step. I'd asked her more than once to take them straight into the kitchen so no one will trip over them, but she claims to be afraid of Nin's eyebrows. Who can blame her?

As I leaned down to pick up the basket, I caught a whiff of strawberry perfume, and then someone came up behind me and yanked my braid. I reacted with a lifetime of skipped self-defence classes by screaming like a girl, and slamming the basket of eggs behind me and into the face of my assailant.

'What the—!' she exclaimed in disgust, and let go of my hair.

Oops. I turned around to see a tall, glamorous woman in black. Not black like a Goth, but black like Emma Peel in *The Avengers*, circa 1966. 'Is that actually a catsuit?' I asked, impressed. Even if I had a stomach as flat as hers, I doubt I'd have the nerve to wear something like that, and I have (almost) no shame when it comes to fashion.

'It was,' said my assailant. Egg and shell dripped down over the black catsuit in question, and down into her fitted leather boots.

'It looks great,' I offered.

'Thanks.' She crossed her arms, elegant and menacing despite wearing twenty dollars worth of smashed free range egg. 'So where is he?'

'You're going to want to get in a shower really soon. Raw egg does bad things to hair, when it goes hard...'

'I'll keep that in mind.' She paused meaningfully. 'Tabitha? I'm in a hurry here. Your landlord. The arsehole. Where is he?'

Ah, well that made more sense. She was looking for Darrow. 'Does he owe you money? Or are you planning to hurt him?' Both possibilities were more than likely.

'Both. Hurry up, I can feel my hair hardening as we speak.'

'I don't know where he is,' I admitted. 'Honestly, haven't seen him for weeks. But he's Darrow. He'll stroll back in, sooner or later.'

She gave me a filthy look, and somehow managed to still look gorgeous in the process. 'You wouldn't lie to protect him, would you?'

'Of course not.'

Yeah, I probably would. There's something about stupidly attractive men. They smile, and your knees turn to honey, and suddenly you're doing things you never thought you would, like giving false witness, or accidentally learning how to poach quail eggs. But I wasn't lying today. 'If you must beat the information out of someone, why not try his white-haired, old grandmother?'

She smiled tightly. 'Good suggestion. I'll keep it in mind.'

I didn't feel guilty. Darrow's white-haired old grandmother was more than a match for either of us. 'Okay, then. I have to go inside and call my egg supplier. And evict twenty police officers from my café.' I backed away from her, until I reached my kitchen door. 'Oh—Xanthippe?'

'What?' she said, sounding tired.

'Good to see you back.'

She glanced down at her egg-streaked outfit. 'Yep. Just like old times.'

Back in the kitchen, Nin had put the focaccia in our little pizza oven to toast, and was making salad rolls so that the breakfast crowd could take their lunch away with them. When I was growing up, a salad roll was a confection-like sticky bun filled with cheese, tomato, lettuce, beetroot and sliced egg, all glued together with a mock-mayonnaise. Good old Australian corner shop tucker. Now, if it didn't have cranberry sauce, gouda or red pesto on it, our customers whinged the roof down. Oh, and ham wasn't good enough for most of the hipster lunch set, even if it was triple smoked and carved off an organic local pig. Fat-free turkey and smoked salmon were where it was at—with a growing interest in grilled mushrooms and haloumi.

I realised I had reached the point of no return when I put 'tofu and ricotta salad roll, deconstructed' on the menu, and it became my biggest seller. After that, I started really having fun. If food isn't creative, what's the point?

Unfortunately I still had a very vocal (if minority) group of customers who were firmly attached to the Good Old Days,

LIVIA DAY

and relied on me to provide the basic staples of Man Food. Steak, fried potato products and pies. I never had this much trouble with the uni students when I was working at the café on campus. At least students appreciated an ironic sprout when they saw one.

Well, no more. The old guard were going to have to find their pies somewhere else. I had hipsters to feed.

The customer bell twanged loudly in the café.

'In a minute,' I protested as Nin's eyebrows became stern and judgemental. 'Egg emergency.'

As I picked up the phone, a tall, dark and handsome police officer in street uniform put his head through the swinging doors. 'Tish, the natives are getting restless.'

I rolled my eyes at the old nickname, and handed the phone to Nin. 'Call Monica. We're going to need another three dozen. Might require grovelling.'

She dialled, knowing a good deal when she saw one.

'So,' I said to Senior Constable Leo Bishop, 'by natives, you mean the usual gang of reprobates?'

Bishop grinned his gorgeous grin at me. 'The accepted term is still *police officers*, you know.'

We went through to the café together. Two customers sat at a window table, enjoying plates of muesli trifle and plum honey toast. The other fourteen customers—sprawling on tables and generally holding up the walls—were mostly over forty, uniformed and slightly dangerous. Even the detectives were so painfully plain clothed that their police credentials were obvious.

Bishop was pushing thirty, but the other adjectives still applied. Uniformed and dangerous. 'One of these days,' I warned him in a low voice, 'you're all going to get bored with keeping an eye on me.'

'Duty is never dull,' he shot back, with that look in his eye. That look had made my stomach jump somersaults when I was sixteen and still innocent enough to be impressed by cute men in uniform. Good thing I got over that particular fetish.

I circulated, smiling my best smile at a horde of middle-aged men who thought of me only as Tabitha, Geoff and Rose Darling's precious little girl. 'G'day all. Seen my new breakfast menu?'

Inspector Bobby tapped the pretty laminated pages. 'No pies on there, Tabby love. How'm I going to start my day without one of Rose's steak and bacon glories?'

My smile got brighter. 'Come on, Bobby, this isn't Mum's café. It's mine. And I'm pretty sure your wife told me that eating those steak and bacon glories for breakfast is what led to your heart attack last year. I can't have you on my conscience any more.'

'Come on, Tabby,' said Superintendent Graham in a genial voice. 'Your pastry's a work of art. Can't go wasting skills like that.'

This is true. Excellent pastry is the one tangible thing I gained from running off to Europe with a French landscape artist instead of going to uni. Phillipe parked me at his mother's farm in the Dordogne for six months, where I learned about soups and sauces as well as melt-in-the-mouth pastry before I found out about the other women he had waiting for him in Paris, Marseilles and Berlin.

'I'm not wasting anything,' I said patiently. 'I have tomato-pear tartlets and vegan quiche on my Specials Board. And the mochaccino special comes with dunking profiteroles.'

The collective weight of the local police force muttered amongst themselves, and glared at said Specials Board.

'What exactly is *in* vegan quiche?' said Bishop in a low voice.

'Bok choy,' I told him.

'And?'

'What do you mean, *and*? I know you all miss my mum's cooking, but she doesn't run the police canteen these days. And, in case you haven't noticed, neither do I.'

It's not that I don't appreciate their business. Loyalty's a nice thing. But if you had fifty-odd honorary uncles and brothers constantly hanging around your place of work, you'd start to crack too. I never dreamed when my parents split up and Mum abandoned the police canteen to make lentil burgers at meditation retreats and folk festivals that I'd end up inheriting her old clientele.

Pies and chips are fine, but I'm not going to spend my life heating them up. This café was supposed to be a fresh start for me, and it was time for me to stand my ground.

'So, no sausage rolls?' asked Detective Sergeant Richo, from his little island of denial.

'I haven't served sausage rolls in six months.' They were the first to go, and it hurt to do it. But every revolution has its casualties.

'Yeah,' Richo said sadly. 'Rose always made great sausage rolls. But yours were better,' he added.

I crossed my arms. 'If no one orders the focaccia with tempeh and pepperberry dressing in the next thirty seconds, I'm going to have to ask you all to leave.'

There was a strangled pause. The effort that it took each of them to not say something patronising was monumental. I could practically see the steam coming out of their ears.

'All right. Tabby,' said Inspector Bobby. 'We'll be in later for coffee.'

'Yeah,' agreed one of the sergeants, brightly. 'Those low-fat muffins of yours are almost as good as real ones.'

One by one, the officers trooped out of the café. I sagged a little. It wasn't working. Possibly it wouldn't work if I served nothing but flavoured oxygen. I was doomed to run a café under constant police surveillance.

'Reckon you were a bit hard on them,' said Bishop, who had stayed behind.

I gave him a dirty look. 'Do you know how good my side salads are? In the year since I started this place, I've had three reviews that specifically mention how awesome my side salads are. I've turned side salads into a work of art. So the day that one of you bludgers actually *eats* one of my side salads, instead of pushing it to the side and ordering another slab of pie, is the day that you get to have an opinion about my menu.'

He folded his arms. 'Do you really think we come here for the food?'

'Thanks,' I said, stalking behind my counter. 'Nice to know.'

A couple of people came in to collect lunch bagels. I served them, ignoring Bishop the whole time. My muesli customers finished their breakfast, and paid for their meals.

'You know I didn't mean that in a bad way,' he said, when they were gone. 'We keep an eye out for you, that's all. Since your dad…'

'I know,' I said between gritted teeth. And boy, did I. Good old Superintendent Geoff Darling, my beloved dad. In the days between his retirement party and eloping to Queensland with his soon-to-be second wife, he took it upon himself to ask every single member of Tasmania Police to keep an eye out for his precious girl. Imagine how grateful I was for that now. 'I feel very safe and warm and protected.'

So protected that most days it's hard to breathe.

The café door clattered open, and a uniformed constable walked in—one I didn't actually know.

'Are you advertising in the police department foyer now?' I complained.

Bishop ignored me. He was good at that—he'd been

practising the art since he knew me only as his boss's teenage daughter, and his sister's bratty best friend. 'Looking for me, Heather?'

The constable gazed around at my colourful pop-art tables, my wall of vintage *Vogue* covers, and my 1960s frock posters. 'They said you'd be here,' she answered, as if not quite believing it.

Yep. The décor had been my first assault in the War against Tasmania Police, long before I went to the lengths of taking red meat off the menu. Sometimes I glue glitter to the windows.

Lesbian lunchtime poetry readings were only a phone call away.

'Constable Heather Wilkins, meet Tabitha Darling,' said Bishop.

I waited for the spark of recognition, but there wasn't one. 'You haven't heard the name, Constable Heather?'

'Should I have?' she asked politely. 'I only started a few weeks ago.'

I smiled happily at Bishop. 'There's my answer. I just have to out-wait you dinosaurs. Thirty years and you'll all be replaced by bright young things who've never heard of me or Superintendent Darling.'

Bishop made the sensible decision to ignore me again. 'What's up, Constable?'

'Burglary in this building—the top floor.'

'Crash Velvet?' I said. 'I'll come up with you.' I leaned into the kitchen. 'Nin! The cavalry are gone. Come mind the front, and bring me the blue muffins for upstairs.'

'Crash Velvet?' It meant nothing to Bishop.

'A rock band,' said Constable Heather.

'Not just a *rock band*,' I said. 'Crash Velvet are the new wave in formal kink. The latest YouTube sensation, right here in Hobart.'

Bishop tilted his head at me, as if I was speaking Mandarin. 'You can't come with us,' he decided. 'This is official police business.'

Nin came out from the kitchen with a basket full of bright blue muffins and a particularly expressive eyebrow lift.

'Thanks, hon.' I made a face at Bishop. 'As if I'm interested in your burglary. I have food to deliver.'

2

There are people who should be trusted with ownership of beautiful old sandstone buildings, and people who shouldn't. I'm not entirely sure where our Mr Darrow fits on the scale. He's rich as all hell, and owns several almost-heritage listed buildings around Hobart. But instead of doing the sensible thing—installing yuppie apartments with skyrocketing urban rents—he fills the rooms with artists and other oddballs, at bargain lease rates.

It's probably a tax dodge of some kind—but what can I say? Darrow came to the uni café for years after he graduated, because he liked my gateaux. He claims that he stole me because I was going to make his fortune, but I don't buy it for a second. There's not much profit in cafés, too many staff to support. Wouldn't surprise me if he moved me in here because it's not far to travel for his daily slice of mocha hazelnut hummingbird cake.

Not that I'm complaining.

I missed Darrow since his latest disappearance. I was used to him hanging around with his stupid laptop, bugging my customers and having pointless, batshit weird conversations with me until I felt the need to bounce cookies off his beautifully-groomed hair.

He'd be back, eventually. Unless Xanthippe was hunting him down to kill him, which was not one hundred percent unlikely. Theirs had been a bad break-up.

Our building has two roomy flats above my café. The first floor is occupied by the Sandstone City mob, a gang of twenty-somethings who blog about weird stuff in Hobart, in the hope of making the place look cool. Bizarrely, it kind of works. Someday the government will stop giving them grant money, but this is not that day.

Then there's the top floor, and Crash Velvet.

A tiny purple-headed rock chick answered the door. Her eyes slid straight past the two police officers to focus on my basket of bright-blue muffins. 'Oh, excellent. Just what I wanted. Any chance you can repeat the order every morning for … oh, the next three months or so?'

'Well, I could,' I said. 'Why would you want me to?' Don't get me wrong, they were fabulous muffins—the savoury ones were parmesan and onion, with a hint of Tabasco, and the sweet ones were blue velvet with cream cheese frosting and silver sprinkles—but it wasn't like they'd ordered them for the flavour. When they phoned down the order, all they said was *blue*. I did consider just using food colouring, but imported blue cornmeal is such a pretty ingredient and I can rarely justify using it. Since they were paying through the nose anyway…

She had the grace to look embarrassed. 'It's a publicity thing. Our new PR manager has us ordering the weirdest food we can, all around town. We're aiming for, when people google "weird" and "food", our band is in the top ten hits. Do you have a Tumblr? Twitter? Facebook?'

I think I was the last café in town not to have a Facebook presence. It was bad for my hipster image, but when you get up at 5AM most days to bake, something has to give. My compromise is to hire trendy teen art students as waitresses who tweet their little socks off, sometimes while pouring cappuccinos. 'Not officially, but we've got a few ways to boost the signal. You should come down and eat the muffins in the café sometimes. We have big windows.'

Really, blue muffins? I'm pretty sure rock bands are supposed to be slightly edgier than that. Still, hard drugs and trashing hotel rooms is such a cliché these days. If they wanted to make their reputation through eccentric baked goods, who was I to judge?

'Excellent idea. Every bit helps.' She took the basket and smiled past me to Bishop, apparently unfazed by his uniform. 'I'm kCeera. Small k, big C.'

'Senior Constable Bishop,' he said, trying not to look offended at how much muffin talk had taken precedence over his own business. 'There was a burglary report from this address.'

kCeera looked genuinely startled. 'There was?' She backed into the apartment, making room for us all to come inside. 'Tabitha, I'll write you a cheque for the first month. Hey Owen, did you call the police?'

The place was a mess—it must have been a long time since Darrow sent his army of cleaning ladies to make an inspection. Towers of junk, CDs and musical instruments were stacked haphazardly against every wall. The only items of furniture were two unmatched Tip Shop couches, a kick-ass stereo system with enormous speakers, and a widescreen TV that probably cost more than my car. It was certainly about the same length as my car.

The best thing about the room was a window with a clear view of the mountain, silver grey against a bright blue sky. Hobart sits squarely between the enormous Mount Wellington, and the mouth of the River Derwent. Water views are all very well, but I'd take our mountain any day. Just looking at the thing makes me feel all Zen and at one with the universe. Plus it helps with urban navigation. If you can see the mountain, you know pretty much where you are.

Fabulous view aside, the most salient feature of Crash Velvet's flat was that it smelled of feet. In the middle of the crappy chaos, two lean and long-haired blokes in paper-thin t-shirts stood playing laser hockey on a Wii system. A pair of boots attached to a fourth member of the band stuck out from one of the couches.

kCeera cleared her throat loudly. 'Guys? Police? Standing in front of me?'

'Oh, right.' One of the blokes paused the game, and elbowed the other. 'Owen. Mate.'

'Yeah,' said the one called Owen. 'Burglary. All our stuff got stolen.'

'Stuff, what stuff?' kCeera demanded. Obviously she was the brains of the outfit. The other two didn't have enough spare brain cells between them to brew a cup of tea. 'Why didn't you tell me when I got home?'

'Mate, laser hockey,' said the one not called Owen. 'Priorities.'

Constable Heather took out her notebook, looking all official. 'Perhaps you could tell us exactly what was stolen?'

'Everything, babe,' said the not-Owen. 'All of it, gone.'

Bishop looked around at the expensive stereo system, big screen TV and CD collection. 'All of what, exactly?'

'The clothes, mate,' said Owen. 'The hats and belts, even.'

'Shoes,' not-Owen added.

'What the hell are you talking about?' asked kCeera. 'I packed the gear away in the spare room this morning.'

'Not there now,' said Owen with a shrug. 'Some wanker nicked it all, didn't they?'

'Someone stole … your clothes?' said Bishop.

'Wearable Art Treasures,' I explained in an undertone. 'The name of their first album. They collected a stash of unusual costume items from museums, antique dealers, artists … the photos looked great. They still wear a lot of the collection at their gigs.'

'Why are you still here?' Bishop asked in a grouchy voice.

'I'm waiting for my muffin cheque. Excuse me for being helpful.'

'So is that all that was taken?' Bishop asked the guys.

Not-Owen looked at him mournfully. 'All? Mate, isn't that enough? What are we gonna wear to the next gig? Just turn up in *plain* tuxedos without leather gauntlets and vintage lace collars and spiky things around our legs? That's not cool.'

'Have you guys been smoking something?' kCeera demanded. 'I was gone for like two hours. You were here the whole time. How can someone have broken into our spare room and taken all the Wearable Art Treasures? Were there ladders involved? Is Rapunzel our prime suspect?'

Owen shrugged. 'See for yourself, mate.'

kCeera marched across the room, flung open one of the doors, and stared through it. Then she turned around, and headed out of the flat.

'Where are you going?' not-Owen called after her.

kCeera flung her head around. 'I'm going to get the guys from Sandstone City. Because when they arrest you for wasting police time, I want to make sure someone bloody well blogs about it!' She slammed the door behind her.

'Okay, then,' I said, in the silence.

Bishop headed for the spare room. I followed him, because—oh, what the hell. It was none of my business, but when has that ever stopped me? If I never found out any gossip, my afternoon Coffee & Cake sales would halve overnight.

Inside the room, Bishop swore under his breath. Very unprofessional—not like him at all. I skidded to a halt at his elbow.

'Tish—no,' he said, but it was too late.

Mostly what I saw was net. It hung from the ceiling, supported by wooden beams, ropes and four upright poles, like a four-poster bed. There was something in the net, weighing it awkwardly. I recognised an arm.

What was it? A dummy?

But the long mop of dark hair hanging down looked real enough, and if it was a dummy, why would Bishop be feeling for a pulse, sliding his hand along the neck, searching for signs of life?

It began to sink in that I was in the presence of an actual dead body. I stepped back to let Constable Heather through, and my foot caught on the strap of a bright green sports bag. A violin case was leaning against it, and I only just stopped it from crashing to the floor.

'Oh, yeah,' said one of the blokes from the doorway. I'd lost track of whether he was the Owen or not. 'Whoever nicked our stuff, they left that thing there. The net. And the body.'

'The violin's not ours,' said the other maybe-Owen. 'But, you know. If no one wants it…'

3

Bishop steered me out of the room. 'Heather, call for Anderson's team to get over here as a priority. Then call Clayton and tell him this is one for the Crime Management Unit. Suspicious death, probable drug overdose. Make sure no one goes into that room.'

As Heather made the first call, Bishop kept moving me through the flat, and out on to the landing. 'Are you okay?' he asked, when we were alone.

I nodded, a bit too fast. I wasn't okay. The most drama I see in one day is a fallen sticky date sponge, or a yard full of smashed free range eggs. 'I'm good.'

'Did you recognise him? Is he from around here? From the café?'

I shook my head, not quite trusting myself to speak.

Bishop gave me one of those 'she'll be right' awkward bloke pats on the arm, and then ducked back into the flat to do his job.

I stood alone on the landing, breathing in the musty air. After a minute or two, I pulled myself together and headed down the stairs.

kCeera charged up past me, dragging one of the Sandstone City bloggers with her, and a large camera. 'Have they been arrested yet?' she asked breathlessly.

'Well, not for wasting police time,' I replied.

About ten seconds after kCeera reached her front door, I heard a yell. 'What the fuck?' Which probably meant she had been informed it was a real dead body in her spare room.

At that moment I could see nothing but that horrible image of the man hanging in the net. He was young—maybe my age. I gripped the banister. 'Real girls don't swoon, Tabitha.'

That was good, because I was pretty sure I was going to throw up instead.

I clattered down the stairs so fast that I didn't see another person step out of the Sandstone City flat, and we collided. The world spun.

'Whoa,' said a male voice. A hand caught my elbow. 'Are ye all right?'

I stared at him, still not really seeing him, though I was dimly aware of a Scottish accent, and stubble. 'Yes. Fine. Really very fine.'

'Good,' he said, which proved he was male and didn't understand anything. 'Did ye see which way our Simon went?'

I pointed to the upper floor.

'Thanks,' the accent continued. It was soothing, actually. I could pretend we were in a gritty Glasgow crime drama on TV. People hardly ever throw up in those, unless they're crack addicts. 'And ye are all right, then?'

It occurred to me that if I had to be asked this many times if I was all right, then maybe I wasn't. 'No,' I said clearly. 'Not.' And I bolted down the last flight, scrabbling to open the back door.

In the side yard, confronted with a burst of sunshine and fresh, crisp March air, I stumbled over the steps and sat down in a hurry. Probably, now I came to think of it, in a mess of congealed raw egg. I covered my face with my hands.

'Are ye planning tae throw up?' The Scottish accent had followed me. The last thing I needed was a nervous breakdown in front of someone who sounded a bit like Ewan McGregor. 'Because I'm bad at holding hair. I often miss.'

I looked up, peering through my fingers. He was an ordinary looking bloke, a bit on the skinny side, a lot on the scruffy side. 'Um, no. Thanks for the offer.'

He grinned at me, and his face lit up in a way that made him a lot more interesting. 'I dinna believe I did offer.'

'Well, thanks for caring.'

'Pretty sure I dinna care.'

I pointed a finger at him. 'I'm going to stop thanking you in a minute, and then you'll be sorry.'

He sat on the steps beside me, stretching out long legs in old grey jeans. 'Dae your worst, kid.'

'I just saw my first dead body,' I confessed.

'Bummer.' The Scotsman nodded seriously. 'Dead bodies are never good. Except, ye know, in Raymond Chandler novels. Anyone ye knew?'

'No. Just random deadness.' Deadity. Was deadity a word?

'Thank Christ for that. My crack about Raymond Chandler wadna been very sensitive, in that case.' He held out a hand. 'Stewart McTavish. Comforting in times o' crisis. Only no' very.'

I shook it. 'Tabitha Darling. Screams, runs away, hides head in sand.'

'Ye look like ye need a cuppa,' he announced. 'Which is to say ... any chance o' a cuppa?'

Lara, one of my teen art students, had joined Nin for lunch prep, and there were only a few customers front of house, so I felt vaguely justified in sitting out in the yard with a steaming teapot, fresh lemon slices, my own neuroses and a Scotsman I was starting to think might be a bit cute. When the world sends you a morning like the one I had just had, you welcome all the distractions you can get.

'Simon was saying I should talk to ye,' Stewart said, inhaling a second long black while I sipped my tea and basked in the adorableness of his accent. 'I've started at Sandstone City this week—the outsider's view of Hobart—and he reckoned that wha' Tabitha Darling doesnae know about this place isnae worth knowing.'

I laughed. 'Simon didn't say that. He said something like, "If you can't find anything, go pick Tabs' brain. She'll do your work for you, mate."'

'That daes sound more like him,' Stewart said sheepishly. 'Any ideas? I'm still finding me way around.'

I finished the last of my tea. Distractions. Distractions were good. Anything to stop thinking about the dead body upstairs. 'I have to drop in on an old friend after the lunch rush. I think you could benefit from meeting her. She's an artist.'

'Art is good,' agreed Stewart. 'Half the grant money comes in because we depict Hobart as a seething den of artistic talent.' I could practically hear the sarcastic inverted commas around his words.

'Her art is somewhat unconventional…' I warned him.

'Even better. Do ye think she'd let me take photos?'

I smiled, feeling a little better about the world. Almost completely distracted. 'I think she'd be offended if you didn't.'

4

'Tabitha,' said Beverly Darrow with a wide smile when she saw me and my new Scotsman on her doorstep. 'Great timing, luv. The cats are just cooled from the oven.'

The Great Australian Nanna is a dying breed. It's seriously difficult to find yourself a lamington-baking, apron-wearing, CWA-registered grandmother, now that the recent crop of 50-plus women are keeping their power suits on and ordering takeaway pizza just like everyone else, while the 60-plus ladies invest all their cash in bungee jumping and life-drawing classes.

Bev is a Nanna in the good old traditional sense of the word. More or less. She bakes, and knits, and dotes on her grandchildren. Luckily for me, she also dotes on her grandchildren's friends. I was deprived of a real Nanna growing up, and I'm not letting go of this one now that I've found her.

Besides, my customers love her wares. Why spend hours cranking out batches of biscuits when you can buy the best?

'Cats?' said Stewart, after I introduced him to Bev, and she cooed about how much his accent sounded like that actor on the TV. 'In the oven? What kind of café are you running, Tabitha?'

I smacked him lightly on the arm. Did inappropriate touching mean that I fancied him? Answers on a postcard. 'Meringue cats. What do you think I am, crazy?'

'Oka-ay,' he said. 'And that would be because meringues shaped like cats sell faster than meringues no' shaped like cats?'

He was catching on. 'That's right. Do you know how many obsessed cat-lovers there are in this city? Cats always sell. *Diabetics* who love cats will buy these meringues.'

We stepped into Bev's breezy, bright yellow kitchen and I helped her pack the cute little sugar kittens into a wide cardboard box. Another box, laden with plate-sized cookies, platter-sized cheesecakes and a mighty slab of brownies, was already done.

'Isnae that on the unethical side?' Stewart suggested.

I looked sternly at him. 'You're fretting that I brought you all the way out here to the suburbs to photograph cat cakes.'

'I dae have that fear,' he admitted.

I bumped hips with Bev. 'Stewart here needs to discover a wacky new artist for this blog he writes for.'

'Oh,' said Bev, with a not-quite-cackle. 'You'll be after the erotica, then, my love.'

Stewart blinked twice.

'You're in luck,' Bev added. 'I've just got a new display all ready for the CWA fundraiser.'

'Are they going to make you put fig leaves on them this time?' I asked.

Bev winked. 'I've whipped up a batch of very flimsy ones. The slightest breeze will send them flying.' She beckoned to Stewart, and led him to her dining room. 'My beauties,' she said with great satisfaction.

I peered around Stewart. Bev had outdone herself. An extravagant display of nude figures spilled over the tabletop, each crudely shaped out of meringue, and decorated with snippets of red fruit and generous blobs of whipped cream.

Meringue's a bitch to work with, and there was something very abstract about the figures until you looked closely, and then you really couldn't look away. They were mostly curvy mother goddess types, but there were a few bulging blokes scattered around, putting Barbie's Ken to shame with their anatomical correctness.

'Bloody hell,' said Stewart.

'My cake stall always brings in the most money,' said Bev with pride. 'Though I do have to wrap them in brown paper for the ladies to take away.'

Stewart slid a professional camera out of his bag, and started setting up a tripod. 'This could get us more hits than the fellae who taped bacon tae his pets.'

'That's good, is it?' said Bev.

I gave her a hug. 'Stewart's going to make you an internet porn star.'

'Well, it's about time someone did, dear.'

Stewart pulled the curtain open to let the natural sunlight into the room. 'Who's that?' he asked.

I followed his gaze. 'Oh, crap.' A familiar female figure was leaning over the back fence, sunshine bouncing off her reflective sunglasses. She was wearing another one of those form-fitting catsuits, this one in purple.

'Xanthippe Carides,' said Bev. 'I haven't seen that girl in ages.'

'She looks like something out of a Bond movie,' said Stewart. He lifted his camera, and took a few shots as if it was his automatic response.

His reaction annoyed me way more than it should have done. 'She's probably casing the joint,' I muttered.

'Invite her in for tea, darl,' Bev suggested. 'I've got the jug on.' She crossed to the table, scooped one of the nearest bare-breasted beauties on to a plate, and cut into it with a bread knife. Baked sugar crumbs exploded around her. 'Some pav with your tea?'

Stewart took her photo. 'Ye're brutal, Mrs D.'

Bev grinned at the camera. 'I also make dioramas using French pastry, marzipan and lollies. I've got a delicious *Lord of the Rings* battle in the outdoors fridge-freezer. You haven't lived until you've tried to put elf ears on an army of jelly babies.'

I slipped out and headed for the garden.

When Xanthippe saw me, she ducked back behind the high wooden fence. She still smelled of strawberries. Expensive ones. Maybe with a little guava thrown in for good measure.

'Hey, Zee,' I yelled. 'When I said to beat the information out of his grandmother, I was actually kidding!'

She popped her head back up, her face unreadable behind the mirrored glasses. 'Darrow owes me.'

'So what, you're going to interrogate Bev to get to your ex-boyfriend? Very sad, Carides.'

'Maybe I was trying to find out if he's hiding here.'

She sounded innocent, but I knew her better than that. Xanthippe was built of stubborn. This was a woman who had devoted the last ten years to locating and wearing fruit-flavoured perfumes in order to prove a point. (Yes, after arguing said point with me.) If she wanted to find Darrow, nothing would stop her.

I crossed my arms, well aware that we had three different schools of martial arts between us, and she had all of them. 'He's not.'

'Checked all the rooms, have you?'

'I don't know what Darrow's done to piss you off lately, but he went to ground ages ago. He was working on one of his mad projects, spent more time than ever banging away on his laptop in a corner of the café, and then poof! No Darrow. If he's really done something wrong, you think he's going to hang out here, where Bev and her Supernanna Telepathy can worm his secrets out of him over a single cup of tea?'

Xanthippe hesitated. 'You have a point. I'd better find out what she knows, the old-fashioned way.' She looked past my head, and waved cheerfully.

Bev stood at her flyscreen back door. 'Tea's ready,' she said, in one of those firm voices they teach at Nanna School. 'Come on in, you two.'

Xanthippe vaulted the fence so fast that my muscles twitched in sympathy.

'No funny stuff,' I warned, and she laughed at me.

I so have to learn a martial art. This was getting embarrassing.

I have never been able to sit in a room with Xanthippe Carides without being uncomfortably aware of the differences between us. I was jealous of her thick, glossy dark hair and legs that went on forever even when we were best mates at school. She's even more gorgeous now, but it doesn't bother me as much as it used to. Nope, not at all. Good to be a grown up.

I have a figure that I'm perfectly fine with, thanks very much, even if it's more suited to vintage hand-me-downs than low-rider jeans. Who wants to wear low-rider jeans (or freaking *catsuits*) anyway? A cook who doesn't eat the food is a suspicious thing. Also, I fill a bra better than she does.

My hair needs serious help of the chemical variety to make a shiny honey blonde ponytail (or ginger or chestnut or um pink, but blonde right now) instead of something that straggles on in a charming shade of mouse, but hey—I like to play with colour. Art is fun.

In short, I'm not remotely jealous of Zee's effortless grace and glamour. Also I hadn't *at all* locked away in my brain the priceless image of her covered in raw egg to relive over and over. Because I'm a good person.

Once Stewart could be dragged away from photographing Bev's masterpieces, we all sat down in a very floral living room, balancing cups of tea and plates piled high with meringue boobs and coconut cookies.

The cups and saucers were real china, but not matching sets. Bev loves antique shopping, but will only buy one piece at a time.

'I was looking for your grandson,' said Xanthippe, sipping from a porcelain cabbage.

'That's easy, love,' said Bev. 'He's staying with me while his mum's on the mainland.'

Xanthippe coughed. 'He's here?'

'In his room, working away. Home schooling,' Bev added in a loud whisper. 'Don't believe in it myself, but his mother has funny ideas about him being a genius.' She went to the door. 'Kevin! Come and have some bikkies, luv. Cordial's in the kitchen.'

'Right,' said Xanthippe, slumping back into the chair. 'I was probably thinking about a different grandson.'

I gave Bev a hard look, wondering if she was doing this deliberately. Dotty oblivious old lady was one of her favourite disguises.

An extremely short Harry Potter lookalike entered the room, glanced at us all with disinterest, and selected a heavy book from the shelf. 'Sugar's unhealthy, Nan,' he said from behind his oversized glasses. 'I'll have a banana.'

'If you like, darl,' she said to his back, as he shuffled out of the room.

'I didnae think children were called Kevin these days,' said Stewart.

'Well, my daughter-in-law is very old-fashioned,' said Bev. 'Or incredibly trendy. I can never remember which. But of *course* you meant my older grandson, Xanthippe. I know the two of you were … close.'

Close like a forest fire and an arsonist.

'He hasn't been around the café for weeks,' I said helpfully.

'I did want to catch up with him, while I'm in town,' gushed Xanthippe, all bubbly and innocent. Pfah.

'He'll turn up,' said Bev. 'I'll let him know you were asking, love.'

Xanthippe put her cup down, running out of polite. 'I'd better be going. Thanks for the tea, Bev.'

'I need to get my goodies back to the café,' I said. 'Bev—there's an American cruise ship in dock tomorrow. Any chance of some shortbread kangaroos?'

'No problem at all, luv,' said Bev. 'I could throw you in some convict kisses as well.'

'Brilliant.'

'Thanks for the story, Mrs D,' said Stewart, shaking her hand politely. 'I'm gonnae hae a hard time topping this one.'

She smiled at him. 'You just come back at Christmas, my darling. My gingerbread brothels have to be seen to be believed.'

As I collected my boxes of goodies from the kitchen, I saw Kevin Darrow tapping away at something on a laptop. He reminded me of his older cousin, drilling away at a keyboard when his enthusiasm was firing on all cylinders, like he couldn't download the information fast enough from his brain. 'What are you writing?' I asked.

'How comic book merchandise insults the intelligence of nine-year-olds,' he said.

'*Tank Girl* was always my favourite,' I said, awash in happy nostalgia.

Kevin gave me a look that clearly said: 'I do not get your pop culture references, strange old lady,' and I backed away quietly under his scornful gaze.

5

Stewart spent the drive back to the café thumbing through the memory on his camera. 'These came out great. I owe ye one.'

'No problem,' I said. 'I've been telling Bev for years she should get a website and go into the Hens Night catering business. Maybe this will give her the right push.'

'Well,' Stewart said as I parked my little blue Renault in my favourite loading zone. 'It's nae quite a mysterious murder, but it's a good start.'

Oh, yes, the murder. I hadn't forgotten, but it'd been nice to pretend for a little while.

'If you want to thank me properly, you could do a story on the eating habits of a certain kinky formal wear rock band, and throw in a plug for the café.' I batted my eyelashes at him. 'Crash Velvet order a dozen blue muffins from me every day. What's that about?'

He laughed, and kissed me on the cheek. Friendly and yet intimate. I resisted the urge to put on a Jane Austen frock and swoon. 'I'll see what I can do. Great meeting ye, Tabitha.'

'Yeah, you too.' I lifted my meringue boxes out of the car, and watched him head back towards my building. Nice arse. Probably gay. So it goes.

'And where the hell have you been?' barked a voice, as I carried my load into the café courtyard. Bishop.

I looked at my boxes with *Bev's Cakes* printed across the top. 'Obviously I was working my other day job as a strippergram.'

'You're a witness in a murder inquiry. You can't go swanning off without telling us.'

'I'm sorry, they didn't cover that in murder witness school. Anyway, who says I'm a witness? I had my eyes closed the entire time I was looking at that dead body.'

This wasn't Bishop and I being particularly cranky with each other because of the dead body in my building. This was how we always were with each other.

Bonking, shagging, screwing—all things that Bishop and I should have done years ago. There was no bonking him now. He had never quite got over the fact that, once upon a time (ten years ago!), I was sixteen years old while he was one of my dad's constables at the incredibly grown up age of twenty. For some reason, he's never given me the credit for growing up.

When Dad skipped the state for his new life of blissful retirement, things between Bishop and me went from bad to worse. The past three months had been particularly dire. I don't *need* an older brother figure, especially one that I want to lick honey off. It's bad for my psyche.

'Are you going to leave your car there?' he demanded as I walked past him and let myself through the kitchen door, balancing boxes on my hip.

I sighed. 'Parking inspectors get free coffee. But they have to pay for their own cake. Otherwise, it would be bribery.'

It was a good line, and I was hoping he would let me end on it. But Bishop hates not having the last word.

I nodded to Nin as I set the boxes down on the table, and she fetched clean biscuit jars from the cupboard so we could store our loot. The cheesecakes went straight into the fridge.

'Who's that bloke you were with?' Bishop demanded, filling my doorway.

I stacked melting moments into a jar, while Nin did the jam drops. 'You're the police officer. Detect me.'

'Stewart McTavish, resident of Melbourne until a week ago,' he rapped out.

I paused. 'Don't know if he's into women, do you? Because you could save me some time…'

'He's only been here a week, Tish, and there's a suspicious death in the building where he works? I can't believe you just went driving off with someone you'd barely met. Aren't you smarter than that?'

'What can I say? He has a cute accent, it made me giddy.'

'Are you actually trying to make my job difficult?'

'No, I'm naturally difficult. The job thing is an unexpected bonus. How is my love life or distinct lack of it anything to do with you?' I glared at him. 'Why are you in my face? No leads? Been taken off the case? Wait—did Constable Heather get promoted over you already?'

Bishop sighed, and looked very tired. 'Can you try and stay out of trouble for a few days?'

'That's lovely. You're the one who goes finding dead bodies all over the place, and I'm supposed to stay out of trouble? I was delivering muffins.' I finished with the biscuits and started slicing brownies, possibly with more violent knife action than was actually required. Nin, who usually did that job, sensibly stayed out of my way.

Bishop looked as if he was trying not to put a fork between his eyes. He gets that expression around me a lot. 'Anderson will need to see you,' he said finally, writing a number on one of my many sticky note pads, and attaching it to the fridge. 'Some time today. He needs to take DNA samples to eliminate any bits of you they find at the scene.'

'Technology,' I said, slightly impressed. 'Hey, if I was the murderer, it would be the perfect crime. You'd have to cross me off the suspect list.'

'You'll always be on someone's suspect list, Tish.'

'Fine,' I said as he made his exit. '*Be* a policeman.'

Half a minute later, Stewart McTavish popped his head in

the same door. 'He seems a mite pissed off, that copper o' yours,' he observed.

'Lack of chocolate,' I said, tossing him a brownie off-cut. 'Shouldn't you be blogging about naked meringue ladies?' I tried not to be quietly smug about the fact that Bishop would have passed him on his way out.

'Need coffee first. Coffee is the essential fuel tha' keeps any good journalist on his toes.'

'Didn't we just have tea?'

'Tea is not coffee. Tea is a thirst quencher and occasional calming agent. Coffee is a lifestyle choice.'

He seemed twitchy, but I'd known plenty of caffeine addicts in my time, so that seemed normal. 'Help yourself,' I said, gesturing to the always-full staff coffee pot on the bench.

Stewart found a mug and filled it. 'That's the stuff. Should ye no' be charging me for these beverages?'

'Did we not discuss how you were going to plug my café in your widely-viewed tourist blog?' I said in mock-surprise. 'Oh, wait—we did!'

He grinned around his coffee, and caught my sticky note as it fluttered off the fridge. Bishop may solve crime, but he's lousy with stationery. 'DNA testing. Dinna believe in it, meself.'

'Is this a religious objection?'

'Cultural. I blame forensics for the death of the good old-fashioned detective novel. Wha's the point of crime fiction when they feed all the details into a computer and it prints out the name of the murderer?'

Nin, who loves all those sexy forensic shows on TV, made a little strangled noise at the blasphemy.

I took Stewart's coffee from him, which made him whimper. I filled his arms with bikkie jars, and pushed him through the door to the public part of the café before bloodshed occurred.

Lara, working at the counter, stopped fiddling with her butterfly-tipped blonde dreadlocks long enough to smile flirtatiously at Stewart. He eyed her, and they exchanged a few words while he figured out where to put all the jars. Hmm. Further evidence that he might not be gay. On the other hand, I was now going to have to fire Lara.

Stewart frowned at my posters and my collage of *Vogue* covers.

'What's wrong?' I said defensively.

'You need a mural there,' he said, nodding at the feature wall. 'All this paper—it's a bit scruffy.'

'Do you have any idea how hard it is to find a reliable mural artist in this city? Not to mention the expense.' I checked out his dog-eared grey jeans and rumpled hair. 'Anyway, if you want to talk scruffy…'

'Och, don't get personal.' He was eyeing my walls in the same way that the dental technician I dated last month had eyed my teeth—like he was longing to fix them up. 'I'm sensing a theme in your posters here. Did ye not hear about the 1960s being over?'

'The 60s are eternal,' I gasped.

'And the 50s too, I suppose? Ye havnae even settled on an era or a single style—it's a mess.'

'Vintage fashion fusion isn't a mess,' I said, gritting my teeth. 'It's a spiritual philosophy.'

'Fusion, you say?' He didn't sound convinced. 'Ye need real art, to get an idea like that across.'

'And I suppose you know a great mural artist who knows his fashion history and works for coffee and crumbs, possibly the occasional sandwich?'

A sideways smile this time. 'As it happens…'

'Oh, no.' I gave him a push back towards my kitchen. 'I've hung out with writers and artists before. You are *so* procrastinating. Go back to your computer and blog the porn meringues. I am not your project.'

'I was thinking maybe after that…' Stewart said, as I pushed him through the kitchen, slapped his mug into his hand, and kept pushing him out the back door. 'I need more coffee,' he called pitifully.

I closed the door on him. 'If he comes back here with a paintbrush,' I warned Nin, 'don't let him in.'

I like my vintage posters. If I get bored with them, I can change them. I was *not* getting roped into feeding stray Scotsmen in exchange for wall art.

'Your new bloke?' Lara asked as I carried the last of the bikky jars into the café.

'No,' I said, more emphatic than I had intended.

'Good,' she said with a smirk. 'Nice arse.'

Between three and four in the afternoon, it gets almost as hectic as lunchtime. The whole city's blood sugar and caffeine levels plummet at the same time, and the workers and shoppers cram into the cafés with wild eyes and handfuls of money.

The meringue kitty cats were a hit as usual, and sold out long before the Coffee & Cake rush eased off. I had Nin and Lara working flat out at the counter and espresso machine, and I still had to let the phone ring about twelve times before I could get to it. 'Café La Femme, can I help you?'

'Have you googled him?' Bishop said, without even a hello.

'Bishop, I'm up to my eyeballs in customers right now. Crazy people need cake. Must cake the crazy people.'

'Your new little friend. McTavish. Google him before you get into a car with him again.'

'Google this.' I hung up, and loaded a tray with lattés.

'Hi, Tabby,' said a fresh voice.

Constable Gary, bright as a button in his zip-up police jacket, smiled at me with his usual mix of desperation and hope.

'Hey, Gary. With you in a minute.' I circulated, dropping off the coffees and clearing two tables before I made it back. Nin relinquished the counter to me, and went out back to fetch another cheesecake or four. Gary was at the front of the queue by then, beaming at me.

He's a sweetheart, really—all sandy hair and freckles, and he'll probably look eighteen right up to his fiftieth birthday. 'What can I do for you, sweetie?'

I love to make him blush. He turns into one whole freckle. 'Um, a vegan quiche, please, Tabby. With extra side salad.'

I lost a little bit of respect for him. 'So Bishop sent you.'

'No,' he protested. 'It's what I fancy. And I haven't had lunch yet.'

If ever a bloke needed a special someone to feed him up, it was Gary. 'Sit down, and I'll get you some lasagne. Don't tell Inspector Bobby I made one today, I promised Cheryl he gets no more béchamel from me.'

An hour later, the café had quietened down to a dull moan, and Gary was still sitting at his corner table.

'I've never seen anyone take so long over a plate of lasagne,' Lara said in an undertone to Nin.

Nin's eyebrows arched a little. 'Hoping Tabitha will honour him with another smile.'

I gave them both my bitchy boss expression, which they ignored. Apparently, I am not an authority figure. 'He does *not* have a crush on me. He's hoping I'll go over there so he can talk about that girl he fancies who works at the newsagency.'

Okay, he had a teeny crush on me, but pretending I didn't know was the best possible way to deal with it.

Lara handed me a flat white mocha, sprinkled with cinnamon the way I like it, and a latté for Gary. 'Well? You've made greater sacrifices to rid the café of uniforms.'

Too true. I put a couple of brownies on a plate, to give me strength. 'Gary,' I said brightly, joining him at his table. 'Don't mind if I sit here do you? Have a brownie. What's on your mind?'

'Hi, Tabby,' he said again, with a little happy sigh.

I gave him his coffee and passed over three sugar packets. If I'd asked, he would say he only took two. People are odd like that. 'Have you asked Veronica out yet?'

'Nah,' he said, looking embarrassed. 'We're really busy in the Crime Management Unit this month. And, you know, she wouldn't be interested in me.'

'We talked about this, Gary. Stop selling yourself short.'

'We really are busy. Bishop's had me running around all day, following up leads on the new murder case.' He looked impressed with himself.

'He should let you break for lunch when it's actually lunchtime,' I said firmly. 'There is still a canteen at the station, isn't there?'

Gary munched happily on his brownie. 'Yeah, but everyone says it hasn't been as good since your mum left. Wow, these brownies are really great. You're so talented.'

I didn't bother explaining that I hadn't done the day's baking—why break the illusion? 'It's been five years, Gary. You boys are going to have to learn to live without Mum some day.'

I paused, sensing that this moment of total chocolate overload was my best chance to pump Gary for information. 'So, what's Bishop's problem? He seems more shouty than usual. Or is it the effect that I have on him?'

Gary was the best gossip in the district, apart from Constable Marie who went off to have babies but still posts Twitter updates about who's shagging whom (she's usually wrong, which is half the fun of it, and the codenames she uses are hilarious). 'Oh, that'd be Inspector Clayton. He's down from the mainland, and he's in charge of our unit—but even though it's supposed to be CIB and uniform working together, he keeps dismissing Bishop's opinions, because he's not a detective.'

Trust Bishop to end up working under the one inspector in the district who didn't think the sun shone out of his arse.

'Yeah,' Gary continued. 'Inspector Clayton has been giving him heaps for ignoring the other traps earlier, but that's really not fair because no one took them seriously.'

When grilling people for gossip, I find it's best to nod and smile a lot, as if you know exactly what they're talking about. So I nodded and smiled. 'Wait—what traps?'

Gary finished his last bite of brownie, and I waved at Lara to fill us up. She gave me the finger, and went back to cleaning the cappuccino machine. Fair enough, really.

'It looked like stupid pranks,' Gary went on, without the extra lubrication of a second brownie. I pushed mine in his direction, just in case. 'The cat stuck up the tree, then the postman who fell into a cage. No one thought it actually meant anything. But then there's this net with a dead body in it, and no one knows how it got up there. Those rock band blokes turned out to have some Super-lawyer, and we can't prove they were involved, so who could it be? The body was some junkie busker, but still … Inspector Clayton reckons that finding the Trapper could be really important now. Pivotal to the case.'

'The Trapper,' I said encouragingly.

'I came up with the name,' said Gary, puffing up a little. 'And everyone around the station picked it up—he's sort of sneaky and cunning. And he sets traps.'

'Clayton,' I said, thoughtfully. 'Is that Des Clayton? I think my dad knew him, years ago.' Big surprise there. There aren't many senior officers in the country who don't know Dad, one way or another. 'Ran the training college in Adelaide?'

'On active duty now,' said Gary. 'Anyway, that's why Bishop's all cranky. So don't take it personally.' He smiled at me. 'That was really good lasagne, Tabby.'

There was a firm cough from Lara, and I glanced at the clock. Quarter to five—that's time to start looking inhospitable and wave chairs around, so we don't get any customers sneaking in at two minutes to closing. 'Great seeing you, Gary. Pop in again soon.' I cleared the plates briskly, leaving him to give a little wave on his way out.

No sooner had he left than the bell jangled as he stuck his head back in. 'Hey, Tabby. If you're interested, there's stuff about the traps up on your friend's blog.'

'What friend?' I said. 'Wait, what blog?'

6

Sandstone City. I'd contributed a few stories to the blog over the last few months, mainly due to the fact that Simon, Head Geek, spent a lot of time hanging hopefully around our coffee machine until he figured out that Nin really isn't into blokes. Also, I talk a lot. Apparently some of the things I blurted out randomly were worth writing down.

I'd never actually looked at the site, though.

Once the kitchen was halfway clean, I sent Nin and Lara home and cracked open my laptop. The blog came up in Google easily enough, and the top post was one of Stewart's glamour shots of Bev Darrow and her meringue erotica. He'd asked her some interview questions, and the whole thing came across pretty well.

Underneath was a post by **simoning** reporting the dead body found swinging in a net in Crash Velvet's spare room and that police were considering it a suspicious death. There was also a bit of a blurb about the Crime Management Unit handling the case, with a link back to the Tasmania Police website about how the unit was made up of general officers as well as members of the Criminal Investigation Bureau (CIB). No mention of the body being a junkie busker, as Gary referred to him, but Simon had published interviews with all the band members about how shocked they were and how weird it all was.

The final tagline of the post was: Publicity Stunt Gone Wrong, or has the Trapper Gone Homicidal? Have your say on our forum!

The word 'Trapper' had a link to an earlier post by **random_ scotsman,** so I clicked through.

WHO IS THE TRAPPER?

Margarita of Margarita's Pre-Loved Fashions (Bellerive) discovered her missing cat hanging in a net from a tree. Bizarrely, it seems that this was part of an elaborate contraption set up to catch a passerby. What kind of sick puppy are we dealing with here?

[UPDATE—in answer to the huge number of comments and emails that crashed our server this morning, the cat was fine. No damage to the cat. Is it morally wrong to play practical jokes on animals? Have your say on our forum!]

'Such a hack,' I sighed, but kept reading.

This is not the first mysterious trap sprung upon the citizens of Hobart. Two days previously, an employee of Australia Post returned

to his Dynnyrne home only to fall through a hole in his entrance hall, and land in a steel cage. Using a mobile phone, he called a locksmith to secure his release. When interviewed, the postal worker (who wishes to remain anonymous) said, 'I don't know how that bastard got all that in there so quickly. I only went out for milk.'
Have you heard any more stories about this Trapper? Has anyone you know been caught in one of his contraptions? Comment!

Sometime later, I lay in wait for our resident Scotsman.

'Tabitha,' said Stewart as he stepped out of the office to find me sitting on the stairs. 'Wha's up?'

I smiled winningly. 'Fancy painting my walls?'

He gave me a suspicious look. 'According to my sources, when ye smile like that, I'm supposed tae start running.'

'Where would be the fun in that?'

Apparently I had a good point.

'The meringue erotica story is daein well,' Stewart said as we went through to the café. 'Bringing a heap of readers to the site. I could do with a few more like that.'

'More hits than the cat-in-a-net story?'

'Are ye kidding me? Real news versus patisserie porn? No contest. Though cats do rule the internet.' He gave me a knowing grin. 'Have ye been reading my blog, Ms Darling?'

'Maybe a little. Looks like we've got our very own Trapper here in the building.'

'Aye, maybe.' He didn't look convinced. 'Can I really take those rubbish posters down?'

'Be my guest.'

Stewart removed them carefully and meticulously. 'See, much better already.'

I think he meant soulless and boring, but I was still trying to tease information out of him, so I kept that opinion to myself. It only hurt a little. 'So, who's this anonymous postal worker?' I asked.

'I'm nae daft,' he said in a tone that said 'sprung'. 'My sources are protected, Darling.' Or was it 'darling'? My last name leads to such emotional ambiguities.

'We don't have Freedom of the Press in this country.'

Stewart removed my Twiggy poster, and added it to the stack. 'I've been in Australia long enough. Ye cannae fool me that way.'

'Bugger.'

He laughed. 'I'm gonnae need a pencil.'

I brought him a handful from behind the counter. 'You don't have to paint my walls. I only used it as an excuse to talk to you.'

Stewart took the pencils from my fingers, then leaned around and pecked me on the cheek. 'I know. Now back off and let me work. I've got plans for this wall of yours.'

That shouldn't have sounded quite so sexy ... right? 'Hungry?' I said in a squeak.

'Oh weeeell, if you're going to feed me, I suppose I'd better start singing like a canary. No, wait, journalistic integrity ...

giving me indigestion…' He faked a messy death scene in front of me.

'I've read your stuff, McTavish. As a journalist, you make a great photographer.'

'Och! You're a hard woman, Tabitha Darling.'

I resisted the urge to swoon upon hearing my name rendered in a Scottish accent. 'I try.'

He started making little gasping noises. 'So very hungry, cannot make art…'

Reader, I fed him.

An hour and several plates of leftovers later, Stewart had cleaned off my walls with the diligence of a true obsessive (the paint job was recent enough that he wasn't insisting on an undercoat, though he had then lapsed into arty jargon about what he was going to do with the layering of paint, leaving me to nod and smile). He was now covering my wall in blocky pencil marks that made no sense to me. 'Um, when you said you knew what you were doing?'

'Shush,' he said. 'Genius at work.'

'Right. So who put you on to the story about the Trapper, anyway?'

'Can't tell. Would hae tae kill ye, and then there would be no more pasta salad for me. Did I mention how exceptional this pasta salad is?'

'Secret's in the dressing. What if you know something that the police need to know?'

'So ye feed me, I spill my sources, and then it gets passed straight on to your grumpy uniformed boyfriend. It's all strangely unappealing.'

'Bishop's not my boyfriend.' I felt the need to share this information purely for the sake of accuracy.

Stewart was still thoroughly amused at himself. 'Do ye think solving this crime will make him fall into yer womanly arms?'

'Oi!' I couldn't help laughing at that. 'I'm not looking to solve a crime here. Leaving that to the experts, thank you very much.'

'Just nosy, then.'

'Basically.'

Stewart went back to work. 'I wouldnae worry about it. The police know everything I know—more, probably. I got nothing out of the mad cat lady. She waved her arms a lot, and howled about how cats were the ultimate pinnacle of creation. And it was one of yer cop friends who put me on to the story, in any case.'

'Oh.' I wasn't sure why I was disappointed.

Stewart gestured at the walls. 'How long can I hae on this tonight?'

'Don't you have anywhere else to be? Someone to be with?' Really subtle, Tabitha, nice one.

'Me, I like walls. They offer so much, yet ask so little in return.' I might have thought he was joking, but he was gazing at the blank surface pretty intensely.

'You can have an hour. It will take me that long to finish cleaning the kitchen, and wiping down in here.'

'Aye, all right.' Stewart paused. 'And will ye be talking to me the entire time?'

'I'll try and resist,' I sniped, and headed for the kitchen. Mopping and scrubbing awaited. Fun fun fun.

Friday morning, after fulfilling my crime witness obligations, I drove across the river to my favourite berry farm. They can deliver, of course, but I like to look at their stocks for myself every now and then. I wanted a new dessert for the Saturday shoppers and was hunting inspiration. The clear air, sweet smell and thick greenery of the farm was exactly what I needed to let my brain do its best work.

Hobart is a small city, as Australian state capitals go. The back of beyond, especially if you listen to anyone under twenty. But when adventuring in the big wide world gets old, it's nice to have somewhere comfy to return to. A boutique city on the edge of a wide river, within a stone's throw of farmland and fresh produce ... oh, yes. There are worse places in the world to settle down.

Raspberries are one of my favourite things in the universe. I loaded up the car with a pallet of them, more than I'd actually planned to buy, plus a bonus box of the last cherries of the season. If I marinated them, they would last me all winter.

I was thinking about mini-trifles as I drove away from Sorell, surrounded by bushland and clear blue water. I love trifle, but it's messy as hell to serve. It would have to be done in individual portions, and that's a lot of faffing about. Plus, as desserts go it's chalked up on the old school blackboard. Shades of Nannaland.

I reached the turn-off to Bellerive, the prettiest and poshest of the eastern suburbs (which is the charming local way of saying 'suburbs on the opposite side of the river to the real city') and before my conscious brain kicked in, I was heading in that direction, scanning the main street for Margarita's Pre-Loved Fashions, the home of the netted cat.

This was unreasonably nosy, even for me. What did I care about some lunatic setting traps around Hobart, even if one of them had netted a dead man in my building?

I spotted the boutique, and a handy parking space right beside it. Behind a police car, as it happens. The shop window was full of cute vintage frocks, which officially made it my kind of place.

Inside, a forty-something, henna-haired drama queen was being interviewed by a uniformed senior constable. Who was, of course, Bishop. I ducked behind a rack of faux fur stoles and feather-wool scarves, pretending great interest in the garments.

'You lot weren't interested in my poor Moonshine when it first happened,' Margarita said to him, waving her arms at a ratty old Siamese cat who was asleep in a basket of lace gloves and doilies. 'I called three times, and none of you came to see for yourselves. One of your little receptionist madams said I was wasting police time.'

'I do apologise for that,' said Bishop between gritted teeth. Sounded like this conversation had been going around in circles for some time. 'Matters have since escalated...'

'Because a human has been killed,' said Margarita, with a fanatical gleam in her eye. 'My Moonshine could have starved in that net! He was three streets away when I found him. Someone thought it was *funny*.'

'If you could just answer a few questions,' Bishop said.

A gaggle of girls came in, laughing, and went straight to the counter.

'You don't mind if I deal with my customers first?' Margarita said, and started talking to the girls before Bishop could answer her.

My eye was caught by a cabinet of glassware and cheap jewellery. 'Shot glasses,' I said aloud. Tiny trifles in shot glasses. Perfect. 'Ow!'

A large hand came down and grabbed me by the shoulder, and pushed me out of the shop. 'Police brutality! I object.'

'Why are you following me, Tish?' Bishop said, his face all thundery.

I resisted the urge to be turned on by his dominant personality. 'It's not always about you, Leo sweetie. Sometimes, it's about shopping.'

He gave me a very suspicious look. 'You're not playing girl detective again, are you?'

'Again? That's so unfair. There's supposed to be an amnesty about stupid things you did when you were sixteen.'

'Tabitha…'

I held up my hand. 'Guide's Honour. No girl detective. I happened to be in the area, and I remembered reading about this place on Stewart's blog, and I thought, ooh, a secondhand clothes boutique I didn't previously know about. You know my lust for pre-1980s cocktail wear is ever and eternal.'

Bishop sighed. 'To my shame, I do know that about you. Also, that you were kicked out of the Girl Guides.'

'Well, then.' I smiled brightly. 'Any leads on the murder?'

'*Tabitha.*'

'I'm interested. It happened in my building. I saw the body. I'm still kind of creeped out by the whole thing. I would like to know that my favourite police officer is going to make an arrest soon, so I don't have to think about it any more.' I paused. 'So does *Sandstone City* have it right? Does your presence here mean there is a connection between the dead busker and the Trapper?'

Bishop looked as if he had eaten something horrible. Not my cooking. 'You're still hanging out with that Scottish bloke, then.'

'Didn't we already have this conversation? And before you ask, I don't google my friends. You know, unless I'm bored. Don't think I didn't notice the way you evaded my question about the murder.'

'It probably wasn't a murder.'

'You said murder inquiry,' I reminded him.

'We were considering the possibility, but he died of an overdose. Needle was still in him. Accident and suicide are looking the most likely. And I'd better not see any of this turning up on your friend's blog,' he growled. 'But … you don't have to worry about murderers running around your building.'

I got that he was trying to be comforting, but was he kidding me? 'Swinging in a giant net in a building where nobody knew him? How do you get from that to accident? Is that Inspector Des' big theory? And where does the Trapper fit into that anyway?'

'Tabitha, you talk too much. Do I come into your café and start telling you what to serve?'

'Yes, actually. All the time. It's very annoying.'

Bishop stopped looking like a human being and started looking like a big angry police officer again. 'I've got work to do. Go home.'

I didn't want to argue any more, and my berries would be getting warm in the car. 'Fine.'

'Have you seen Anderson?' he called after me.

'Yep, this morning. My DNA is officially no longer a suspect.' I made a face at him, as I opened my driver's side door. 'He wouldn't tell me anything interesting about the case, either. Bastard. Like I *didn't* introduce him to his last two boyfriends. Like I *didn't* get him tickets when The Cure came to town.'

Bishop looked pained. 'Just try and keep your nose for gossip in check during the investigation, okay?'

I blew him a kiss, and headed for home.

Except, I didn't. I drove along to the dock, and ate a punnet of raspberries beside the bright blue water, watching the little white sailboats dart back and forth in front of the postcard-pretty city of Hobart. When I had allowed enough time to pass for Bishop to interview Margarita and head off to solve crime elsewhere, I went back to the shop.

Because, you know. Shot glasses.

7

By the time I made it back to the café, it was nearly time for the lunch rush. I took the counter, left Yui (my other art student) driving the cappuccino machine, and Nin in charge of the kitchen. That's usually the best way to do it—Nin isn't overly compatible with customers.

I also had to throw marshmallows at Stewart until he got down off my wall, and put the tables he had been standing on back the way he found them.

'I need painting time,' he protested.

'I have customers! We're closed on Sunday, if you can wait that long,' I told him. 'You can have the place to yourself most of the day, and we'll have time for the paint fumes to clear overnight. Don't you have an actual job, in the meantime?'

'If I use acrylic there won't be much smell—sealing the final result might stink the place up for a few days but it's not essential—means the work ages more naturally.' Stewart grinned at me, and then an even wider grin at Yui as he accepted a cup of coffee from her. I was going to have to fire both of them. 'Also, I blogged the blue muffins this morning. Slow news day.'

'You're going to get typecast as the food reporter,' I said. 'Thanks.'

Stewart shrugged. 'Simon's away covering the comics convention at the Town Hall, so he asked me tae hang around and keep an eye on the police investigation for follow up posts.'

'Do mysterious deaths really make Hobart seem like more of a happening place?' I suppose it beat landscape pictures of the mountain and cartoon Tassie Devils.

'Sadly, it does.' Stewart leaned in, regarding me closely. 'So, Tabitha Darling. What do ye know now that ye didnae know yesterday?'

'Do I have Nancy Drew written on my knickers now?'

'I wouldnae be shocked if ye did.'

'I'll show you mine if you show me yours.'

He grinned and shook his head. 'Think ye can tempt me with modern literary references and yer underwear? I'm no' that easy.'

The trickle of customers suddenly swelled to a torrent, and hardly any of them were police officers—except good old Gary, of course, who had probably been sent ahead to check the menu for pies and report back to his superiors. 'Come back after two,' I told Stewart. 'I'll bribe you with food.'

'I feel oddly cheated,' he replied, with a wicked grin.

As soon as the lunch crowd eased, I abandoned Nin and Yui to immerse myself in the possibilities of custard combined with berries, cherries and other sources of deliciousness. I left some sponge cake soaking in homemade lemon-and-raspberry juice jelly, with a good splash of limoncello. I had a cherry curd chilling in the fridge. The new shot glasses were freshly scoured, washed and gleaming on a tray.

Oh, and I had already eaten my own body weight in fresh fruit. It's a bad thing to skip lunch on experimental recipe days.

It wasn't working. The shot glasses made for great bite-sized trifles, but you could hardly squeeze enough fresh raspberries in to make the enterprise worthwhile. By the time Stewart turned up, I was depressed about the whole thing. Also a bit queasy, and craving salty things.

'So what do ye have for me?' he asked, from the doorway of the kitchen.

'Margarita talked to me. Of course, she talked to Bishop first, which makes it less of a victory.'

'I have no objections tae the police being as well informed as I am,' said Stewart, stealing a handful of cherries I was about to drown in three different kinds of brandy. 'They're no' exactly our main competition.'

'Which police officer gave you the information about the Trapper in the first place?' That was one thing I had been wondering about. Bishop would not be happy about one of his people spreading rumours.

'Called himself Victor,' Stewart shrugged. He sat on Nin's favourite stool, and ate more cherries. 'Constable, I think. Youngish.'

'I don't know a Constable Victor.' But then I didn't know Heather, either. Things were looking up. I might eventually become a total unknown to Tasmania Police. When I was fifty. 'What happened to protecting your sources?'

Stewart gave me a funny look. 'He didnae ask to be anonymous. The postal worker in the cage did.'

'But you didn't quote Constable Victor directly in your stories?'

'I'm no' stupid. Even saying "a police source" would have yer Bishop breathing down my neck. Giving Constable Victor's name would make certain I get no more information from him, ever. Tabitha, why on earth are ye putting jellied sponge in those perfectly good shot glasses?'

'It's supposed to be teeny weeny trifle,' I said. 'But there's no room for whole raspberries or cherries.'

'Does it hae tae be trifle?'

I stared at him. Brilliant. Thinking outside the box. 'Truly, you are a prince among Scotsmen.' I started another jelly, only this one was made from raspberry juice, lemons and—after a moment's thought—some champagne left in the fridge from the last private party I'd let Lara and Yui hold here.

The cherries could go on top. Where else would they go?

'Wasnae difficult,' Stewart said, around another mouthful of my precious, precious cherries. I took the bowl away from him. 'I loathe trifle. My granny used to make it slimy and gritty at the same time.'

'She was doing it wrong.' Stewart's granny had to be a pretty special person to make trifle both slimy and gritty.

'So…' he said now, pretending to be casual. 'What did this Margarita say?'

Ah, the metaphorical mutual flashing of underwear. 'She said Bishop was a Spanish bull in a previous life, which I really couldn't argue with. Then she said that cats were the superior species and they're just waiting for us to die so that they can become the super-species of the planet, and I was going to run away very fast at that stage, but she distracted me with some Jackie Kennedy pillbox hats until I calmed down. Then she started telling me all about how some bastard set up a trap in the street, and her cat got caught in the net. She said it was about the right size for a person, but it was under a tree, not done with poles like the one upstairs.'

'Does she hae any of the pieces?' Stewart asked quickly.

'Nah, she cut the cat free and took him home. The next day, when she went back, the whole thing had been dismantled.' I hesitated. 'Do you think Crash Velvet are in on this? I mean, is it some freaky publicity stunt?'

'Killing some bloke is gaein a bit far,' said Stewart. 'Even metal bands don't tend to be that hard-edged.'

'Bishop said…' I swallowed, remembering Bishop telling me that Stewart wasn't to be trusted. 'And this is totally off the record, but it probably wasn't murder. The busker died of an overdose, and they're thinking it was accident or suicide. Which suggests that his death was drug related, though Anderson wouldn't confirm that for me. Maybe…Crash Velvet had a party or something and the guy overdosed and they thought they'd use it to their advantage.' That was the creepiest train of thought I'd had in a long time. Never mind cherries—it was time to start eating custard straight from the bowl.

'Maybe,' said Stewart. 'But they're pretty damn clean-cut as rock bands go. I mean, blue muffins and Facebook? That was their big plan to conquer the internet? Also, I don't think they have parties up there. They rehearse during daylight hours, but I've pulled a couple of late nights at *Sandstone City*, and they don't even turn up their telly loud enough for us tae hear it. I've known Boy Scouts who were less considerate neighbours.'

I ate some more custard. 'Maybe the traps are … random. And the dead body is just a dead body.'

'Could be,' said Stewart. 'So we have three traps, one in Bellerive, one in Dynnyrne, and one upstairs. Randomly.'

My spoon hovered halfway between my mouth and the bowl. 'The postman's trap happened in Bellerive?'

'No,' he said slowly. 'That's where Margarita's was, aye? The postman lives in Dynnyrne. Parliament Street.'

I stared at him. 'Margarita's shop is in Bellerive, but she lives in Dynnyrne. Well, Sandy Bay, but the street where her cat was netted is, like, just around the corner from Parliament Street.' And about thirty seconds from my house. Holy crap.

'Are you all right?' he asked.

'I … this is starting to feel kind of personal. Margarita and this postman of yours both live close to me. And the busker in the net was here upstairs.'

'So,' Stewart said slowly. 'What do ye want tae do?'

Throw myself into Bishop's bed until the danger has passed. 'I think,' I said, licking my spoon. 'I think maybe it is time to start playing girl detective.'

Stewart took the bowl away from me. 'Too much sugar, lassie. I'm cutting ye off.'

'No, I'm serious. I want to know what's going on, especially if it's in my back yard. I am a genuinely nosy person, and Bishop's never going to tell me.'

'This isnae a murder mystery like in a book. Red herrings, and the suspects called to the drawing room for tea and revelations.'

'I know,' I said. 'But I'll help you with your story. Maybe we can make sense of it together.' I had to do something. Standing still was not a very appealing idea right now.

'I'm no' denying I could use yer help. Native guide and all that. But … can we no' tell Bishop about this? I like my balls where they are presently.'

'He's not that scary,' I protested.

Stewart was sceptical. 'Tabitha, he looks at me like he wants tae kill me. Every time he sees me in the same room as ye. The man has homicide on his mind, and I dinnae mean because he's a detective.'

For some reason, that made me a tiny bit happy. Was that wrong? 'I can keep a secret if you can. We have a while before my jelly sets. Fancy hunting some buskers?'

Some of my earliest memories are of the Hobart mall—back in the day when kids were let loose on wooden play structures while their parents were shopping. The place has had a few revamps since then, though for all its café tables with big umbrellas and strange plexi-glass sails over the top, it still has that small town vibe about it.

Not small town enough for me to feel safe walking through the mall alone at night, or anything. But ... small.

Mid-afternoon is shopping time in the city. There were people everywhere. Where people congregate, so do buskers.

I wasn't expecting it to be quite so easy, but buskers love attention, and most of the ones we met were happy to pose for Stewart's camera when he mentioned the *Sandstone City* blog.

When I asked—casually—if any of them knew a male violinist with long, dark hair, most of them knew whom I was talking about. Apparently, our corpse was pretty memorable.

'Sure. Morris.'

'Haven't seen him around today.'

'You want to find him, ask his girlfriend.'

I lit up at that clue, but it didn't lead anywhere. 'You know his girlfriend?'

'Nah, just keep a look out for red-haired chicks.'

At least three separate people confirmed that Morris always dated redheads, but none of them were able to supply a second name, the contact info for a specific redhead, or any tangible information. Stewart gave out *Sandstone City* business cards, and we left handfuls of spare change in a dozen different instrument cases.

'Stewart,' I said as we gave up and headed back, 'keep an eye out for redheads.'

'Ye always give me the difficult jobs,' he said, not sounding like he minded.

'*Cherchez la femme.*'

'How do ye even know there's a *femme*?'

'There's always a *femme*. Luckily, I have a job that allows me to listen out for gossip. Speaking of which, we have to speed it up before Nin takes out a hit on me. I promised I'd let her go early today.'

As we approached the café, I spotted a drug dealer on my doorstep. 'Oh, hell.'

Tim Lockwood and I were at college together—he was the kind of guy you always saw at parties selling weed, but never actually saw in class. It shocked the hell out of me when he turned up in Film Studies and turned out to be amazingly knowledgeable about Audrey Hepburn and Elizabeth Taylor as well as 80s schlock horror.

Locks used to look scruffy and disreputable ... but these days, he looked like crap. So thin he was practically translucent, wrapped in a stinking stockman's coat even on the warmest days, and always sucking a cigarette. I glared at him. 'I have the local police in and out of my café on a daily basis, and you reckon it's a good idea to sell dope on my doorstep?'

Locks' bright eyes glittered out at me from behind round glasses. 'You know I don't sell out in the open, babe. Give me some credit.'

'No, you go across the road to the cathedral instead. Very classy.'

He shrugged. 'Any chance of a coffee? Nin wouldn't let me inside.'

'I don't blame her. That coat smells like something died in it.' I sighed. I was a soft touch, and he wasn't a bad source for gossip. 'Go round to the courtyard. I'll be out in a minute with your coffee. But I'm not going to feed you.'

'Good decision, cutes,' Locks said, inhaling the last of his cigarette down to ash and flicking it into the gutter. 'Do that, and you'd never get rid of me.'

8

It had never occurred to me that Stewart had anything in common with Bishop, but there was a look on his face when I brought out Locks' coffee ... mildly fierce and protective, and very familiar. Fair enough. I didn't trust the dealer too far either—though it is difficult to think of someone as all bad when you've heard them ranting about the inherent sexism of 1960s Brit cinema.

'Good coffee,' Locks said, as he drank it hot from the cup.

'Five sugars,' I sighed. 'You may as well put marshmallows in and be done with it.'

'Don't tempt me.'

'I was wondering if you knew anything about a busker called Morris?' I took a deep breath. We hadn't told any of the buskers about why we were looking for the guy. 'He was found dead upstairs, yesterday. Probably an overdose.'

Locks gave me a wary look. 'You asking if I sold him anything?'

'As if I'd ask that.' If he had, I didn't want to know. 'I wondered if you knew anything about him? All we have is that one name, and that he fancied redheads.'

'Come off it,' said Locks around another mouthful of coffee. 'You know him better than me.'

That startled me. 'What are you talking about? I don't know any buskers.' I thought about the limp form hanging in the net, all that hair everywhere. Bishop had asked if I knew him, and I'd said no without hesitating. 'He didn't look familiar.'

'Nuh,' said Locks.

'What do you mean, nuh?'

'I mean nuh. He was at college with us, Tabs. You knew him, all right. Remember when Katie Feldham's dad came in and stalked the corridors because she thought she was pregnant?'

I laughed at that, remembering. 'Eight guys in the Com Sci Department fled the state.'

'Yeah, well she was mates with that girl Kelly, and Jen, you know, Jen with the freckles?'

'Kelly, my ex-housemate Kelly?'

Locks nodded. 'Yeah, didn't know she was ex.'

'She moved out the other week—swanned off with her boyfriend and stuck us with an extra third of the rent, selfish cow.' I could see Locks filing the damn information for future reference—however deeply he might sample his own stash, it's never affected his memory.

'Morris was going out with Kelly for about five minutes. He

couldn't get her to dye her hair anything but green, so he got it together with Jen instead.'

I was lost. It all had a vague ring of authenticity, and I definitely remembered Kelly's green hair phase, but I still couldn't see where the long-haired dead busker fit into the picture.

Locks rolled his eyes at my obvious stupidity. 'He's Ange Morris's little brother.'

The sandstone walls of the courtyard swam around me, and I had to sit down.

'Tabitha,' Stewart said, sounding a long way away. 'Are ye all right there?'

I had lost count of how many times he had had to ask me that. 'Morris is *Julian* Morris? I went out with him,' I said in a dim kind of horror, remembering a wet, not overly satisfying kiss up against a wall. 'His hair wasn't long, then.' How could I not have remembered him? How could I not have recognised him, dead in a fucking net?

He was my age, and he kissed me once, and now he's dead.

'I thought he only went out with redheads?' said Stewart.

I gave him a dirty look. 'My hair was pink that year. I guess it was close enough.'

Locks pushed himself to his feet, and I could almost hear his bones creaking with the effort. 'You going to the glam party Sunday night?'

'Are you invited?'

He laughed. 'I wouldn't invite me if it was *my* party. I'm supplying.'

'I'll make sure to avoid the punch.'

'Might be a plan. See you around, cutes.'

When Locks was gone, Stewart came to sit on the steps beside me, and for a minute I let myself forget that I didn't know him that well, and that Bishop kept telling me not to trust him. I just leaned on him.

'So,' he said awkwardly.

'So,' I said. 'Basically, if I need any detective work done around here, I can go through my back catalogue of boyfriends until I find the relevant one. Freaky Mt Wellington ley lines.' At his blank look, I said, 'Not real ley lines, just—things connected to other things. Coincidence is a common thing around here. It's a small city. Everyone is everyone else's ex-boyfriend, or girlfriend, or significant-other-of-non-specific-gender. We have about one and a half degrees of separation and we blame the mountain, because—it's there.'

'My family's from Dundee, I get the concept of a small population. The mountain ley lines thing is a bit obscure, though.'

'In-jokes usually are. A mate of mine...' Well okay, Xanthippe, 'used to say that it would be dead easy to be a private detective in this city. If you want to find something out, you walk around downtown and chances are you'll bump into someone entirely relevant to the case. Or a jilted lover with a grudge. Knowing her, probably both.' I was babbling, which probably meant I was upset. 'I can't believe I didn't recognise him. Julian. Somebody I *pashed* is now dead. That's so weird I can't think about it.'

Stewart sounded uncomfortable. 'Is this a bad time to remind ye that my shoulders are awkwardly unsuited to being cried upon?'

I shoved him. 'I'm not going to cry. It's not like he was someone I liked. Well, obviously I did for the three days we were technically going out. Well. The first day. Then I was just trying to shake him off.'

'So, what now?'

I stood up. Enough whingeing, Darling. Work to do. 'I want to make coffees for the afternoon crowd until caffeine fumes explode out my ears. Thanks for the shoulder.'

The good thing about being the boss is that, while your staff may heartily resent you for ducking out on them for an hour on a whim, they can't actually do anything about it. Unless they are Nin.

'Ow!' I complained. 'Don't kick me.'

'You were supposed to be making experimental trifles in the kitchen.'

'I stepped out for one minute.'

Nin glared at me. 'You gave him coffee.'

Ah. Well, yeah. She has this thing about not being kind to drug dealers. It's a reasonable attitude, I can sympathise with it. But giving people coffee is what I do.

'I swapped it for information.'

Nin's eyebrows told me exactly what she thought of that, but at least she stopped kicking me.

'I'll woman the cappuccino machine for the next hour,' I offered.

'Done,' said Lara, relinquishing her position at light speed.

It was nearly two hours before the murder (*suspicious death*) collided with my life again. I almost missed the moment. I was loading up a tray with half a dozen variations on the latté when I heard Lara saying, 'Back out the door and around the corner, and there's another door with a staircase. They're one floor up.'

And as I reached for the cinnamon shaker to use over the skim mocha latte, I saw a flash of red hair heading out of the door.

'What did she want?' I asked.

'*Sandstone City*,' said Lara with one shrug of a shoulder. 'She had one of their business cards.'

A redhead with a *Sandstone City* business card. Coincidence? Around here? Hell, no. 'I have to run upstairs.' I glanced around, but Nin was in the kitchen. 'Tell her that the aliens kidnapped me.'

'Hot sex aliens with extra arms,' said Lara with a smirk.

'If you must.' I served the lattés fast, and made my exit.

Simon has been trying to get Darrow to replace the *Sandstone City* door with a glass one for months, so they can pretend it's a proper office. Until that happens (which, according to our esteemed landlord, will be never), they keep it propped open with a brick when one of them is in the office. Stylish.

Ruth, the only female Sandstone Citizen, was leaving as I arrived. 'Come to save him, have you?' she asked, and clattered down the stairs.

I stepped inside, and immediately saw the problem. Stewart was leaning against a messy desk with an armful of wailing redhead. What is it about this man that invites physical contact from strange women?

He saw me over the heaving feminine armful, and looked pitiful.

'Stewart McTavish,' I scolded him. 'Are you letting other women cry on you? I want a divorce.'

'Tabitha,' he said loudly. 'Come in. Great to see you. This is Morris's flatmate, Claudina.' He gave Rose Red a push, and she unwrapped herself from him to stare at me through a haze of mascara and snot.

'Oh,' she said, sniffling. 'Hello.' Excellent, she was one of those women who hates to lose control in the presence of other females. That would save time. 'Were you the girl asking about Julian?'

'That's right,' I said drawing her attention while Stewart backed away to a safe distance.

'Coffee?' he suggested, indicating a manky coffee pot with his elbow.

'Ew, Stewart, I have standards,' I said automatically. 'Um, I mean—Claudina, would you like Stewart to make you a lovely cup of coffee?'

'No thanks,' she said. 'He's dead. Julian. The police told me yesterday.'

'We know,' I said awkwardly. This was all starting to feel like a whole lot of none of my business. 'Hence our interest.'

'I had to identify his body,' she said, scrubbing at her face with the back of a hand.

I went straight to Ruth's desk, and found a box of tissues. Men never have the really useful office supplies. 'Why you?' I asked when I gave them to her. 'Why not his mum, or his sister?'

'His mother is a mess about the whole thing,' Claudina said, blotting her eyes. 'Ange agreed to do it, but she asked me to come with her.'

'So,' said Stewart, more comfortable now there was a desk between him and the crying woman. 'Why come tae us?'

Claudina put the box of tissues down, and flicked her hair. 'They think he's some kind of drug addict. The police. It's so stupid. I mean, it was Julian.' For a minute, she seemed to have forgotten she was talking to strangers. 'Sami said you were giving cards out at the mall, asking about him, and I checked out your blog. I want you to do a story about how the police have got it all wrong.'

Stewart winced at that. 'Your Bishop is gonnae kill me, Tabitha.'

'It was inevitable,' I told him. 'He has deep sexual jealousy issues.'

'I mean,' said Claudina. 'No one who knows him would ever think that. Julian wasn't into drugs and stuff—he's a vegetarian.'

'Okay.' I was prepared to let that one go, though I knew enough vegetarians to find her premise dubious. 'When did you last see Julian?'

'The day before yesterday,' she said. 'He went out after breakfast, and didn't come home. I didn't think much of it, until the police came around…' She took a deep, shuddery breath. 'We weren't together, you know. Not a couple or anything. We just shared a place.'

That surprised me. 'I thought—'

'Yeah,' Claudina said. 'Everyone thinks that. Because of the hair. Even his mum thinks we're a couple. Mine's not natural, anyway.'

'Really?' That did impress me. 'What do you use?'

'Henna, the real stuff. It works great, but the roots are just starting to come out, look.' She leaned in, and I smelled chamomile as I saw the tiny glimpses of ash-blonde amongst the red.

'Excellent,' I said, then noticed that Stewart was giving me a funny look. 'What? You ask a question, then.'

'All right,' he said in his low burr. 'Why would Morris come here, tae this building?'

Claudina was startled. 'Here? What do you mean, here?'

'The next floor up,' I said. 'You didn't know?'

'This is where he *died*?'

'It's where he was found,' Stewart said.

Claudina's freckles stood out brightly on her pale face. 'Is that the only reason you're interested in all this? Because it's your building?'

'I think plenty of people would be interested,' Stewart said slowly. 'I'm covering the story for *Sandstone City*, and yer perspective on Morris could be very valuable.'

She looked uncertain. 'I've got to get back, now. To see his mum. I promised I'd go straight after work. But you can call me, if you want.'

Stewart handed over a notebook, and Claudina scribbled down her details. 'I'm glad someone cares,' she said before she left.

'Right,' said Stewart, letting out a long breath after we heard her footsteps disappearing down the stairs. 'Clearly I need tae hire ye as my bodyguard.'

'You can't help it if you have a face that makes women cry.' I looked at my watch. 'Damn, it's almost closing. Nin's going to kill me.'

'Can I draw on your walls tonight?' he asked as I made a scramble for the door.

That surprised me. 'It's Friday night, you don't have anything better to do?'

'With tha' big empty wall calling me? Ye must be joking.'

'I'll be cleaning until about seven. If you really want to stay later than that, continuing your hot love affair with my walls, come by after closing and I'll give you the back door key.'

Call that security? Bishop's voice thundered in the back of my brain, but I ignored it. I wasn't talking to him right now. And it was hard to be suspicious about Stewart after rescuing him from a soggy damsel.

'Ceege, are you home?'

There was silence as I let myself into our share house. Sandy Bay is half fancy beautiful mansions and restored cottages owned by shiny rich people, and half dodgy falling-apart student residences. Guess which I lived in.

Sure, I was getting a bit old for the share house thing, but I wasn't ready to accept the title 'independent businesswoman' and turn it into a mortgage in the suburbs yet. If ever. Also, I could never afford to live this close to the city if I wanted to buy. Location, location. There are definite benefits to living like a student, especially when you can afford to eat better than baked beans and ramen every night.

I heard a little *pad pad thump*, and Kinky Boots came trotting out of the kitchen, his usual pissed-off expression plastered across his face.

'Good cat. I brought you your favourite.' I waved a bag at him. 'Sashimi!' Mine is a very urban cat. I've had to take him off latté and aioli for the sake of his waistline, but as long as I don't skimp on the raw tuna, he's prepared to forgive.

I gave Kinky Boots his dinner, and lay on the couch with my eyes closed. What I should do was climb up the stairs to my room and commune with my doona for a good ten hours or so. What I wanted to do instead was put on a cute frock, spray something colourful in my ponytail and run down to the Salamanca courtyard to spend hours and hours around people and music and vodka shots.

As if I could work up the energy. Geez, I really must be getting old.

I wasn't feeling up to the usual gossip and dancing. Not because my feet hurt like four kinds of hell—they always did on a Friday night, and that had never stopped me before. I'd known Stewart McTavish for two days, and I'd left him in my café with a door key and a drawer full of pencils. It niggled at me.

Ceege's computer loomed from the corner. The benefits of having a gamer for a housemate is that he pays the broadband bill. It was rare to see the computer without my pet engineering student attached to it like a limpet.

And Google *is* a girl's best friend.

I hated myself for giving in to Bishop's paranoia, but hey. Who doesn't screen new friends these days?

I swung myself out of the comfy couch, swatted a stack of *Doctor Who* novels out of Ceege's office chair, and got online.

Two hours later, I was still reading.

9

The absolute suckiest thing about running a café is working on a Saturday. I can't avoid it. Sundays, the town centre is legitimately dead, and that's the one thing that makes me glad Darrow didn't set me up in Salamanca, or the espresso strip of North Hobart. My weekly sleep-in is sacred.

But everyone shops in the centre of town on Saturdays, and they need their foamy Fair Trade vanilla mugaccinos, oh yes they do.

So every Saturday, from 5AM when I get up, 6AM when I start the day's prep to 8AM when I open the doors, I hate everybody. I think that's legitimate.

Today I hated everybody slightly less than usual—I had spent a ridiculous number of hours in Ceege's precarious office chair before crawling to bed with Kinky Boots and a trashy novel, but at least I hadn't been downing over-priced cocktails until after midnight. I hadn't had to rinse purple glitter spray out of my hair, and I was able to do that complicated braid that kept my hair out of the side salads on the very first try.

I got to the café fifteen minutes early, and Nin had still managed to beat me to the kitchen. 'How do you do that?' I complained.

She shrugged and smiled a little, her hands busy with what could only be her chocolate scone recipe.

There is no universe in which chocolate scones should work, but—well, Nin has her own universe, and sometimes she lets others visit. 'Mm,' I said happily. 'Chocolate scone days are always good days.'

'You gave your Scotsman a key, then,' said Nin, breaking her cardinal rule by speaking before ten in the morning.

'How did you know about that? Did he steal the furniture?'

Nin had a definite smirk on her face. 'Go look at your wall.'

I went out to the café, switching on the lights as I went. It wasn't the brightest of days outside—it looked like we were in for winter a month or two early this year. Climate change has a particularly menacing sense of humour when it comes to Hobart.

I'd seen some of Stewart's artwork as part of my Friday night Googlefest. There was a mural at a high school in a Melbourne suburb, and a couple of graffiti-style pieces in Dundee and Glasgow from his teen years. There was a web-comic from a couple of years ago that cracked me up with its surreal characters and offbeat sense of humour—displaying much better writing skills than his *Sandstone City* 'journalism'.

But then, there was this.

It's a total cliché to have a café mural that depicts people in a café. You know the sort of thing—cartoony umbrellas and stick-thin girls sipping coffees in Paris haircuts. Blank, static faces.

This wasn't anything like that.

This was a glorious, giant sketch of overturned tables and damned cheek. My favourite poster girls and boys were squabbling for room at the central table, the only one still on its feet. Wonder Woman was arm-wrestling with Holly Golightly. Sean Connery as James Bond was slipping something into Ursula Andress's drink, while making eyes at Barbara Windsor. Doris Day rolled her eyes at them all as she texted a friend. Elizabeth Taylor's Cleopatra flipped through an authentic 1965 issue of *Vogue*. Steed and Mrs Peel snogged in the corner.

Hobart was there too, in the background. The bright water, cloudy skies, the looming mountain, the little patchwork suburbs and winding streets. The shiny metal office buildings jammed up against colonial architecture.

'It's like he can see right inside your shallow but stylish soul,' remarked Nin, as she came through the kitchen doors to join me.

'Ssh, don't talk. I'm bonding with my wall.' The artwork was all still in outline, though there was a promising splash of candy pink across Cleopatra's frock. I couldn't wait to see what it would look like when fully painted. 'This wall,' I said finally, 'is made of pure awesome.'

'Also, he locked up properly,' said Nin. 'The boy's a keeper.'

Even Senior Constable Bishop couldn't spoil my mood on a day like this. Not that he didn't try.

Before the late morning shopping crowd reached fever pitch, I took a basket of chocolate scones up to Crash Velvet, along with their regular order. kCeera was so happy to see a baked good that wasn't blue, she dragged me in to drink a wheatgrass concoction with her.

'*Sandstone City* is *fantastic*,' kCeera said through her second scone. 'We've been trying for years to get the newspapers to give us some publicity, but can they be bothered? They didn't even get the name of the band right when they reported the murder. Bloggers care about the details.'

'I thought the police weren't calling it a murder,' I said carefully.

'Well, they say suspicious death,' she admitted. 'But, you know what I mean. Hey—guess what? That blue muffin thing is totally paying off.'

I blinked. 'You are kidding me.'

'I'm not. Since Stewart's post went up, our YouTube hits went through the roof. Facebook too. Someone even set up a Tumblr for fans to speculate about recipes. Check it out.' kCeera opened one of her kitchen cupboards to reveal two shelves stacked deep with watermelons. 'I've been sending Owen out to get one of these from the local grocer's every morning. Do you reckon

Stewart would do another post about our eating habits?'

'Depends how desperate he is. You can try.' I eyed the water-melons. Mmmm, watermelon slushies. 'I could take some of these off your hands for the café? Smuggle them out secretly. Not that I want to deprive you…'

'Oh, please. Take, have.'

I picked a couple out happily. 'I'll give you a discount on your next month of muffins. Watermelon is a valid currency around here. Heard about your stolen gear?'

kCeera looked a little uncomfortable at that. 'Nah. The police can't be stuffed with that, they're all distracted with the dead bloke business. Owen and the others are off with our PR manager today, going through the op shops to see if any of it turned up. We're playing a glam party tomorrow night, and we're going to look pretty stupid without our costumes.'

'Maybe it's time for a new look.'

'Yeah,' kCeera said, trying to sound enthusiastic. 'Hey.' She pulled a stack of folded papers from her back pocket. 'Do you want one? It's a flyer listing all the missing items. If you come across any of them, we've got a reward posted.'

I eyed the list. 'Well, if anyone is likely to happen across a lace crinoline or a set of hand-forged handcuff accessories with foot-long spikes in their day-to-day life, it probably *would* be me.'

I was going to ask more about their PR manager, and maybe get in a question or two about whether any of the band had been acquainted with Julian Morris, but there was an official-sounding knock on the door of the flat, and I guessed before kCeera opened it that it was Bishop. I have a sixth sense that is entirely devoted to cranky police officers.

'I'd like to ask you some more questions,' he said in a tight voice. 'But if you don't mind, I'll have a few words with Ms Darling first. *Outside!*'

The second that the door closed behind us, Bishop was yelling at me. 'Are you interfering in my investigation again?'

'Not again, not ever. No!' I headed down the stairs with my arms full of watermelons, making him damn well follow me if he wanted to rant face to face.

He did, stomping with those long legs of his. 'So what were you doing up there?'

'Being neighbourly. Delivering scones. Drinking tea. Being normal. Shit!' The heel of my cute vintage boot snapped off, and I fell two steps before I hit the *Sandstone City* landing.

Bishop grabbed my arm to steady me. 'You okay?'

'No! These boots were a bargain. That's *worse* than if I'd spent serious money on them.' I breathed hard, staring at him. 'I'll report you for police harassment.'

'Bully,' he said.

'Brat,' I shot back, and we both laughed at ourselves in the same moment, breaking the tension.

Bishop still hadn't taken his hand from my arm. 'Why do I put up with this shit from you, Tish?'

The old nickname made me feel warm this time around, which was ridiculous. I resorted to flirting in order to make him go away. (We're so messed up.) 'Because you love me, of course.'

'In what universe?'

'All the universes. Look—I'm not trying to screw with your investigation, really. If anything, it's screwing with me. I hear gossip all the time, and Stewart's working on the story, and then Claudina asked for my help, well, our help…'

'Who's Claudina?'

I glared at him. 'Remember taking two cute redheads to identify the body? His sister and his flatmate?'

'Contrary to your belief, I don't do every piece of police work in this state, or even on this case…'

'I knew him,' I blurted out. 'Julian Morris. We were at college together.'

Bishop stared at me. 'I didn't know that. You said you didn't recognise him—'

'I didn't. I only found out who he was afterwards. How is anyone supposed to recognise anyone when they're dead and hanging in a *net*? It's worse than a passport photo.'

He touched my cheek with the flat of his hand. 'Breathe. It's okay.'

'He was my age, Leo. It's not okay.' I turned my face into his hand. 'Claudina doesn't think Morris was a drug addict.'

'I think she's wrong,' he replied. 'You're going to have to trust me on this. I can't tell you any more than that.'

'But what if it was murder? What about the Trapper?'

Bishop pulled his hand away at that, face darkening. 'That bloody stupid name. And that blog—the so-called Trapper was just an urban myth circulating the police station until Kilt Boy got his hands on it. The newspapers have got on to it now, and the TV cameras are circling. Are you still seeing him?' That last bit came out as something of a bark, and it was a few seconds before I realised he was talking about Stewart.

'Not exactly seeing...' Not this morning, anyway. Though I did owe him a great big smooch for the beautiful thing he had done to my wall.

'Good, stay away from him.'

'I'm sorry, I saw your lips move just then, but I can't have actually heard you forbid me to see him? What the hell business is it of yours who my friends are? Stewart's a good bloke.'

'Yeah, tell that to Diana Glass,' Bishop growled. I didn't manage to conceal my reaction fast enough, and he was on me. 'You did google him, then.'

I hated him for making me admit it. 'I happened to be bored.' Plus, policeman's daughter. Old habits die hard.

'So you know what I'm talking about.'

'I didn't find anything that made me change my mind about him. He wrote a bitchy article about a stuck up romance novelist. So what?'

'A series of articles and reviews, and blog entries, and forum comments. He had a vendetta against that woman, like he was out to destroy her. Is that the kind of man you want to spend time with?'

'I don't know that I want to be held accountable for everything a stranger could find out about me online. That footage of my top falling off at Becky Sumner's party is still doing the rounds. There are animated gifs. I was a *meme*.'

He winced at that. 'I'm just trying to protect you.'

'Well, stop it. Stop it right now. Even my dad never pulled crap like this, and they don't make dads more over-protective than him. You have to stop treating me like I'm sixteen and ridiculous.'

'I don't think you're ridiculous.'

'Well, I don't need a big brother watching over me.'

'So what the hell do you want?' he asked.

'Work it out,' I hissed, and made for the second flight of stairs. My uneven heels made me unsteady, though, and Bishop grabbed for me, pulling me back towards him and into him and, oh shit, he was kissing me.

Didn't see that coming.

So, right. Bishop and kissing. Can't deny it's one of those things that I've thought from time to time. Since pretty much the first time I dropped Dad's sandwiches off to him at work, and found him lecturing one of his new recruits about correct evidence procedure. Ten years ago.

And now Bishop's mouth was hot and wet, and for a moment I let him swallow me whole. I'd always imagined he was far too uptight to do interesting things with his tongue, but there was a hard sweep along my lower lip, and a graze of teeth that just about undid me altogether.

Possibly it was a good thing there were two large watermelons preventing his body from pressing too closely to mine, or I would have been ten seconds away from ravishing him right there on the staircase.

My brain shrieked in protest as I pulled away from the omigod-so-hot-I-could-die-right-now kiss. But what the hell else could I do? 'Wrong answer,' I said breathlessly, and limped away as fast as I could on my cute little busted-up boots, back down to my kitchen.

The nice thing about kitchens is they tend not to have unexpectedly passionate police officers cluttering up the place. I took a few deep breaths, set down my melons and flung open my fridge. Where were the vodka mixers when you needed them? I drank half a litre of milk instead, and threw the carton away.

Cooking. Can't go wrong with cooking. I stared at my oven for some minutes, trying to remember the menu I'd planned for the day.

Quiche. I can make quiche in my sleep, let alone during a major emotional trauma. There was smoked salmon and

Virginia ham in the fridge, four kinds of cheese, spinach, olives. Quiche was a definite option.

Eggs.

I opened the back door to check if our usual free range basket had been delivered, and found Stewart talking to Xanthippe Carides.

When I say 'talk', I mean, 'imagining having sex with'. Seriously. They weren't close enough to touch, but he was smiling as she murmured to him, and they were mirroring each other's body language.

She looked amazing too, the wench. All in black again, this time a leotard under jeans that showed off her sleek arm muscles. Was it fair for someone to have so little body fat *and* muscles? Her hair was all shiny, in dark waves. I could use three times the safety recommendation for hair conditioner and still not get my hair to look like that. 'Morning,' I called out, as I picked up the eggs.

Stewart threw me one of his warm smiles, not looking the least caught out, and Xanthippe waved. She said something in an undertone to Stewart, flexed her triceps at him, and left.

'Morning,' he said then, loping over in a grotesquely good mood. 'I don't suppose ye have any more Bev Darrows up yer sleeve? I could do with another quirky profile between all our buskers and murders.'

I sighed, letting him follow me back inside the kitchen. 'My old primary school teacher is setting up a Romantic Poets Wine

Tasting in Battery Point. "Have your merlot poured by a theatre student pretending to be Byron or Shelley." I'll write down the address.'

'Brilliant, thanks.'

I scribbled it on a Post It. 'Tell Suze I said hi.'

Stewart hesitated as he took the note. 'Xanthippe said something just now.'

'Oh, were you two talking? I thought I caught a whiff of artificial fruit.' Smooth, Tabitha. Didn't sound jealous at all, there.

He grinned at me as he stuck the note in his jeans. 'I think she was trying to figure out if I knew if ye knew where that Darrow bloke was. Subtle woman.'

'Her wardrobe does scream subtlety.'

'She implied he might be in on this Trapper business, or know something about it.'

That surprised me. What was Xanthippe up to, implicating her ex like that? 'Interesting thought. Barking mad, obviously.'

'Obviously,' Stewart said, and hesitated again, by the door. 'Have ye seen the wall yet? I mean, it's nae finished, so ye probably cannae get the whole effect—'

'Oh.' I'd forgotten. How could I have forgotten? I crossed the two steps to him, put my arms around his neck and hugged hard, smelling coffee and wool jumper and man. 'It's the best thing ever,' I said into his throat. 'You must paint more, immediately. I'll clear the place out, send everyone home with their food wrapped in foil swans.'

'I can wait til tomorrow,' Stewart laughed. 'I still get Sunday, aye? Ye could come keep me company. I'll need yer advice on what colour nail polish Ursula Andress would wear.'

I leaned back, and beamed at him. 'I've been waiting my whole life for someone to ask me that question.'

10

Café La Femme closes an hour early on Saturdays, which is the least the universe owes me, quite frankly. Hobart falls asleep at about 4PM on a weekend, and I was looking forward to my precious Sunday off. I headed home with a box of leftovers and a happy glow. The half-finished mural had been cheering me up throughout the afternoon, and I had almost avoided thinking about Bishop all day.

Two big questions: why did I let him kiss me, and why did I stop kissing him back? Pfah. Thinking—so overrated.

I let myself in the front door, and remembered all over again that both of the Trapper's first efforts had been within a couple of streets of my house. Bad, bad thoughts. Very unhelpful.

What was Xanthippe on, to spread rumours that Darrow was the Trapper? Why was she out to get him? Sure, they were the world's worst couple and when they broke up the earth basically trembled with the fallout, but that was years ago. I thought they were back to being friends.

Zee and I had a difficult relationship. We hated each other at school, for the first two years. It was loathe at first sight. We tripped each other, bitched and snarked at every opportunity, and on one memorable occasion got a detention for a slapfight in the quadrangle. But then … gradually we figured out that the school was full of girls who were top-of-the-class smart and good at netball, and girls who were destined to be dumb and popular and still pretty good at netball. And there were the girls who tagged along with whatever crowd they could, sucking up like crazy. And then there were the really netbally ones.

At the end of it all, there was Xanthippe Carides at one end of the classroom and me at the other, with absolutely nothing in common except that we kind of liked insulting each other, and other people, and we were the only ones who hated netball. Enforced group sports in track pants, no thank you. Then in Grade Nine, after the slapfight and a month of silence, Zee came over and sat next to me at lunch. The next day, I sat next to her.

When the next athletics carnival rolled around (running in *circles*? I think not), we hid behind the gym together, reading martial arts magazines (her) and the history of Coco Chanel (me). I made her watch classic movies, and she made me help her restore a vintage car.

We went to the same college for Grades Eleven and Twelve, but there was a wider assortment of cool people available by then, and we needed each other less. She took off soon after, running full tilt for the mainland like everyone else, returning for occasional bursts only to vanish again. She seems to have a different job every year—she's been a PR rep, bodyguard, karate instructor and barmaid, among other things.

I didn't even realise she and Darrow knew each other until that time I saw them arguing, snogging, breaking up and getting back together at a zombie theme night Darrow had set up in one of the more karaoke-friendly local bars, a few years back. It didn't surprise me. Even if we didn't live in a place dominated by those good old Mount Wellington ley lines, threads of connectivity binding us all together… Darrow is one of those people who knows everyone and if he doesn't, he'll strike up a conversation. They'll be his new best friend within minutes.

Possibly I'm that sort of person too, which is why we get along so well.

I made myself a cup of tea and switched on my dad's beloved old police radio. To most people, it's just a heap of static and codes, but for me it's about picking up on all the gossip.

My housemate Ceege came home from his shift at the call centre, yawning in yesterday's grey t-shirt. I waved at him, and he made a peanut butter sandwich before logging on to his computer, and *World of Warcraft*.

I lay on the couch, and toyed with a knitted cupcake cushion. 'Ceege?'

He didn't respond.

I sighed loudly, to let him know it was serious. 'Cee-eege…'

LIVIA DAY

'Hush, woman,' he said, not looking up from his screen. 'My guild's about to meet at the tavern, and I'm figuring out what to wear.'

'But I'm having a crisis,' I wailed. 'Can't you leave your gay elves for a minute to come and talk to me?'

'We're not gay, we're metrosexual. I can talk to you from here. What's your trauma?'

'I snogged Bishop today. Well, he started it. But I wasn't exactly a helpless bystander.'

Ceege laughed softly.

'It's not funny.'

'It's *so* funny, Tabitha. Have you told your mum yet?'

'Shut up.'

'She's gonna book the celebrant.'

'Shut up, shut up.' I buried my face in the cushion. 'I need more girl friends who don't work for me. Boys are useless at this.'

'Tabitha's in lurve with a policeman...'

'Police officer,' I corrected, the cushion muffling my voice. 'And I am not hooking up with a man in uniform. No way.'

'You are so hot for the uniform,' he chuckled.

'One more word, and I'll tell Katie about your Harry Potter fanfic. I'll give her your pseudonyms...'

There was a cough from above me. I peered up, around the cushion. Ceege was holding a packet of Tim Tams, just out of reach. 'I'll make you a deal. We stop talking about your sick, twisted love life right now, and I'll give you the biscuits.'

'I could make my own biscuits if I wanted biscuits,' I said prissily.

'You're fooling no one. I'll give you the Tim Tams, and I get to kick uninterrupted dragon butt with my metrosexual elf friends. Okay?'

'Eh, works for me.' I accepted the bribe for what it was, and ripped the packet open with my teeth. 'I do *not* have a thing for men in uniform.'

'Whatever helps you sleep at night, Tabs.'

Several Tim Tams later, I staggered off the couch (whoa, chocolate rush) to have a shower. The police radio was still squawking as I walked through the kitchen, and I gave it a kick as I went.

Hot water solves almost any stress. Baths are best, but if I make the mistake of having a bath during daylight hours, I'm there until bedtime. Couldn't afford the time today, so a shower it was. I turned my neck into the hot spray and thought, blissfully, about nothing at all for at least ten minutes.

'Tabs.' Ceege rapped on the shower door.

'Perve! What are you doing in here?'

'Like I care about your wet bits. You left your radio on.'

'Turn it off yourself.'

'It's not that. There's something major going on over in Landsdowne Crescent. Like an armed siege kind of thing.'

The water didn't feel hot on my skin any more. I turned the tap off, trying not to panic. We're a little touchy about sieges, here in Tasmania. 'And?'

'Your Bishop is right in the middle of it.'

I leaned my head against the glass door. I was never going to trust chocolate scone days ever again.

Of course I went. Where else was I going to go? I spent my teens working alongside my mum, making sandwiches at bushfires and soup for crisis victims. It's what Darling women do. Well, Darling women who don't rebel at fifty and start wearing tie-dyed skirts with bells on.

I didn't take sandwiches. He didn't deserve them. If Bishop came out of this alive, I was going to kill him.

West Hobart is a steep, multi-hill suburb between our little city and the first bushy slopes of the mountain. Most days, it's green, leafy and cheerful, despite the freezing wind that cuts straight from Antarctica. Most days, West Hobart isn't full of police cars, ambulances, incident tape and red-faced, irritable women in sweaty tank tops and track pants who had been rudely interrupted in the middle of their yoga, pilates, step-aerobics and pole dancing classes.

The press had surrounded the aerobics centre by the time I got there—TV crews, a few newspaper journalists, and two very indignant bloggers who were trying to convince a couple of police officers that they were legitimate press. I waved at Stewart, but he didn't see me. Neither did Simon. I tried to catch the attention of Inspector Bobby, who came right over.

'Hello, love. Don't worry, all sorted. Bishop's fine.'

'Who's worried?' I said. 'Do I look worried?' I ignored the fact that he was acting like I was Bishop's girlfriend—most of the station had been doing it for years. My only consolation was that it annoyed him way more than it annoyed me. 'What's going on?'

I resisted the urge to ask how close it had been.

'Come on, Tabby, you know I can't tell you anything.' Inspector Bobby patted my arm. 'It wasn't guns, thank gawd. I'll send Bishop over when he's got a minute.'

'Don't do that,' I said in a panic. 'I'll catch up with him later. In fact, don't even mention I was here. *I was never here.*'

Stewart and Simon weren't part of the gaggle of press any more. I found them behind one of the ambulances, Simon keeping a lookout while Stewart took discreet pictures on his smart phone.

Several paramedics came out of the aerobics centre that was apparently named the Jiggle It Fitness Hub (it amused me no end that the press would have to repeat that name with a straight face over and over again), pushing a uniformed figure on a gurney. I tried to see who it was, but I was distracted by the sight of a grim-faced Bishop walking alongside. He looked like he was having a really bad day.

What I *didn't* do was cross the police tape and throw myself into his arms. So proud of me.

'So,' I said, tapping Simon on the shoulder and scaring the hell out of him. 'How do you have an armed siege without guns?'

'She used Olympic standard archery equipment,' Stewart muttered, leaning out a little further to get clear shots. 'Luckily, she's not an Olympic standard archer. She's one of the instructors here, resident expert on something called Bellycise.'

'Completely barmy, then.'

'I wouldnae care to judge.'

A woman was brought out next, flanked by police on both sides. She had apricot hair under the towel they were using to cover her face from the cameras. She wore a Jiggle It Fitness Hub t-shirt, harem pants and designer sneakers. A third uniform carried a large evidence bag with a bright green bow and several arrows inside.

Stewart pulled back before the paramedics reached the ambulance. 'We should be away. Action's done. I've got crowd reaction, and some contacts to follow up.'

'Excellent,' said Simon. 'It's like the city put on a bizarre crime spree this week, just for us.'

'So glad you're having fun,' I said crossly. The two of them skipped around the ambulance before the paramedics reached the back doors. I didn't move fast enough, and the sight of the figure on the gurney slowed me down. 'Gary!'

Bishop's head whipped around. 'Tish, what are you doing here?'

I ignored him, my eyes on my favourite hungry constable, who was pale under his bright freckles. 'Gary, did you get *shot*?'

'Just a bit,' Constable Gary said, looking sick. His arm was heavily bandaged.

'Out of the way, please,' said one of the efficient paramedics, and I stood well clear.

'I'm not happy, Gary,' I called as they loaded him into the ambulance. 'Heroics are very unsexy. Don't do it again!'

He laughed weakly. 'I'll try not to.'

I blew him a kiss, then turned to look at Bishop. There was no avoiding it, really. 'I happened to be passing by.'

'Uh-huh. That radio of yours is not supposed to be used by non-police personnel.'

'I don't know what radio you mean, except the one my dad left with me, which is in storage. Don't even know which box it's in.'

Bishop nodded slowly. 'You okay?'

I punched him lightly on the arm. 'I heard "armed siege". What do you think?'

'It wasn't exactly that.' Bishop shook his head, thoroughly pissed off, though not with me for once in his life. 'We were brought in by a hoax call from someone who said she had information on the Morris case. As soon as she saw us, that fitness instructor turned around and went into a storeroom. We were about to send someone in after her when she came out with her bows and arrows. No one even knows what her issues are.'

Bishop rolled his eyes in the direction of the ambulance, as they closed the doors. 'I was talking her down, nice and calm. Gary didn't say a bloody word to her, and halfway through, she shot him for no reason! Poor bastard didn't even twitch. Lucky her hands were shaking, she only got him in the arm.'

I couldn't stop looking at him. He was weirdly calm, like this was the sort of thing he dealt with every day. Which, I guess it was. There he was in one piece, all dark and chiselled. Apparently I did have a thing for men in uniform. Damn it. I reached up and put my hands on his face, and kissed him.

Probably the most chaste kiss I've given anyone since I was about fifteen, I might add. No tongues. Barely even mouth. But then Bishop leaned his forehead against me, and I sighed a happy little sigh. This was nice. It felt right.

The ambulance rolled away, leaving us in full view of all remaining members of the press.

'They just took pictures of us, didn't they?' Bishop said, his face still touching mine.

'Pretty sure they didn't.'

Of course they did.

So, yeah, our paper's somewhat parochial. Local weather girl gets married, it makes the front page. Anything to do with Princess Mary of Denmark (born around here, went to Taroona High school, don't you know) is more important than federal politics. I don't think I know anyone who hasn't been worthy of at least a half page spread in the Hobart *Mercury* at some time in their lives, whether it's winning a science prize at school, or picking up litter on the beaches for Clean Up Australia Day.

Still, it was a shock to the system to see my intimate embrace with a certain Senior Constable plastered in colour across the front of the *Sunday Tasmanian.*

Too late now to wish I'd blowdried my hair before running out to make a fool of myself in public. I looked like a drowned rat, cradled against Tall, Dark and Uniformed.

All I could do was close my eyes and pray that my mother didn't see this newspaper. I would never be able to convince her that Bishop and I weren't an item now.

We weren't. We really weren't.

I did force myself to read the actual story—mad arrow lady wasn't named, but the paper said she was the wife of a respectable local dentist, and her lawyer was refusing to let her make any statement to the press. It couldn't be that hard to find out who she was with a bit of judicious Google Fu (or at the very least, checking the Jiggle It Fitness Hub website to see how many apricot haired Bellycise experts they had), but I didn't feel up to finding out. Stewart would probably know.

It was just after ten in the morning. I couldn't get a park near the café, and had to walk a couple of blocks. I was standing at the lights near the GPO when I saw something that almost made me swallow my own tongue: an orange taxi turning a corner, with Darrow at the wheel. My prodigal landlord.

There was no mistaking him. He was even wearing one of his horribly expensive designer suits. 'Hey!' I screamed, waving an arm at him, but he drove smoothly away without giving any impression he'd seen me.

Stewart was waiting on the steps in the courtyard behind the café when I arrived in a foul mood, the Sunday paper tucked under my arm. 'Didn't I give you a spare key?' I demanded.

'Thought I'd wait tae see if ye were talking to me,' he said, a little sheepishly.

'The rest of the mural had better be freaking good.' We went inside together, and I threw the paper on the kitchen table.

'I didnae actually take the picture they printed in the paper,' he offered as a possible white flag.

'Mm.' I switched on the lights in the café and booted up the computer. When I typed in the *Sandstone City* URL, Bishop and I filled the screen, snuggling intimately.

'See?' said Stewart. 'The one I took is far more flattering. Ye can hardly tell how bad yer hair looked.'

I narrowed my eyes at him. 'I'm going to spend the morning experimenting with trifle-free trifles. I may talk to you by lunchtime. But don't count on it.'

Hours later, the smell of paint was warring with the scent of raspberries, custard and brandy. We had the doors and windows open, and it was freezing cold despite the bright sunshine outside.

While Stewart glued sequins to Mrs Peel's boots, I lay on the café counter, sucking custard out of my third shot glass and reading the flyer of stolen Wearable Art Treasures that kCeera had given me. 'You should blog this, it's hilarious. Where did they even get a pair of ruby glass slippers with seven inch spiked heels? I want to shop where they're shopping.'

'Mm,' said Stewart. 'Might get us further than your so-called murder mystery.'

'Don't tell me you're bored?'

'The arrow-happy belly-dancing fitness instructor is a lot more newsworthy than the dead busker in a net. Not that our readers don't prefer meringue porn any day of the week.' He glanced over at me. 'Ye know there's a connection between Robinette Hood and Julian Morris, right?'

'You mean that she—or someone—made a hoax call to get the police to good old Jiggle Bits yesterday?'

'No, not that. Apparently this woman—Natasha Pembroke—runs local charity events to sponsor and promote health issues. Everything from dental health in third world countries to depression and suicide in local teens. Six months ago, she hired the Tin Man Tossers to provide the music for one of her soirées. That was Julian Morris on violin, his sister Ange on cello and someone called Misty Heavens playing the tambourine.'

'Sounds vile,' I said. 'Good detective work, though. How did you find that out?'

'Only good? I was hoping for brilliant,' said Stewart. 'Or maybe, masterful.'

'I'm prepared to downgrade you to competent if you keep going on about it...'

'Ange Morris emailed me after she saw the Fitness Hub story, and gave us the scoop. Not sure what that means, if anything. But it's a start.'

'See, it *is* a real murder mystery,' I said cheerfully. 'This is what we call a clue.'

'Mysteries in books have the decency tae provide properly spaced out clues that lead tae a well-plotted resolution.' Stewart shook his head. 'I think I'll stick tae Hobart's arty citizens. Fighting crime hurts the brain. Got any more for me, by the way?'

'A girl I was at school with is going to protest the tuna fishing industry by chaining herself to the Tasman Bridge wearing nothing but a mermaid tail.'

'Excellent!'

I rolled my eyes. 'Honestly, Stewart, you really do believe anything that comes out of my mouth, don't you?'

'Oh.' He sounded disappointed. 'Ye made it up.'

'Yeah, it was last week. You missed it.'

'Bugger.' He leaned back, and regarded Mrs Peel's boots with satisfaction. 'Glue guns are most excellent devices.'

'So,' I said. 'If we were trying to solve the mystery of Julian Morris's death…'

'Which we're not.'

'Which we're not, because your blog readers aren't all that interested, and the clues don't make sense.'

'And even making the attempt would piss your boyfriend off no end…'

'He's so not my boyfriend.'

Stewart made a cough that had the word 'denial' firmly lodged in it.

'Shut up. Anyway, what would we do?'

'Pool our information, re-interview witnesses, maybe start up some kind of spreadsheet tae compile the evidence…'

'Might have known you'd be a spreadsheet geek.' I seized on the most interesting thing he'd said. 'When you say pool our information…'

'Aye?'

'Going to tell me who your sources were for the Trapper story?'

'Nope.'

'Even if I promise to swap it for a really hot lead?'

'How hot?'

'Smoking hot.'

Stewart gave me a suspicious look. 'I'll give ye one source.'

'The postal worker.'

'No. Constable Victor. I think he gave me a fake name,

though, which is why I dinnae feel I'm compromising anything to share it with ye.'

I'd already figured that. I might not know all the constables in Tasmania Police, but I knew a good eighty per cent of them, and had never heard of a Victor. 'What makes you think it was a fake name?'

'Because when they took him away in the ambulance, ye called him Gary.'

I almost dropped my shot glass. 'Gary gave you the Trapper information?' I mean, yeah, he's the biggest gossip tart in the station, but normally just for me. I felt cheated on. 'Bishop would roast him for *dinner* if he knew.'

Stewart laughed. 'No, he'd blame it all on me.'

'This is actually true.'

'So...'

'So, what?'

'Smoking hot lead, Tabitha. Ye promised me smoking and hot.'

'Oh, right. I saw Darrow today.'

Stewart spun around so fast he almost fell off the table he was standing on. 'Yer landlord.'

'My *missing* landlord. Yes.' I frowned. 'Usually when he vanishes for weeks at a time, it's because he's off somewhere exotic. He's been gone weeks, so I was expecting at least a bottle of duty free when he got back. But instead, he's driving a taxi around Hobart. A *taxi*.'

'What's odd about that?'

I waved my hand. 'Darrow has more money than God. He doesn't need to work a job like that. He's hiding.'

'From Xanthippe? Her teeth did get rather snarly when she talked about looking for him.'

I knew exactly what he meant. Zee had a snarl that could scare wild animals. Men probably found it hot. 'Maybe from Xanthippe. But he vanished long before she came sniffing around.'

'She thought he might be involved. In the Trapper business.'

'I've been saying the word "weird" a lot more than usual,' I sighed. 'Hobart isn't usually like this. Buskers in nets, and postmen in cages, and strange women holding up corner shops with compound bows.'

'So it's usually … perfectly reasonable weird with meringue porn and mermaids chained to bridges?'

'Exactly. But when something bizarre does happen, like the Penguin Appreciation riot at the Antarctic centre, or Miss Drag Queen 2007—well, usually, Darrow has something to do with it. He's like the muse of odd. He was definitely working on something big before he went away—whenever I asked him what he was tapping away at on that laptop he would act all mysterious. Said he wanted to surprise everyone. But if he's hanging around Hobart in a taxi, why hasn't he come by to pick up his rent? I owe him six weeks. Don't ask me why he can't do electronic funds transfer like a normal person…'

Stewart gave up any pretence of working on the mural, and sat cross-legged on his table. 'Let's assume Darrow is behind the Trapper thing. Theoretically.'

'Okay.' I was in no way convinced, but I could entertain the theory.

'Margarita's cat was practice. That's logical, aye?'

I agreed. 'He wanted to see if the net system worked, before setting it up in Crash Velvet's spare room. To which he probably has a key, as he does own the building…'

'Getting ahead of ourselves. Next came the postman.'

'Aha!' I sat up. 'You said postman. Not postal worker. That narrows it down.'

'Stop tha' right now. Think about how the postal *worker* fits into it.'

'Hard to do that if I don't know who he is…'

'Hush.'

'Well, you said he was based in Dynnyrne. A street or two from my place, which is so creepy I can't think straight. And Margarita lives near there, too…' A thought struck me, and I stared at Stewart. 'Hang on, a postman living in Dynnyrne? In Parliament Street?'

'Maybe,' he said cautiously.

I was squeaking now. 'Danny Masterton?'

Stewart looked at me in outrage. 'How dae ye dae that? It doesnae count as revealing my sources if ye use telepathy!'

'I used to have a thing with his brother. Plus, he's shacked up with my stepsister Amy. Or he was last time I talked to either of them.' I fished for my handbag, which was somewhere on the floor, and found my mobile phone.

'I really hate this city,' Stewart muttered.

'Accept that you will never again have any secrets, and you'll survive.' I got the recording, and left a short message for Amy to call me back. 'I think it's an inside job,' I said as I hung up.

Stewart didn't look up from where he was glueing glitter across Wonder Woman's corset top. 'A bit cold to suspect yer stepbrother, isn't it? Or is he a particularly suspicious postman?'

'Stepbrother-in-law. Without the law. And no. I think it's got something to do with Crash Velvet. I mean, I love them dearly, but they do seem a bit obsessed about self-promotion.'

'A PR stunt,' said Stewart in a tone of voice that made it clear they were also his prime suspects.

'Maybe. If the cat and the postman—Danny—were practice, then Morris in the net is the main event. And there haven't been any more traps since he was found.'

'Ye really think the band killed a stray busker to get extra hits to their YouTube channel?'

'Can't be the first time that's happened,' I scoffed, only half serious. 'I don't know. Maybe he was a junkie after all, and they found him dead and decided to make use of him...'

Stewart looked at me blankly. 'Where do ye get ideas like that? I've read about a thousand detective novels, and I dinna come up with dead junkie theories.'

I pointed my phone at him. 'Obviously you're not pulling your weight in this relationship. Do you want to come to a glam party tonight?'

The first reaction that flitted across Stewart's face was suspicion. Interesting. 'Why?'

'Because Crash Velvet is playing. Maybe we can find out something useful. Plus: party. A party is an end without a means.'

'Is this some kind of elaborate plan to get me murdered by a jealous senior constable?'

Ah. Hence the suspicion. 'Trust me, it's not his kind of party.' I was momentarily distracted by the question of what kind of party would be Bishop's kind. Possibly, it would involve lamingtons. And square dancing. I went a little cross-eyed at the image.

Stewart's voice broke my train of thought. 'If I say aye, will ye stop making that face?'

I uncrossed my eyes. 'Yes?'

'Then, aye.'

'Excellent.' I slid off the counter, and rummaged around in my bag for the spare key. 'You can have this back. I need to go stock up on berries for tomorrow. Come by my place at five.' I scribbled the address and a few vague directions on one of my Post Its, and stuck it to Stewart's table.

'Isn't five a tad early for a party?'

I blinked innocently. He was going to look so cute in glitter.

'I was planning to dress you up.'

Normally a threat like that has most straight boys sweating, but Stewart looked past me, through the window. 'Is that … a goth in a bustle?'

I went to the glass, and pressed my nose to it. 'Why, yes it is. And there's a bloke in a Red Riding Hood costume, carrying a basket of vintage boots.'

Stewart joined me at the window. 'It's an anti-fashion riot.'

Dozens of people converged on the café from all directions, some wearing costumes and others just carrying them. There was a tall woman with a silver sequined top hat and a giant plastic bag full of petticoats. There were several men in drag, and at least four women in fishnets. 'Someone set up a fancy dress flash mob, and no one told me?' I said aloud. 'Why would no one tell me?'

'They're all coming *here*,' said Stewart.

'Not quite here.' I heard the outside door opening, and people crowding into the stairwell. 'Crash Velvet.' I ran to the counter and looked properly at the flyer that kCeera had given me earlier. 'Oh, hell. The idiots offered a reward. This damn thing says they'll be taking calls on Sunday afternoon.'

'They didn't publish their address, did they?'

'This is Hobart. Plenty of people know where they live.' I gazed out at the stream of helpful Crash Velvet fans. 'Okay, there's a bloke in fairy wings, and an old age pensioner in a corset. This is officially a happening.'

'They're between me and my *cameras*,' said Stewart, running for the door.

'Use your phone,' I called after him, but that obviously wasn't good enough.

I didn't see any ruby stilettos or glow-orange fur boots out there. But hey—even if this shower didn't provide any genuine info about the stolen Wearable Art Treasures, at least the band would get some new costumes out of it.

I tugged at the cream lace hem of my vintage skirt, and checked my rosebud stockings for holes. It's a rare day when I feel underdressed to walk the streets of Hobart.

11

'Were any of them genuine?' Ceege asked later.

'Not one of them had any of the stolen gear,' I laughed. After my berry run, I had found kCeera hiding out in my kitchen with Stewart—of course he'd taken the opportunity to interview her. 'There was some sort of altercation over the ownership of a bedazzled Grateful Dead t-shirt, though. So that was fun.' Thank goodness it hadn't got bad enough to warrant calling the police—there was a special kind of sarcasm Bishop reserved especially for that sort of situation.

I hadn't seen Bishop since we were plastered across the Hobart media as the latest supercouple, and I was planning to keep it that way for as long as possible. Bad enough that Mum had already called to demand I buy her a few extra copies of the paper, and to sigh about how dreamy young Leo looked in his uniform. Luckily she lives a couple of hours away, or I might have had to accept the Sunday lunch invitation on his behalf. 'Back to the important issue. Does peach go with silver?'

Ceege gave me a sidelong look. 'You can probably get away with it.'

'I can, can't I?' I tilted a hand mirror away from my mouth, and applied an Outback Peach lip crayon. I was going to look excellent tonight, with my new comb-through silver wig, and a go-go dress to die for—assuming I could a) find the dress and b) it still fit me after my recent chocolate biscuit frenzy. It was somewhere in the piles of clothes and dry cleaning bags on the floor of my room, and I was wrapped instead in one of my many quilted dressing gowns.

Ceege stared at his own reflection in the full length mirror that we'd taken out of his wardrobe and leaned against the fridge. 'Well, you got away with it at the last glam party.'

I stared at him in horror. 'You are kidding me. Damn.' I grabbed a handful of wet wipes and scrubbed at my mouth. 'What about silver and magenta?'

'Last October.'

'Damn.' I threw the little mirror on the table. 'Do you think it's time I moved away from the silver thing? Am I getting predictable?'

Ceege shrugged. 'There's always silver and silver.'

I forgave him instantly. 'With sparkles?'

'Dude, do you have to ask?'

Someone pushed our front door open. 'Hello?' Stewart called.

Ceege lifted his eyebrows. 'Accent.'

'I *know*,' I said, giving him a girlie squeal-face. 'Back here,

Stewart.' I scrabbled through my lipstick shoebox. 'Cee-ege, I can't find my tube of sparkles.'

'The pink sparkles?'

'No, the sparkle sparkles.'

'That's the Italian shoebox,' he grunted. 'Try the French.'

I blew him an air kiss. 'Genius!'

By the time Stewart made it through the mess of our main hall to the kitchen, I was on my tippy toes, trying to lever the French shoebox down from the top of the fridge. Stewart reached over me, lifting it down easily.

'Thanks,' I said. 'This is Ceege, my housemate. He's an engineering student, but don't hold that against him.'

'All right, mate,' said Ceege. 'Beer?'

'Thanks,' said Stewart. He didn't seem freaked out that Ceege was wearing a bugled orange mini-dress, a shoulder length wig in the same shade, and make up that could only be described as Drag Queen Chic. So that meant we could keep being friends, good to know. 'Tabitha, when ye said you wanted to dress me up for this "glam" party...'

I brought the sparkles out of the shoebox in triumph, along with two canisters of spray glitter. 'Yes?'

'I have three sisters, and I've still never been more worried in me life.'

I gave him my best smile. 'Don't worry, it won't hurt a bit.'

I've always loved dressing up. I may have a shade too much boob or hip to fit perfectly into half the clothes I fall in love with (my 1920s phase was ... unsatisfying) but that just adds to the challenge. Maybe I'm getting too old for fashion play, but ... hell, life's too short to be a grown up.

Dressing up other people is even more fun than dressing myself. Stewart had given me something easy to work with, starting off with white jeans and a close-fitting black t-shirt. He fought me on swapping the t-shirt for a sequined tank top, but allowed me to use my glitter spray on the jeans. I also managed to work some pink enamel and sparkles on his sneakers while he was distracted.

I was allowed free rein over his hair, and happily broke out four kinds of gel for the occasion, giving him sparkly spikes that caught the light when he turned his head.

He let me decorate his face, too. I highlighted the planes and angles with streaks of black and silver. He gave me a suspicious look when I broke out the mascara, but allowed it.

Friendship eternal, then.

Ceege found my dress—finally—in one of the overstuffed downstairs cupboards, and zipped me into it. 'Sure you can breathe in this thing, Tabs?'

'Don't need to,' I gasped. 'Party dress.'

'You so should have laid off the Tim Tams this week.' He's so judgy. We don't all get our party frocks made to measure.

Stewart shook his head, grinning at us both. 'I warn ye,

Tabitha, if we get to this party and everyone's wearing ordinary clothes, I'll be most displeased.'

Stewart needn't have worried. When we fell out of our taxi some time later, the streets of Taroona were filled with gaudy butterfly people, all heading for the same place. It was a big, fancy house—all windows and water view and shiny black furniture. The music poured out of it like the house itself was a huge, pulsing stereo.

'Wow,' I said. 'They must have really bribed their neighbours.'

'Or drugged them,' said Ceege.

The second we stepped in the door, we were pounced on by a vampire in gold earrings and a few wisps of satin. 'Tabby, sweetie,' she hollered in my ear.

'Hi, Meryl,' I shouted back. 'How's the band tonight?'

She gave me a funny look. 'There's a band?' Then she saw Ceege. 'Oh, C.J. *darling*, look at you, all fabulous. Come and have a champagne cocktail with me, they're to die for.'

Ceege scowled at her under his day-glo makeup. 'Mez, you couldn't get one of those ponced-up wank drinks down my throat if I was tied to a bed and unconscious. Where's the beer?' He nodded briefly to Stewart and I, then elbowed his way through the crowd in search of drinks, applying a spiked heel to anyone who didn't move out of his way fast enough.

We weren't making as good progress through the glam

costumes and pressing bodies as Ceege had managed. As we squeezed through the kitchen door I caught a whiff of stale cigarette smoke and saw a familiar figure leaning up against the fridge. 'Locks?'

The drug dealer waved his fingers at me. The only concession he'd made to the dress code of the party was a sparkly gold daffodil stuck into the buttonhole of his grimy stockman's coat.

'I thought you weren't invited,' I said from the doorway.

Locks looked smug. 'I wasn't, cutes. Ask anybody.' He grabbed a handful of jaffas from a nearby bowl, and tossed them into his mouth.

The crowd surged. Stewart and I ended up several feet from the kitchen door. He grabbed my arm. 'Do ye think that Locks fellae is involved in the case?'

At least he hadn't said 'murder' or 'mystery.' Though 'case' wasn't much better. I was starting to feel like a character in a Trixie Belden novel.

'Probably,' I sighed. 'Come on, let's head upstairs. I think the band will be up there.'

I slid and wriggled through the crowd, dragging Stewart after me. I got to the staircase with minimum bruising, but Stewart caught a few stray elbows in my wake.

The upstairs floor was open plan, a huge expanse of floor and glass. It wasn't quite dark yet, and I could see the sharp grey-blue of the Derwent filling the windows along one whole side of the house.

The music was louder here—I could feel the beat through the soles of my high heels—but I couldn't see the band.

The room was full of glammed-up dancers. There was glitter and hairspray and leather corsets everywhere—like a David Bowie theme party if Bowie was going through a modern goth phase, and had possibly mated with Austin Powers. 'How are we going to get to the band?' I yelled at Stewart.

'We could dance!' he yelled back, not sounding overly enthusiastic.

'I thought you'd never ask!' I said, and threw myself at him.

Twenty minutes—or three hours or something—later, we clawed our way to one of the ocean windows and leaned against the glass, hot and sweaty and basically stuffed. 'What were we doing here again?' I gasped.

Stewart looked as dazed as I felt. 'I d'know. There was definitely a plan.'

'I vaguely recall a plan…' I leaned on his shoulder. 'I used to have party stamina. I think I'm getting old.'

'Yeah, it's all downhill once ye hit yer thirties.'

I gave him a Stare. 'I'm twenty-*six*.'

He bumped his head gently against mine. 'Lightweight. Age is no excuse. Ye aren't even trying to do this in jeans.'

I spotted something odd out of the corner of my eye. 'Stewart, did you read that Wearable Art Treasures flyer, where it listed all the missing items?'

'Sure, I blogged it this afternoon, to go with the pictures I took of all the phoneys that responded. Had to do a round up of all their tweets. This city takes its fashion very seriously.'

'Do you remember the details about the gold spiked belt?'

'Handmade by a local artist, gold leaf embedded in the handwoven fabric, gold leather spikes at a forty-five degree angle,' he said as if he had the flyer right in front of his eyes.

'That's the one,' I said. 'One of a kind. And it's over there, moshing.' I pointed, and the belt in question swung in and out of view, surrounded by corseted women.

'Hey,' said Stewart. 'The same fellae's wearing those steel-capped boots with Elizabethan spurs, too. Or something tha' looks exactly like them…'

'Get him,' I said, and lunged forward into the crowd. Stewart came after me, but I was faster because of being shorter, and having the ability to crawl between people's legs. I latched on to the knee of the Wearable Art Treasure Thief, and climbed up.

'Hello, Owen,' I said, as Stewart caught up to us.

The Crash Velvet guitarist stared at me. 'Café Babe! Love the magic blue muffins. I'm like, addicted now!'

'So, ye found yer Wearable Art Treasures then,' Stewart shouted at Owen's ear.

The guitarist looked alarmed. 'Well, you know, turns out they weren't stolen,' he said. 'They were … lost, right?'

'I expect the drummer had them in the back of his ute, and forgot about it,' I yelled above the music.

Owen brightened noticeably. 'That's, yeah! Exactly what

happened. Or something. No, wait, that wasn't the story. They were returned. In a parcel, right? All good.'

'Uh-huh. Can you spell "insurance fraud"?' Though that didn't make much sense. Unless it was an incredibly stupid attempt at insurance fraud.

'Dudes,' Owen said, shrugging. 'I've gotta get back to the band. We're about to start the second set.' He smooched a couple of the nearest corset girls, and sidled off into the crowd.

I sagged against Stewart.

'Can ye spell "red herring"?' he asked against my hair.

'I'm so depressed,' I moaned. 'No wonder Bishop is pissed off all the time if he has to deal with this sort of thing every day.' I gave Stewart a meaningful look. 'No more girl detective. I'm through. The police can solve all the mysterious deaths they want. I want to go home and make apple strudel and forget all about postmen and Trappers and Wearable Art Treasures.'

Stewart laughed, hugging me. Which I didn't mind, actually. 'Ye can forget about all that and still enjoy the party. Come now, we got all dressed up. D'ye really no' want tae dance any more?'

'Did the glitter go to your brain?' I teased. 'I think you're enjoying yourself.'

'Is that a crime? Less whining, more shaking yer thing. If yer thing wants to be shaken. It's an entirely voluntary exercise.'

Well, when he put in like that...

'Drinks first,' I said firmly. 'Sissy girlie drinks with bubbles. Then the shaking of things.'

Some time later, we finally moved close enough to get a good look at the band—not that I was feeling all that friendly towards them now. They were bloody good, I had to admit. Of course, I was plastered by that point, having downed several of what Ceege would refer to as ponced-up wank drinks mainly consisting of lemonade, vodka and pretty swirly colours.

The boys of the band were all in formal suits, and kCeera wore an ankle-length black satin gown. Their outfits were modified with the usual spiked, glittering and antique augmentations, wrapped around them like jewellery. Owen and one of the not-Owens played guitar, and the second not-Owen (the one usually asleep when I visited their rooms) was covering electronics, keyboards and drum tracks.

kCeera sang in a clear, smooth scream that dominated the whole sound:

Do you want to wear me in your skin, open up your mouth and let me in...

'Hey, Stewart,' I said, grinding against him as we danced. 'Is that a camera in your pocket, or—'

'It's a camera,' he said, his eyes on the band.

I looked at him. 'You're not just here to party, are you? That's why you wanted to stay.'

I'm the source for all your pleasure, I'm a wearable art treasure...

One woman with bright platinum blonde hair stood right up against the makeshift stage, her whole body swaying in a tiny black leather dress which showed off long legs. I glanced back at Stewart and realised he'd been watching her for a while, keeping her in line of sight, even as he danced with me.

I leaned up, and grabbed his chin to make him look at me. 'What the hell is going on?'

Kiss me quick and kiss me slow, stab me in the back and go...

A jolting sound came through the speakers as the band stopped playing. Someone screamed, but that was nothing new at this particular party. I swung around.

The platinum blonde was on the stage, brandishing a huge kitchen knife. The band members fell back in a tangled heap together, dragging their instruments with them. The automatic rhythms from the keyboard were still pulsing out through the speakers.

The woman with the knife couldn't reach the band, because people were grabbing, hauling her back. She lashed out with her feet and hands, and twisted free of their grasp, all without actually using the knife.

Stewart was taking photographs, his hands steady on the long-lens camera. I resisted the urge to kick him. Instead, I wormed my way through the crowd towards the woman with the knife—or at least, to a position between the woman and the door at the far end of the room.

Sure enough, when she started running for the exit, I was smack bang in her way. She shoved me aside and kept going through the door, leaving nothing behind her but a trailing fragrance of limes and coconut.

Stewart reached me a few minutes later, looking angry and worried. 'What was that?'

'Did you know?' I yelled at him. 'Did you know that was going to happen?'

He didn't answer straight away. 'I knew something was going tae happen.'

'Because she told you.' I had guessed even before I saw her face under the platinum blonde wig. Legs like those don't come along every day. Xanthippe fucking Carides.

'Aye.'

'Damn it.' I shook his hand off, and stood up on my own. The band announced that they would play on through the party, and the whole crowd started cheering and yelling. 'I need a drink.'

'Tabitha…'

I glared at him. 'Go away. I'm going to find Ceege and my actual friends.'

I found Ceege with some mates of ours, and the kitchen, and the tequila, not necessarily in that order. A few hours after that, I stumbled out of the party in order to preserve my dignity and/ or life. Never try to outdrink a bunch of engineering students.

Stewart was lying on the grass in the front garden.

'What are you up to now?' I demanded.

'Waiting for ye.'

'Hmph.' I sat down on the grass next to him, and called a taxi on my mobile. 'I'm not feeling the trust right now, Stewart.'

'I should have told ye. I wasnae thinking. She told me nothing, just to be prepared with the camera. I sure as hell didnae know there would be a knife involved. Is Xanthippe totally insane?'

'Unfortunately not,' I sighed. 'She'd be less of a danger to society if she were.'

'It was a publicity stunt.'

'Oh, you've figured that one out?'

'It's no' difficult. Xanthippe's been hanging around the building for days—says it's tae find yer precious landlord, but that doesnae hae tae be the only reason. We know the band have some new PR manager encouraging them tae dae daft things tae get media attention—hell, I've been blogging most o' them.'

'Feeling used?' I asked.

'Just a tad.'

'Will you post the story anyway?'

'Fuck aye. Knife-wielding woman attacks band? How can I no'? Tempted to run it with a "band stages dodgy publicity stunt" headline, though.'

'Wouldn't blame you if you did.' I yawned. The grass was snuggly. 'We'll think about it tomorrow.'

'Still angry at me?'

'No, I'm over it.' I rolled over on one elbow to look at him. The gel spikes had softened in the heat and sweat of the party, and there wasn't much makeup left on him, though his skin still glittered. 'Your lipstick's smudged,' I told him. *Very strong hands. Deep grey eyes.*

Stewart grimaced and put a hand up to his face, stroking glitter on to his fingertips. 'Imagine tha'.'

Oh, and sexy accent, I added sleepily to my list of Stewart's good qualities. *Even when sarcastic.* 'Want me to remove it?'

'Given that the only preferable option is for ye not tae have put it on in the first place...'

I looked speculatively at him for a moment, then leaned in to remove the last of his lipstick by my favourite method.

For the first split second, Stewart's mouth tasted of surprise, and then he relaxed and kissed me back, warm and soft. I sighed happily, and let my face drift down to his neck.

'Tabitha, how drunk are ye?'

'Very,' I murmured, burrowing close. *Mm. Sleep.* He wasn't overly comfortable, and his shoulders were kind of bony, but it would do.

'Taxi's here.'

'Hmm?'

But Stewart was up on his feet, and holding my hand, and somehow we made it to the taxi without me losing consciousness again. 'How's the lipstick?' I asked him as he put my seatbelt on.

'Cured,' he said with a wicked grin, and I heard him giving the taxi driver my address as he slid into the back seat beside me.

12

I woke up very slowly, unwrapping myself from a nest of doonas, sheets and novelty cushions. The blinding sunlight through the upper windows illuminated a room full of clothes, clothes and more clothes, draped over every available surface. Well, that was something. After a night on the tequila and fizzy lemonade, it's a good thing to wake up in one's own bed.

There was something I was forgetting.

My sheets were full of glitter. I moaned and pulled a few limbs out to peer at them. Obviously I hadn't been in good enough shape to shower before bed. Damn it. I tried to remember getting to bed, and couldn't. Last thing I remembered was the taxi, and getting in the taxi, shortly after I…

Kissed Stewart. Huh.

Speculatively, I slid one arm across the length of the bed, just to check whether I had company. A shape twitched under the doona, and my fuzzy black cat licked my hand. I relaxed. 'We seem to be alone, Kinky Boots.'

Kinky Boots crawled out and stared at me, unimpressed. Then he *mrrowed* at me. A breakfast *mrrow*.

'Keep your whiskers on, puss puss.' I rolled out of bed and peeled the silver party dress off my body. It had left tight creases in my skin, and my waist was all squinched. I draped on an oversized green kimono, the best thing I ever stole from my mum's wardrobe. The fabric was cool and light against my skin, and it felt as calming as green tea, or scones and cream.

If only I could get my eyes all the way open.

I remembered kissing Stewart on the grass outside the party—also, I remembered pashing him again in the taxi, and snuggling up as close to him as the seat belt would allow. I hadn't been blacking out drunk. Did that mean I had fallen asleep before we reached my front door? 'Shit,' I said aloud, combing my fingers through my hair and discovering that the damn silver wig was still partly attached. I didn't have the brain power to remove it yet. It would have to wait until tea and breakfast, and more breakfast. And more tea.

In the kitchen, Ceege looked about how I felt, only he had showered and found some actual clothes (back in jeans and t-shirt, his secret identity).

I eased myself in and sat at the kitchen table very, very gingerly. 'Make me a cup of tea,' I moaned, 'and I'll love you forever.'

'Tell you what, Tabs,' said Ceege as he switched on the electric jug. 'Are you sure you're a size ten? Cause you're bloody heavy.'

'Ten-ish,' I replied, which was almost completely true except when it wasn't. 'It was you who put me to bed last night?' I tilted my head at the fridge, where the big mirror was still resting from our dress up session the night before. 'Of course. Who else would think to remove my eye makeup first?'

'Too right,' said Ceege, lifting the lid of the washing machine and glaring at it, as if challenging it to work better. 'Though your man Stewart did most of the carrying. I was more in the directorial, project management line of things.' He smirked. 'Came home at three and found you two crashed out on the couch. Cosy.'

It was far too early in the morning for me to deal with this. 'I need breakfast.'

'You know where the corn flakes are.'

I made little mewling noises. Pathetic, but I was hungry. 'Waffles?'

'You're a professional cook. You run a freaking café. Why should I make you waffles?'

Shit, the café. 'Nin is going to kill me.'

'You're only about four hours late.'

'I wasn't stupid enough to go to a party last night without rostering Lara *and* Yui on for this morning,' I said defensively. No, it wasn't that. Nin was going to kill me when I told her my new plan to find Darrow.

After the mess with Xanthippe the night before, I couldn't put it off any longer. Darrow wasn't just my landlord, he owned sixty percent of my business. If he was involved with something dodgy, I needed to know. 'If I have a ten minute shower, and I give you unlimited access to my lipsticks this week, will you *please* have waffles on the table when I come out?'

'Take fifteen minutes,' he grunted. 'You look bloody shocking.'

I blew him a kiss as I staggered for the bathroom. 'Love you, Ceege.'

'I wouldn't have you—you're as hard on your blokes as you are on your frocks.'

It was after eleven by the time I had sorted things out with Nin, paid off Lara and Yui, and closed the café for the rest of the day. I left Nin furiously scrubbing the kitchen floor. She only does that when she's really narked at me. I think she pretends it's my face.

I then fled to my favourite hiding spot, the sloping well of trees and greenery that is St David's Park. It's the best park in the city, a huge expanse of grass at the older end of town, surrounded by crumbling stonework. If you go down deep enough into the park, you can almost forget that there are things like cars and traffic lights in the world.

I lay on the grass (trying not to think of a similar patch of grass the night before) and started plotting my campaign against Darrow and Xanthippe.

All right, and I had a snooze. Just a little one. I was woken by a Scottish accent, and the smell of coffee. *My* coffee. Well, Nin's coffee.

'Good morning,' said Stewart.

I cracked an eye open. 'S'practically afternoon.'

'Aye, well I thought it wouldnae be overly polite tae mention that.'

I stuck out my hand. 'Give.'

He passed me one of the Café La Femme takeaway cups, and kept the other for himself.

Sitting up, I blew on my coffee and tasted it. *Mm, latté good, coffee yum.* 'How did you get this, with the café closed?'

'Promised Nin it would annoy ye. And about that—why is the café closed, exactly? I thought her eyebrows were going to explode off her head when I asked, so I didn't push it.'

'And she told you exactly where you'd be able to find me?'

Stewart shrugged. 'She said ye usually come to this park when sulking...'

'I am not sulking.'

'...or hungover.'

'Ah.' I took another long suck of coffee. 'Listen, Stewart, about the kissing thing.'

'Oh, aye,' he said. 'I've been thinking about that.'

'You have?' I squeaked, trying not to sound paranoid. It was important to be very cool about random snogging, just in case the other person a) read too much into it or b) didn't read enough into it. To give you some idea of my state of mind at the time, I had no *idea* which I wanted from Stewart. So that was helpful.

'Mmhmm. Now, Tabitha, when ye were kissing me … were ye imagining Bishop in or out of his uniform? I cannae decide which one's kinkier.'

I stared at him, not sure whether to be relieved or insulted. Then I smacked him. 'I was not thinking about Bishop.'

The horrible truth was that I wasn't. Not at the time, not one bit. But maybe it was better Stewart thought so. Less complicated.

Stewart took a long swallow of his coffee. It looked even stronger than the stuff I make for him. 'Why don't ye throw yerself into his arms and say, take me, ye big manly policeman?'

'It's complicated,' I muttered. 'And that is so wrong, by the way, on many levels.'

'Ye know what I mean. Why no' jump him and get on with it?'

'A lot of reasons.' I couldn't believe I was having this conversation with Stewart, of all people. Especially the morning after I had kissed him. Well. Really, drunken snogging hardly counted at all, right? Apparently not to him. Should I be this irritated that he was dismissing our smoochage as if it was nothing? Possibly I was a crazy person.

'Like?' he said, waving for me to expand on that.

'He still treats me like he's the grown up and I'm the teenager. I was friends with his little sister before I even met him, and he's never reclassified me. He doesn't even think of me as being … adult and beddable.'

'Apart from the snogging.'

'That's a recent development.' I eyed him. 'How do you even know about that?'

'I photographed it.'

'That's sick—oh, wait.' I realised he was talking about the kiss after the siege, and hadn't been spying on us in stairwells. 'Well, okay, then. Then there's the fact that my parents adore him, and have been dropping hints about us getting together since I was seventeen.'

'Parental approval! Doomed.'

I rolled my eyes. I wasn't used to having to vocalise why Bishop and I would be a bad idea—all my other friends took it for granted. 'He doesn't fit the pattern, okay?'

'There's a pattern?'

'It's mine, and I'm very attached to it.'

'G'on, then.' I still couldn't tell if Stewart was making fun of me, and if his eyes should be quite that warm if we were just friends and the kiss had just been a kiss? 'What's yer pattern?'

I slugged down the last of my latté, not wanting to tell him. 'Unreliable men with foreign accents who dump me for other women and whose mothers take pity on me and expand my culinary repertoire,' I mumbled.

Stewart blinked. 'How many times has this particular pattern repeated itself?'

'Eight.'

'Nae wonder yer sae good with pasta.'

I nodded sheepishly. Then a thought occurred to me. 'Hey, what's your mum like in the kitchen?'

Stewart waved a finger at me, sternly. 'No. Bad Tabitha.'

'I've always wanted to learn about bannock and cock-a-leekie soup...'

'No!'

'Sorry.'

Stewart tried not to smile, but I saw it sneaking out the side of his coffee cup. 'So. Why is the café closed?'

I snorted. 'Don't worry, it's not a post-traumatic reaction to kissing you. It's part of the plan.'

'What plan?'

'The plan to drag Darrow out of the woodwork, and find out if me and my business are implicated in whatever dodgy scheme he's up to his neck in, with or without Xanthippe.'

'Oh. Is it a good plan?'

'I hope so. If it doesn't work soon, Nin's going to bake me in a pie crust.'

Stewart said nothing, meaningfully.

It occurred to me that he was expecting me to tell him my plan. 'So,' I said brightly. 'What are you doing for the rest of the day? Need more of my people to blog about?'

'I'm good, ta. Found some people of me own. But if the café is closed, do ye mind if I work on the mural?'

'Not going to stop you.' I stood up, and brushed grass from my skirt. 'I have an expedition tomorrow. You can come along if you like—might be *Sandstone City* compatible.'

'Works for me.' Stewart drank the last of his coffee, and looked bereaved about it.

'You're not really interested in painting my walls,' I teased. 'You just don't want to be parted from my coffee machine.'

'It is the one true love of me life,' he admitted, and held my gaze for a little longer than he had to. Hmm.

So, breaking and entering. Not exactly my area of expertise. But everyone has to start somewhere.

I already regretted having closed the café. Apart from anything else, my staff insisted on being paid for all their regular shifts, because of the short notice. Still, if Darrow was driving around Hobart in that taxi of his, he was sure to spot that the café was closed.

If there's one thing Darrow hates, it's not being in the loop.

I hadn't bought much time. I couldn't afford to keep the café closed for more than a day or two—plus Nin would actually murder me if I carried it on longer than that, using sharp knives instead of eyebrows. I had to find out what was going on, fast. That meant a visit to Darrow's place.

I'd assumed he wasn't there—he hadn't answered the phone or returned a message for six weeks. Either he'd been deliberately avoiding all contact and was actually still at home, or the place would be empty and thus potentially full of clues about his absence.

Which brings us back to breaking and entering.

The way Darrow looks and dresses, not to mention the way he throws his cash around, most people expect him to live in a shiny bachelor pad apartment, maybe with a view of the river.

But he has this fetish about Tasmanian heritage buildings, and his home is one of the collection. It's a tiny, old-fashioned stone cottage that belonged to the mistress of one of the colony's governors, a couple of hundred years ago. The street is so narrow that it can only fit one line of parked Saabs and Land Rovers, and the gardens are all of the tiny, overgrown 'this plum tree has been here since 1808, and these roses have a better lineage than you' variety.

I stood in Darrow's garden, wondering how old the glass in the windows was, and whether it would be a moral and aesthetic crime (as well as, you know, a criminal one) to break it.

It was really, really important that I figured out what Darrow was up to, and whether it was going to endanger my business. But I wasn't sure if I was willing to risk arrest to find out. Particularly not if the arresting officer was someone I knew, and the odds of that were hardly in my favour.

I stood back, and circled the cottage. Along the side, one of the windows was slightly open. Entering without breaking. Much better. I slid my arm into the gap, trying to lever the window up with my shoulder. *Ow. Bruised something.* I pulled my arm back out, and shook it until it stopped feeling numb.

I needed to get into shape. Zee wouldn't have trouble with a titchy little window like this, not with her sleek arm muscles and great self confidence. She'd just give it a little shove, and…

The window flew open, and I screamed. Strong arms hauled the pane of glass upward, and a head appeared. 'Can I help you with something?' asked Xanthippe.

Crap.

13

So yeah, there is a possibility that Xanthippe is not entirely perfect and cool at all times. I mean, she's human. Has to be. I've seen her in mismatched underwear in the school change rooms. I not only witnessed her failed experiment at mixing vodka with Bailey's and half a kilo of blueberries, but I lost a favourite pair of jeans to the hideous aftermath. I was there when she cried for twenty minutes about some boy who shall remain nameless, then pulled herself together and glared at me and said 'We never speak of this again.'

Still, she's such a stylish robot from the future these days that any reminder she is a real person is gratefully received.

I shouldn't have been so delighted that when she caught me trying to break into Darrow's house, she was wearing nothing but a Spider-Man t-shirt, grey knickers and a hair towel. But I was. Gleeful.

Xanthippe placed a cup of tea in front of me.

'Yes, all right, I was trying to break in,' I said crossly. There was no point in lying about it. She didn't have any more right to be here than I did.

Unless … she and Darrow hadn't hooked up again, had they? I lifted the cup to my lips, and tried to think of a tactful way of asking if Xanthippe was boning her ex.

'I've moved in, by the way,' she said, and I almost snarfed the tea.

'Excuse me?'

'Nice place, this. Darrow has taste—for an unreliable son of a bitch who deserves to die horribly.' She gestured around at the sleek kitchen. The outside of the cottage might be all heritagey and historical, but he had spared no expense on modernising the interior. I suspected that the gleaming stainless steel kitchen had never even had a cup of tea made in it before.

'So, why?' I asked, keeping it simple.

Xanthippe gave me one of those 'you are so very stupid' expressions that she specialised in, back in school. 'I was looking for clues. Obviously. And then I got comfy. I needed somewhere to crash while I was around. If anyone owes me crash space, it's Darrow. Well, no. What he owes me is money, and serious grovelling. But I'll take what I can get.'

'How much money?' I couldn't resist asking.

Her face closed over. 'None of your business. Why have you shut the café?'

'None of your business.'

Xanthippe laughed. 'I suppose I deserved that.'

'So … no clues about where Darrow might be?'

'No,' she said. I figured she was probably waiting for me to ask about Crash Velvet, and what the hell she had been doing the night before, with the knife and the drama, and…

'I'd better be going,' I said, with a genuine smile. I so love to mess with her expectations.

'Of course. Party shopping.' I raised my eyebrows at her. 'Oscars day,' she added.

Damn. I'd forgotten. Ceege would never let me live it down if I didn't provide him with an Oscars watching soirée. No wonder the sneaky bugger had made me waffles that morning—keeping me sweet. 'You know me,' I said lightly. 'You can come, if you like.'

'Not really my scene.'

Fine, be like that. I'd been trying to figure out whether we were still friends or not, and I guess that was my answer. 'I thought you *liked* dressing up.'

'Are you going to ask me, or what?' she said impatiently. 'About the party last night.'

Heh. For once in my life, I had outcooled Xanthippe Carides. Winnah and champion. 'Were you at the party last night? There were so many people…'

She smirked a bit. 'Okay, then. Leaving by the door or the window?'

'It's a nice window, shame to waste it.'

'Uh-huh.' She took my teacup, and rinsed it in the sink. 'I like your new sidekick. Figured out all his secrets yet?'

'Who says he has any secrets from me?'

Xanthippe looked amused. 'I bet you haven't even googled him. You're so twentieth century, Tish.' There was the old teenage nickname again, a reminder of how long we'd known each other.

'I have email,' I said, a little wounded. 'I have *broadband*.'

'Yes, how are Ceege and his gay shamans going?'

'They're metrosexual, actually.' I was tired of this conversation. I went back to Darrow's shiny white sitting room, and slid one leg over the window sill. 'If you find Darrow, once you've finished breaking his ribs or making him beg for forgiveness, can you tell him I'd like a word about the café?'

'I'll try to remember,' she said.

I bruised my tailbone climbing out of the damn window, and as I walked away I spent at least five minutes thinking of nothing but how much I hated Darrow and Xanthippe and the stupid pretty house.

Before I got to my car, though, I flipped open my mobile phone and called the café. Stewart picked up on the first ring. 'Café La Femme, it's no' me fault it's closed…'

'It's me,' I said. 'Do you have a tuxedo?'

He sounded a little alarmed. 'Right this minute?'

'No, for tonight. It's an *emergency*.'

'Tabitha, most people don't have tuxedo emergencies. Not getting married, are ye?'

'I need you at our place tonight. Dress *pretty*.' I heard a sound in the background. 'Stewart, do you have a woman there?'

'Yes,' he said. 'I am using your café as a love shack. It's proved remarkably successful.'

'Sponge down the furniture afterwards. Also, bring tequila.'

'Tonight?'

'By seven. Or I cut off your coffee supply.'

'Cruel woman.'

'You love it.'

Ceege rolled home from lectures that afternoon to find the house transformed in a mass of streamers and balloons, with the scent of *hors d'oeuvres* billowing out of my oven. 'You remembered,' he said with delight.

I tried not to look guilty about the near miss. 'Of course. Idiot.' I sat at his computer in a blue ballgown, my hair skewered high in defiance of the laws of both gravity and hairspray. I was also wearing a long strand of fake pearls, and shiny diamante stilettos.

'I'll get dressed,' Ceege said, grabbing a handful of caviar blinis from the buffet table. 'You stay off the internet. I don't want to hear you've already caught up on Oscar spoilers from the live broadcast.'

The downside of celebrating international events of glamour and glory is that they happen at the wrong time of day for us—the Oscars screen live in our afternoon, but we wait until the evening to party because some of us have real jobs.

'I'm doing something else, promise.' Actually, I was busy checking my sources on Stewart McTavish's secret internet life.

I'd come across the Diana Glass story the first time I googled him. There was even a Wikipedia article devoted to Stewart's original article—'Why Romance Novels are Bad for the Soul' in *Vogue*, no less, three pages of snark which served mainly to tear strips off the works of a certain Melbourne romance writer. Some fangirl had scanned and posted the original article, which I had to admit was as funny as hell. I had also read acres of forum comments about the unfairness of the article, mainly from pissed off romance writers, both published and unpublished. Wikipedia linked to a follow up story about an electronic slapfight between Stewart and Diana Glass on Amazon.

In between stuffing mushrooms, blowing up balloons and making myself look fabulous, I had followed up the last few links this afternoon. Twentieth century girl? I'm new Millennium all the way, baby.

It sounded like the Romance Writers Guild had all but declared war on our McTavish, decrying him wildly in as many pixels as they could muster. Still, the deeper I got into the forums, the more comments I found that suggested that Stewart and Diana had known each other while he was living in Melbourne.

It didn't entirely fit together. There was a mystery here, and apparently that was my thing these days.

Finally, in an obscure little lit gossip blog that never quoted anyone's names, I found the final piece of the puzzle. A blurry snapshot suggested that Diana Glass and Stewart McTavish had once—before a certain *Vogue* article—been a serious item.

I could see why Bishop had jumped to the conclusion that Stewart was an outrageously bad ex-boyfriend. But in light of the last few days, I was thinking in an entirely different direction.

And what I was thinking was: publicity stunt.

'Are those stuffed mushrooms?' Ceege whooped from the kitchen.

'Hands off! They're not even grilled yet.'

It was nearly time for the Red Carpet special, and that meant our guests would be arriving any moment. Also, it was time to grill the mushrooms, assuming Ceege hadn't eaten them all raw. Before I finished up on the computer, I clicked on the *Sandstone City* bookmark.

random_scotsman's latest blog entry was at the top of the page—and I made a little *meep* of surprise.

Julian Morris filled the screen.

Hardly surprising I hadn't recognised him dead, as he'd done some growing up since I saw him last. He smouldered lopsidedly out of the picture, one arm looped around the neck of a woman I recognised as Claudina the flatmate. His dark, curly hair tumbled around his shoulders.

Hell, if I'd known he was going to turn out like that, I might not have dumped him so quickly back at college.

Ew, Tabitha. Try to restrain yourself from perving on dead people.

IS THIS THE FACE OF A DRUG ADDICT? screamed the article header.

Julian Morris (26) was found dead under mysterious circumstances in a Central Hobart apartment last Thursday. Police have indicated that the death may have been an accidental overdose, but Morris's family and friends claim differently.

'It's bullshit,' was the candid response of Morris's sister Angela, speaking exclusively to Sandstone City. 'All the police's questions suggest they think he was some kind of junkie, but he never used drugs.'

'I shared a flat with him for two years, and never even saw him smoke pot,' claimed Morris's flatmate and close friend, Claudina Wells. 'He was diabetic and super health-conscious. He never injected anything but insulin.'

These women have embarked upon a public awareness campaign, along with many of Morris's friends, family members and ex-girlfriends, to spread their belief that Morris is being misrepresented by Tasmania Police. The campaign involves posters, distributed around local businesses in Hobart, and an electronic petition addressed to the Chief Superintendent. The Twitter hashtag #cleanmorris has been trending in Australia for the past forty-eight hours, and is gaining international support.

To sign the petition, click here.

To read a scan of the flyer, click here.
Tweet this story #sandstonecity #cleanmorris
Comment!

'Bishop's going to kill me,' I moaned.

What the hell was Stewart thinking? The police were going to be furious about this. I scrolled down to the bottom of the article, and found a group of gorgeous red-haired women, holding armfuls of Clean Morris posters and flyers, and looking pleased with themselves.

Never mind Bishop killing me. I was going to kill Stewart. Not only had he gathered this gang of harpies together to push their agenda, he'd done it in my bloody café. Love shack, my satin-sheathed arse.

'Zip assistance, please!' Ceege demanded from the kitchen. I came out to find him smashing ice for margaritas, dressed in a devastatingly accurate copy of an ill-fitting pink Ralph Lauren ballgown that Gwyneth Paltrow wore to the Oscars a million years ago. He'd matched it with a scary straight blonde wig, and gel tears studded down his cheeks.

'That's hideous,' I said. 'Well done.'

He looked proud, and smashed more ice. 'I know it's a period piece.'

'That's what makes it awesome. Frocking it old skool.' I lifted two cocktail glasses out of the freezer. 'Make mine pink.'

'Don't I always?'

The doorbell rang, and I trip-trapped down the hallway to answer it.

Stewart stood on my doorstep with a bottle of tequila. I stared at him. There's something about black tie on a halfway decent looking man that … wow. More to the point, it was raining outside and his hair was forming damp ringlets around his neck. I was a little dizzy for a moment. When I felt safe to speak, I said, 'I was mostly kidding about the tuxedo.'

'I guessed,' he said. 'But I had this lying around…'

'Uh-huh.' I wasn't going to ask. I really wasn't. But it didn't look like a secondhand treasure, or a squeaky-clean rental. The boy had depths. Then I remembered some of his depths, and hit him quite hard on the shoulder. 'I'm not talking to you.'

'Ow!'

'If you intend to keep quiet about your nefarious activities in my café, you might want to *not blog about them*.'

'Oh, that,' he said sheepishly. 'I did work on the mural today. As well.'

'And interviewed a gang of redheads, and photographed them in my café. Bishop's going to blame me for this. He already suspects me of messing with the investigation.'

'I didnae think of that,' Stewart said, looking alarmed. 'There was more room there than in our office, and the light was perfect for the picture … sorry, Tabitha.'

I scowled at him. 'I want you to know, I'm only letting you into this party at all because you look hot.'

158

'Okay,' he said, somewhere between baffled and afraid. 'Good to know.'

I snatched the bottle from under his arm, and headed back in. 'Tequila's here, Ceege!'

'Excellent!' he yelled from the kitchen. 'Almost killed this bottle.'

'The insulin thing isn't news to Bishop, by the way,' Stewart said in a low voice. 'Claudina told the police Morris was diabetic when she and Ange first identified the body. They have all the information we do—more, probably.'

'Mm,' I said. 'You know, the police only told the papers that Julian Morris died of a suspected overdose. They didn't say what it was an overdose *of*. They didn't officially call him a junkie, either, whatever his precious flatmate screeches about.' Gary had called him that, but not exactly on the record, and he wasn't as involved in the case as Bishop was.'

Stewart looked interested. 'Ye think it was an insulin overdose?'

'I think a lot of things. Some of them are possibilities.' I had a wow of a thought. 'Ceege, is it too late to invite Quinn over for tonight?' I knew a few people in police forensics, but only one who would react positively to a party like this.

Ceege handed me a bright pink frosty drink, and Stewart a blue one. 'Cool suit, mate. Very swish. You kidding, babe? A chance to frock up and eat his weight in Tabitha snacks? He'll be here in a shot.'

Stewart gave me a curious look, but I didn't explain. He could wonder just a bit longer.

It was my favourite Oscars party ever. Lara and Yui turned up in outfits they'd made themselves, all green netting and black leather. Ceege's girlfriend Katie surprised him by wearing an actual vintage frock she had bought cheap on eBay. She normally lives in Sportsgirl, so he was delighted she had made the effort. Nin took over the kitchen the minute she arrived, leaving me free to provide snarky commentary on the Red Carpet frocks. Quinn, one of our ex-housemate Kelly's brother's ex-boyfriends, let the side down slightly by arriving in ordinary jeans and a t-shirt, but made up for it with chandelier earrings, scarlet nail polish, and being almost as much of a bitch as I was when it came to slagging off celebrities.

Nin brought in a tray of my famous anchovy puffs, and smiled at Stewart. She smiled at him again when he refilled her champagne glass.

I dragged him aside at the earliest opportunity. 'What's going on? Nin never smiles at anyone.'

'We bonded over our mutual appreciation for her coffee machine.'

I patted him on the arm. 'Make sure you invite me to the wedding.'

Huh. The two things I could usually count on about introducing new male friends to my life was that Bishop would hate them, and Nin would think they were useless. She tolerates Ceege because they're the same shoe size and he doesn't mind sharing.

A good thing that Bishop didn't like Stewart too, or my world would be officially upside down.

'Oh, come on,' Quinn was yelling at the screen. 'What's with the tasteful black frocks?'

'It's practically cheating,' I agreed, squeezing up next to him on the couch. 'And was there a "no bras" policy this year? Magic tape is not a good alternative to cleavage, ladies.'

Ceege and Katie were arguing in the corner about Angelina Jolie, and whose lips she was wearing. Ceege won by putting a piece of ice down Katie's back, and she hit him with a cushion.

Twice, I fended off my cat, who had developed an obsession with Stewart. 'Back, Kinky Boots, don't you dare get hair on that pretty suit,' I scolded.

Stewart laughed. 'Some people shouldnae be allowed to name pets. I hope yer not planning on children.'

'So,' I said, putting my head on Quinn's shoulder as the scuffles broke out around us. 'How's training going? Solved any crimes from stray hairs and fingerprints yet?' I met Stewart's eyes as he dropped into a chair beside us. 'Quinn's in police forensics.'

'Really?' said Stewart. His mouth twitched a little, as if he was trying not to grin. 'Must be interesting.'

'They don't let me do much yet,' Quinn said. 'I've only just started. It's great, though. I'm learning heaps.'

'So you don't actually—do stuff with bodies yet,' I said, shuddering a bit at the thought. 'Like that man the other day, the junkie hanging in the net.'

Quinn chuckled. 'They don't let me near the autopsies. I'm lucky if they let me observe. But I know the case you mean. Strange bloke.'

'Strange how?' I couldn't help asking. This wasn't messing with a police investigation, honestly. It was chit chat.

'Okay, my supervisor Meg spent ages on his hands, right? He had short nails, pretty good condition—that makes sense, because he played violin. But his fingers were all messed up, scratched and stuff, like he'd been doing manual labour. Carpentry. Ropes.'

'Building the net they found him in?' I couldn't help wondering aloud.

'Maybe,' said Quinn. 'But then there was the nail polish. Not on his nails, right, but on his fingers. Like he painted someone's fingernails, doing a pretty lousy job of it, and then went off to build something.' He shrugged. 'Glad I'm not the detective who's got to make sense of it. Hey—check out that jacket on Clooney, what do we think, is he trying too hard or what?'

We all stared at the screen for a long time. You just don't see Hollywood's ruggedest in purple velvet every day. 'Do you think it was a bet?' I said finally.

'How do ye know it was actually nail polish?' Stewart asked a little while later. 'Could it have been paint or something else?'

Everyone in the room—well, all the girls, and Ceege—looked at him as if he was unhinged.

Stewart blinked. 'I'm the only one in the room who knows nothing about nail polish, then.'

'Actually, you've got a point,' said Quinn securing a handful of miniature chocolate croissants from the plate in front of him. 'Meg thought it was paint too. But I recognised the line. It was *Poison Flesh*.'

'Oh, the new matte range from Gee Bee, with glitter?' Ceege jumped in. 'Sweet.'

'Yeah, mate—the purple with little bronzey flecks. I mean, the stuff's shit—if you take the gloss out of nail polish, it just scratches to buggery, you have to keep repairing it every few hours.' Quinn looked proud of himself. 'So I told Meg what it was, and she was really impressed. Said she'd never have known it was nail polish, if I hadn't been around.'

'Doesn't hurt to impress the boss,' I said lightly. 'More drinks, anyone?'

Stewart joined me in the kitchen, and I handed him the rolling pin to smash some more ice. 'Matte nail polish?' I complained. 'If that's the kind of clue they're having to deal with, I don't envy the police.'

'Not that yer interfering with a police investigation at all,' he said.

'Well, no. I've got enough problems trying to find Darrow.' I frowned at him. 'Had any more cosy chats with Xanthippe lately? I noticed you didn't blog about the glam party, or the stunt with the knife.'

'Got distracted by all the redheads.'

'I can see how that happens.'

'Plus...' Stewart hesitated. 'It felt like putting the boot in. Exposing them.'

'Some reporter you're going to make, with ethics getting in the way. Unless the problem is that you're sympathetic to what they were trying to do?'

He seemed unbothered by the concept. 'Nothing wrong with trying to generate a bit of publicity.'

'Mm. Like you did for Diana Glass?'

Stewart looked startled. 'What are ye on about? Have ye been stalking me on the internet?'

'Obviously. But at least I wasn't trashing some poor debut writer about her books being shallow and pointless! Some of my best friends are romance novelists, you know.'

Stewart narrowed his eyes. 'Mine too.'

'Hah!' I pointed a swizzle stick at him. 'I knew it was a set up. That article and all the follow up stuff—it was just to promote her books, wasn't it? You played the villain, and let her be all innocent and under attack so everyone would rally around her and *spread the word about her books*.'

'Maybe I honestly thought she was crap.'

'You're too much of a gentleman, it's a dead giveaway.' I fetched the tequila and lemonade out of the fridge. 'What I don't understand is why you used your real name for it. I mean—Bishop took one look at your internet presence and decided you were some kind of troll.'

Stewart took the bottles from me, and started assembling the drinks. 'Bishop would think tha' about any man who spent any time with ye.'

I filed that away to think about later, though I was pretty sure I knew Bishop's reasons for snogging me, and it had nothing to do with fancying me. 'Real trolls at least manage to stay anonymous. That's the point of them.' I shook my head. 'She must be special, this romance novelist of yours. For you to be willing to make yourself look like an internet nutcase, just to help her career.'

'I dinnae want tae talk about this,' Stewart warned.

'Tab-beee!' Ceege hollered from the living room. 'Cher's dressed like a grown up, and Miss Piggy turned up in the best frock yet! I'm losing the will to live!'

'I'll bring you some marshmallows to throw at the screen!' I yelled back, and left Stewart to finish making the drinks.

14

Bright and early the next morning, I knocked on Stewart's front door. He lived in a seedy little flat over a shop in Liverpool Street, only a block or two from the café. Ten out of ten for convenient location, but the stairwell was a scary concrete bunker with a very suspicious smell to it. After the longest time, I heard a few shambling footsteps, and jumped back as a bleary-eyed Stewart answered the door. 'Tabitha?'

'Gadzooks, you're a horrible sight first thing in the morning,' I said cheerfully. A total lie—his face and hair might have given a half-dead scarecrow a run for its money, but he'd pulled on a pair of jeans and nothing else on his way to the front door, which more than made up for it.

Stewart peered at me. 'Did ye say, "gadzooks"?'

It's important at times like this to speak the right language. I wafted a fresh cup of coffee at him. 'Rise and shine, princess.'

He grunted, took the cup from me and disappeared into the bedroom. A few minutes later, he yelled from within. 'Tabitha, it's no' even 7AM!'

'Expedition, remember? I'm sure I told you we had to set off early.' Was that between the second or third tequila cocktail?

'Early is … ten. Possibly eleven,' he said. 'Is this café withdrawal? Ye secretly want to be scrubbing floors and toasting sourdough right now, an' I'm the man who has to suffer along with ye.'

'Wimp! Just because you're a blogger doesn't mean it's okay to spend half the day in your pyjamas. It will be worth your while, I promise.'

'I need a shower almost as much as I need this coffee.'

'Be quick.'

While the water ran in the little bathroom, I wandered around Stewart's flat, poking around his stuff. Not much stuff, to be honest—it was mostly cameras, and many boxes. I had to move several of them to sit down on the couch.

Mind you, who am I to criticise someone else's mess?

Eventually, Stewart came back out to the living room with damp hair, buttoning up a half-decent shirt over the same jeans and marginally clean socks. He threw the crumpled paper coffee cup in the direction of his kitchenette. 'Going tae need more of those.'

'Not a problem,' I said, not looking up from a portfolio of photographs I had found on top of one of the boxes. 'Are these pictures all yours?'

'Uh huh. I put it together when I was applying to *Sandstone City*, but it turned out Simon really hates romance novels.

Something tae do with his ex, don't ask. The *Vogue* article and all that fallout meant he'd already decided tae give me the job. All I had tae do was turn up for the interview.' He gave me a mock-stern look. 'And tha's not why I did it, incidentally. I lucked out, that's all. Right place and right internet scuffle at the right time.'

'This one's pretty,' I said, looking at a gorgeous, cheeky young woman with brown fluffy curls hanging in her eyes, hugging a terrier who looked disturbingly like her.

'My sister Sophie. Too dog-obsessed tae hold a decent conversation with. If she could only get over trying tae pick up guys who own Dobermans.'

The next page was a wedding photo—the groom pretending to bite the bride's neck, and the bride giggling hysterically. 'This one's good.'

'Aye,' said Stewart. 'Did ye not say we were in a hurry?'

'A few minutes won't hurt. You still need to put your shoes on.' I looked closer at the bride. 'That's Diana Glass.'

'I shouldnae think so.'

'It bloody is. I saw her author photo online.' I flipped a few more pages of the portfolio, and stopped. 'That author photo, as it happens.' There was Diana Glass, all serious and pouty, her long dark hair beautifully arranged, and a bookshelf in the background. 'You took her author photo. And her bridal photos.'

'Tha' one shouldnae be in there,' Stewart muttered. 'Can we go, all right?'

'Fine, don't tell me.' I closed the portfolio. 'You do know each other. I thought as much.'

'Coffee,' Stewart said, pulling on his last shoe and not looking at me. 'Ye promised coffee, and ye now owe me extra, because of being nosy.'

'Yes, I did.' I took pity on him, and shut up about Diana Glass. For now. 'Grab your cameras. You're going to get some shots for the blog, and I'm going to find Darrow so I can get my café open again.'

'As long as there's coffee.'

'Did I mention? Really not a problem.'

We walked along the grey concrete of Constitution Dock with an Antarctic breeze in our faces, and the smell of fish and chips warming the air. There were boats everywhere, jammed into berths in the harbour. A horde of seagulls were stalking us in the hopes that we had something tasty to offer them.

All I had to offer them was Stewart.

'When ye said expedition,' he mocked. 'I imagined something more than ten minute's walk from my place. Did I really have to get up this early?'

'Do you never stop complaining?' I shot back. 'No wonder we call you lot whingeing Poms.'

'Poms are English,' he said firmly. 'I'm a Scot. The English are our mutual oppressors.'

'Please. Have you seen a cricket match lately? If anything, we oppress them.'

'So where are we away to?'

'Have patience. You'll love it.' I spotted a boy I knew working one of the boats, and waved while I tried to remember his name. *Amos? Emmett? Adam.*

'Hey, Tabby,' he called out.

'Hey,' I called back, hoping a smile would disguise the fact that I had forgotten his name. Couldn't lose my Tabitha-knows-everyone reputation with Stewart now.

'Going to the coffee fair?' the nameless boy asked.

Stewart sucked in a breath.

Oh, *Eammon*. Now I remembered him. I waved and smiled again, and hustled Stewart onward.

'Coffee fair?' Stewart said delightedly. 'Is it true? Tell me it's true.'

'It was supposed to be a surprise.'

'They set it up just for me?'

I rolled my eyes. 'Yes, the city of Hobart conspired to make you happy. As if. You gave me the idea of coming here, you know.'

'Oh, aye? That was bright of me.'

'Your ridiculous caffeine addiction reminded me that when they ran the inaugural coffee fair last year, you couldn't move Darrow out of the place with a gardening fork—trust me, I tried.'

Stewart looked at me with wide eyes. 'So if ye weren't trying to find Darrow, ye might not have bothered tae mention this vital event tae me at all? Yer cruelty astounds me.'

Salamanca Place is one of the most beautiful streets in Hobart—a long stretch of old stone buildings crammed with cafés, art galleries, studios and shops. However high the rents get, it has never quite lost the aura of bohemian grunge. I love Café La Femme's little city corner dearly, but I can never compete with this particular ambience.

On the other hand, did I mention my Sunday sleep in? I'd never get another one if I worked here.

The imposing stone buildings, stuck together with twisty arcades and all kinds of hidden nooks and courtyards, face an avenue of trees. On Saturdays, the whole street is blocked off for the local market, and it fills up with colourful stalls, food vans and abundant produce. During the week, though, the street is a normal thoroughfare for cars.

Except for the Tuesday once a year when the coffee fair takes over, and all bets are off.

Today, Salamanca was full of stalls and people. It was like a condensed version of the market, with one single important difference. It was all about the java.

The mingling scents of a hundred different varieties of a certain beany product wafted around on the cool air. The stalls were laden with sweets, cakes, gelato, crockery, and a variety of products for sale that should really not have coffee connected with them, but did. The soaps and perfumes were unusual. The fashion and the sex toys were downright terrifying, and the street theatre … okay, let's just not talk about the street theatre.

Tasting tables had been set up on the grass under the leafy trees, and people were already filling up the chairs, despite the fact that it was a work day, and barely eight in the morning. Even the seagulls were wired.

'Your eyeballs are twitching,' I said to Stewart.

He looked stupidly pleased with the universe, in a dreamy kind of way. 'Tabitha, this is the nicest thing ye have ever done for me. I've no idea even where tae start.'

I kicked him in the shin. 'Get it together, McTavish. We're not here to sate your fiendish lusts. We're here because Darrow is as much of a coffeeholic as you—though I am starting to suspect that you do have an actual problem—and he is not likely to miss this.'

'Right,' said Stewart, sounding halfway normal. 'That makes sense. Absolutely. So I have no function in this scenario?'

I rolled my eyes. 'Order me a latté and find us somewhere to sit. I'll be with you in a minute.'

It didn't take me long to find Bev Darrow's cake stall. Mocha gateaux, pale brown meringue kittens and all sorts of odd constructions from glued-together chocolate coffee beans were arranged on a trestle table. Most of it was non-smutty, as she saves the really hot stuff for private CWA functions. Kevin Darrow, the eleven-year-old grandson, was handling the money.

'Hi, Bev,' I said. 'It all looks great.'

'Hello, darl,' said Bev.

'Did you get my message about the café being closed? I won't need the usual cake orders this week.'

'Yes, that's fine,' she said. 'It will give me more time to work on my art.'

'Have you … seen your other grandson lately?'

Bev gave me a sly look, as if she knew exactly what I was up to. Nanna's intuition is a scary thing. 'No, darl, but I expect he'll be around today.'

I smiled, and bought two chocolate-coffee-bean echidnas. 'Don't let him know I'm around, Bev. Wouldn't want to scare him off.'

Bev winked at me.

When I caught up to Stewart, he was sitting at one of the acre-long tasting tables, contemplating his breakfast. I assumed that the latté was for me, which meant that the double espresso, the cappuccino and the macchiato were all for him.

'Wow,' I said. 'You really don't like getting up early.'

'Hush,' he said, gazing dreamily at his cups. 'Yer interrupting our forbidden love.'

'Fine,' I said, giving him the echidna. 'But if you see a gorgeous, well-dressed man making similar burbling noises at *his* caffeine fix, let me know.'

While Stewart engaged in silent worship, I scanned the crowds. Darrow wasn't the world's earliest riser, but I wouldn't put it past him to sneak in and out before lunchtime, in the hopes of not bumping into anyone who might be looking for him … and on the other hand, no. This was the coffee fair. No way he'd spend anything less than several hours embracing the love of the sultriest bean of all.

The mocha cream pancakes on a nearby stall were calling to me, and I was on the verge of giving in to their siren song when a familiar voice interrupted me. 'Tabitha? Hi.'

I turned to see a pretty blonde woman with a pram. Amy was a nice enough person that I had had nothing in common with except, two years ago, my dad unexpectedly a) retired, b) skipped the state for sunny Queensland, and c) married Amy's mother.

That, and Amy's partner was one of the recent victims of the Trapper.

'Amy,' I said, delighted to see her for once. 'Sit down and join us. Tell me what's been going on with you.'

Amy was practically dying to spill the details of Danny's encounter with the Trapper, and it only took one cappuccino and a plate of beige melting moments to get her talking.

'You'd think they'd have taken it more seriously,' she said, referring to Tasmania's finest. 'It's not every day you come home to find a giant mantrap has been inserted into your house.' She shuddered. 'If it had been me and Maddison instead of Danny…'

That was a nasty thought. Babies weren't designed to fall ten feet into metal cages. 'But how did it happen?' I asked.

Amy shrugged. 'We don't know. We didn't change the locks when we moved in—you don't, do you? Turns out the place was a rental to a whole lot of dodgy characters before us. The police have a list of about twenty people who could have had access to our basement.' She reached out and touched baby Maddison's hand—she did that a lot, touching and stroking her when she got nervous. Good to know babies were useful for something. 'I'm not being fair to the police,' Amy said finally. 'They did make enquiries—they still are investigating. And Gary keeps us informed when he can. But it's all so frustrating. That someone could just break into our house like that—do that to us.'

'You mean *Constable* Gary?' I asked. Not that I should be surprised by anyone knowing anyone in this town.

'Mm, he was at school with Danny. He babysits for us sometimes.'

'Hobart,' I said, shaking my head.

Amy laughed, knowing exactly what I meant.

Now, to the good stuff. 'So what happened when Danny walked into the house?'

'That's it,' said Amy. 'He walked in, took two steps on to our hall rug, and fell into a cage in the basement.'

'What kind of cage?'

Amy waved her hands a little. 'Just a cage—like something out of a movie. Homemade, the police think, all welded bars and chicken wire. There was an old mattress on the floor, so whoever it was didn't want us hurt—well, I don't know what they wanted. I heard the noise and ran out of the kitchen … and there he was. I couldn't believe it!'

'Hang on, you were in the house at the time?' I repeated, making a face at Stewart for not giving me this vital bit of information earlier. He must have known it, after his interview with Danny.

Stewart looked worried about something. 'Tabitha…'

I waved him to silence.

'Well, yes,' said Amy. 'That's the weird thing. I'd been in all day. I only went out for milk, about noon. I know I'm sleep-deprived since Maddi was born, but surely I would have heard someone building a trap in the basement! It takes five minutes to the corner shop with the stroller, and five minutes back again. I wasn't delayed at all. How does someone break into a house and install a full-sized man trap that involves sawing up the floor in the time it takes me to fetch milk?'

Hmm. Sounded like an inside job. Or something.

'Tabitha,' said Stewart, more urgently.

'What?' I snapped back, not wanting to miss any of Amy's story. Stewart was looking up, above and behind my head.

Uh-oh. I turned around, very slowly.

Bishop stood there, arms crossed.

How does he do that? I mean, really. How is it possible that he is there to witness every little thing I do that he wouldn't approve of? When Melissa Marcus shoplifted a sleeve full of lipsticks and the manager detained both of us, it was Bishop who took the call. When the police were called after Sharni Taylor's seventeenth birthday party went past 3AM, it was Bishop who caught me with Xanthippe and a half-empty bottle of gin. And when a certain undergrad prank on a certain gang of med students went horribly wrong, it was Bishop who found me hiding in the bushes on the Sandy Bay University campus, wearing a Warrior Princess costume and some green jelly.

I tried not to let any hint of guilt cross my face, but I was well and truly sprung.

'Hi,' said Amy brightly. 'It's Leo, isn't it? We met at my mum's wedding. And, uh, the funeral. At Christmas.'

Bishop switched from smouldering, grim-faced policeman to friendly professional in the blink of an eye. 'Amy. Nice to see you again.' He shook her hand, and gave her the warm smile that I never get. He nodded at Stewart, managing to not quite glare at him, and then looked back to me. 'Tabitha, a word?'

I sighed. Tabitha, not Tish. Much though the old nickname irritated me, my real name in Bishop's mouth spelled trouble. 'If I don't come back alive, Stewart, Ceege gets my frocks.'

'I want yer coffee machine.'

'Fight Nin for it.'

Bishop and I walked a little away from the tables. I held up a hand. 'Before you say anything, I want to state that I have done nothing illegal, unethical, or in any way wrong.'

'You were talking about the case. To a witness.'

'I was chatting to my stepsister.'

'You've never been interested in Meredith's family before. You haven't spoken to any of them in months!' He had to have heard that from her. Were the family talking to him about me? Not cool.

'Don't pretend you know anything about me. And stop shouting!'

Too late for that, of course. We launched from there into one of our usual howling fits, neither of us listening to the other, too busy coming up with the next accusation to throw.

To our credit, we walked several more paces from the table first, so our yelling wouldn't frighten the baby.

'I am not interfering in police business!'

'I don't know what the hell you think you're doing—'

'Stop treating me like a child!'

'Stop acting like a spoiled brat. How much attention do you need—'

'Not everything is about you and your stupid police work.'

After about five minutes straight, we both stopped at the same time and breathed heavily at each other. 'Done here?' I said, finally.

'It'll do,' he grouched, and we went back to the tables. Constable Gary had joined Stewart and Amy, and was sharing a bucket of hot chips with them. I kicked my handbag out of the way, and sat down next to him. 'These aren't espresso flavoured chips, are they?'

'I don't think so,' said Gary, pleased to see me.

I prodded his arm. 'Still in one piece, then? Should you even be back on duty yet?' It gave me a whole different excuse to shoot Bishop a dirty look. 'I'd think being shot by a bow and arrow entitled you to a holiday...'

'We can't all dump our responsibilities whenever we feel like it,' Bishop said back, without any particular heat.

'Message just came through from Inspector Clayton,' Gary said, looking nervous.

'What message?' Bishop rapped out.

'You might want to call and talk to him yourself.'

'Right.' Bishop strode away, muttering to himself.

'Wow,' Amy said. 'He gets kind of shouty around you, doesn't he, Tabitha? I always thought he was—you know, ordinary and nice. A bit on the broody side, but dependable.'

'Apparently I bring out the homicidal maniac in him,' I said, stealing some more of Gary's chips.

'Case isn't going well,' Gary said. 'Inspector Clayton has been doing a lot of yelling, too.'

'Oh, really?' I glanced over to where Bishop was talking into a mobile phone. He looked like he was about to punch a tree. 'What's up, then?' I asked, and could have kicked myself. The last thing I needed was Gary telling Bishop that I'd been pumping him for information.

But it's so not fair to get a girl all interested, and then keep secrets. I can't help being a gossip queen.

Lucky for me, Gary's chat gland was already kicking into overdrive. 'Take a walk with me, Tabby?'

I jumped up so quickly, I almost tripped over the bench. 'Stewart, don't eat all the chips. And watch my handbag.'

'I didn't want to say anything in front of Amy,' Gary said in a low voice as he led me away. 'But apparently one of our witnesses has changed her story. That Claudina girl, the redhead who's been sobbing into tissues and yelling to the world that Morris was never a junkie? According to Clayton, she's now ready to make a statement that the victim was taking everything under the sun. She also reckons that he was into carpentry in a big way. Clayton is getting a lot of heat from the Drug Investigation Team, and they're building a case that *Morris* was the Trapper, and he just got tangled up in his last trap due to being high on something that killed him.'

'Right,' I said. 'Why, exactly, are you telling me this? Bishop will take off your head.'

Gary hesitated. 'I wanted you to know that it's almost over. You don't have to worry or anything.'

I patted his hand. 'You're very sweet, but obviously a crazy person.'

Bishop was looking over at us, and, something dark passed over his eyes. He closed his phone with a snap.

'Quick,' I said. 'Veronica at the post office—on with her yet?'

Gary looked startled. 'No!'

'Good.' I smiled tightly as Bishop strode towards us. 'Now you can say quite honestly that I was advising you on your love life.'

'Claudina,' Stewart repeated, some time later. Amy and her pram had abandoned us, and a grouchy Bishop had hauled Gary back to the station. Stewart and I were hanging out at the wishing cauldron (basically an old cast-iron fishing pot, but try telling that to any of the wide-eyed kids who toss five cent coins in for their wish). The giant silos at the end of the street loomed over us, possibly more than they should have done due to us both being strung out on caffeine.

'Claudina,' I confirmed.

'*Claudina* told the police Morris was a drug user?' he said.

'If you keep repeating everything I say, I'm going to have to ban you from the espresso.'

'Tabitha, I spent hours with those redheads yesterday. Claudina is evangelical about Morris being clean. No way she would suddenly change her mind.'

'Unless someone changed her mind for her—or maybe she found something out?'

'Not that yer interested in a police investigation?'

I threw the empty chip bucket at him. 'It's not my fault if it keeps getting interesting in my face. People are practically flaunting the investigation at me. I'm not trying to be involved.'

Stewart gave me an exasperated look. 'Oh, yer not trying at all—Tabitha, have ye considered the possibility that ye *like* Bishop being angry at ye?'

'That's just—that's completely...' A brief image of Bishop's dark, furious eyes flashed through my mind. Not sexy at all. In the least. Oh, hell. 'You have a very twisted imagination.'

'Uh-huh. So when I contact Claudina for a follow up interview, ye don't want to come with me?'

I opened my mouth and then closed it, trying to figure out which answer would be least incriminating. 'If you will excuse me, I have a landlord to stalk.'

'I'll keep meself busy. Pretty photos tae take, moral high ground tae keep.'

'No more long blacks,' I chided him as we went our separate ways. 'They've made you delusional.'

Subtlety was getting me nowhere, so I spent most of the rest of the day helping Bev Darrow at her cake stall while keeping my eye out for her eldest grandson, who failed spectacularly to make an appearance.

By the time the fair was drawing to a close, I was ready to

kick something. Two days, and Darrow had neither responded to my blatant closing of the café, nor turned up to his favourite public event of the year.

Obviously, he wasn't just in hiding. He was going out of his way to avoid me.

Nin came past the stall at one point, and came close to stabbing me with those eyebrows of hers. 'Café still closed tomorrow?'

I swallowed hard. It wasn't working—but what if three days was the charm? 'Yes.'

Nin gave me a look, and I resisted the urge to hide under the cake stall. 'Fine,' she said, in a voice that kind of implied, 'I hope you die.'

'That is a dangerous lady,' said Kevin Darrow, after Nin had moved on. Smart kid.

After 4PM, the road was officially unblocked and Salamanca Place filled up with the cars and vans of stallholders. Bev left Kevin and me to pack up while she fetched her own van. Stewart came over to smile giddily at me. 'Good day?'

Oh-oh. 'Have you been here this whole time? Do I need to take you to have your stomach pumped? How much coffee have you actually consumed?' I had cake on my shoe. How had I ended up with cake on my shoe?

'All of it, I'd say—took some great photos. Gotta go do some blogging. Make some phone calls.' Stewart was speaking faster than usual, the words blurring into his accent. 'Café free tonight, aye? Key please. Want tae paint walls. Many walls. Inspiration has hit.'

'You're not going near my walls until some of that coffee's worn off,' I said, rummaging in my handbag for a tissue to deal with the cake-shoe situation, and not the key to the café because he shouldn't be encouraged.

'Do me best work on high caffeine levels,' Stewart insisted. 'Paint brush moves faster. Ne'er a bad thing.'

My handbag was full of the usual crap. I pawed through scraps of paper, hairbrush, half a dozen abandoned lip glosses, receipts, shiny things—'Ow!' A sudden spark of pain clutched at my fingers, and I dropped my bag.

It was somewhat gratifying, the way that Stewart was instantly at my side. 'Are ye well?'

'Something *bit* me,' I said, sucking my finger.

Half of the contents of my handbag had spilled out on the ground. Stewart picked through them, looking for the culprit.

'Hey, that's private,' I protested, trying to think if there was anything embarrassing in there.

Boys! Give them a crisis, and they turn into amateur forensics experts. Kevin Darrow produced a plastic bag and held it out, while Stewart deposited each item into it. Lip gloss, purse, tissues, tampons, ping pong ball…

Just as I opened my mouth to identify that as an alien object, Stewart picked up the ping pong ball between finger and thumb and gave a little jump, dropping it again. 'We have a winner.'

'I was bitten by a ping pong ball?' I suppose stranger things have happened.

'Ye were no' bitten,' said Stewart. 'This has an electrified charge.'

'Can I see?' asked Kevin, far more interested in this than I had ever seen him around adults before. Which was to say, slightly.

Electrified charge. I had to sit down for a minute. 'I was *electrocuted*?'

'Only a wee bit,' said Stewart.

I was outraged. 'What do you mean, only a wee bit? Someone put an electrified object in my handbag.'

'Calm down, it's nothing serious. More of a practical joke, I'd say.'

'It's not funny,' I growled.

Stewart looked at me, and then nodded. 'No, not funny. But how long has it been in here? That's the question.'

I glared at the sinister ping pong ball, sitting there on the ground all innocent. 'I don't know.'

'When did you last clean out your handbag?' Kevin asked.

I gave him a blank look. 'Excuse me?'

Stewart laughed. 'So young, so much tae learn about girls.'

'I resent the implication,' I sniffed. 'I'm always groping around in there for my keys or whatever. If that ball works every time, it can't have been in there all that long.'

Kevin swept some Tupperware containers off the stall. 'Let's have a look at it, then.'

Using a pocket knife and a couple of toothpicks, my two amateur Boy Scouts dismembered the ping pong ball, analysing the innards with great interest.

'What kind of person could make something like that?' I asked finally. 'How would they even think of it?'

'It's a simple enough idea,' said Stewart. 'We used tae make up stuff like this at school all the time. Like I said, practical jokes. I'm worried about the "who", though. I canna help thinking that whoever did this might also be responsible for trapping cats in nets, or postmen in cages.'

'But why would the Trapper be interested in me?' I protested. Sometimes denial is a girl's best friend.

Stewart gave me an incredulous look. 'Ye work in the same building where Morris was found, ye live barely a street from the other two incidents, one of which involved yer step-sister's partner, and ye were recently photographed in a clinch with one of the police officers investigating the case.'

'Apart from that,' I said weakly. Oh, hell. I didn't like this at all. 'Gary said they think Morris was the Trapper all along,' I added.

'And if not?' Stewart glanced at Kevin. 'What about yer other friend, Tabitha? The one Xanthippe suspected.' He mouthed 'Darrow' at me.

'No,' I said sharply. 'He wouldn't try to scare me like this. The other stuff … I don't know, maybe, but not *this*. I'm the only person in the state he trusts to make caramel briôche.

We're friends.'

'As ye say,' Stewart said, not looking convinced. 'But ye have to tell Bishop about this wee ball. It might be relevant.'

'He'll shout at me,' I said quietly.

'Have we nae established yet that ye subconsciously want him to shout at ye?'

'Caffeine and electric shocks make you *mean*.' I bit my lip. 'This electrocuting ping pong ball—could one of those kill a person? If the charge was strong enough?'

'No,' Kevin said primly, sounding like a university professor. 'The charge you experienced is about as powerful as it gets. An elderly person with a pacemaker who held it in both hands might potentially be hurt, but even then I shouldn't think so.'

'How do you know this?' I accused. 'I can just about take the mystical knowledge of electrical workings from Stewart, but you're a kid. Is there some secret boys club that teaches this stuff?'

Kevin tilted his glasses at me. 'I read books.'

And they say the internet's dangerous.

15

'Is Gladstone Street around here?' Stewart asked as we left Kevin Darrow and his scary little brain with his nanna.

'Sure, it's just up the hill. What's in Gladstone Street?'

'Dr Pembroke's office.'

I eyed him warily. 'How much coffee have you had? I don't think a GP will have a stomach pump...'

Stewart laughed, a maniacal caffeine-laced laugh. 'Dr Pembroke happens to be the well-respected dentist whose wife threw a hissy fit two days ago at the Jiggle Bits...'

'Jiggle It Fitness Hub,' I corrected. The words were apparently burned into my brain forever. 'Stewart McTavish, you're not doing detective work, are you?'

'I prefer the term journalism. Want tae come with?'

'Hell yes!'

'You didn't tell me it was a party,' I complained a little later, as we arrived at the swanky dental offices. What the hell kind of dentist has a ballroom? The reception area looked like something out of a fancy hotel, and was filled with elegant people drinking champagne and orange juice out of flutes.

'Did I not?' said Stewart, snagging us a couple of drinks as he surveyed the crowd. He looked particularly scruffy surrounded by the pretty people. 'Possibly I was afraid ye would add glitter tae the occasion.'

I took my glass of bubbles, and then elbowed him. 'Luckily, I always look good. They might take one look at your last century jeans and kick you out, though.'

Stewart wasn't bothered. 'The trick is to look like ye belong.'

'I belong everywhere.' I eyed the *hors d'oeuvres* platters. There's something very wrong about sushi made with semi-dried tomatoes and pine nuts. Seriously. And the vegetarian sausage rolls looked like something had died inside them. 'Ten to one their caterers are ripping them off.'

'Not the story I'm investigating, but I'll keep tha' in mind,' said Stewart cheerfully.

'Toothpick food,' I said, wrinkling my nose at a platter of chilli prawns and lemon scallops surrounded by abandoned toothpicks. 'They never think about where the guests are going to stash them afterwards.'

The crowd applauded. I assumed it wasn't because of me—it was only a minor snarky comment by my standards.

A very refined looking man had the attention of the crowd. He smiled at them all and—oh. Shiny, shiny teeth. 'Should have brought sunglasses,' I said in an undertone.

'That's our host, Dr Pembroke,' Stewart whispered in my ear. 'Dentist tae the rich and smug. Ye dinnae want tae know how much he charges for a consultation.'

'His teeth are almost *blue*.' I wasn't actually listening to Pembroke talk, but his smile was oddly hypnotic. 'What are you looking for?'

Stewart's mouth tickled my ear, and leaning closer was the only way to hear him under the crowd noise and the booming microphone. 'Suspicious tha' a man whose wife was arrested for assaulting a police officer three days ago is hosting a party.'

'Technically it's a soirée,' I said. 'Once you have semi-dried tomatoes and pine nuts in the sushi and women wearing—bloody hell, that's a fur stole. A real one. Not even vintage or ironic. Who are these people?'

I'd done my share of catering, but mostly for uni students, police officers, hipsters and musos. Even a wedding or two, when I was training. The rare big fancy affairs I'd helped with had been—well. Not quite as *soiréeish* as this.

I'd bet they were paying for each pine nut what I would normally charge for a plate of sandwiches.

'This is officially the other half,' murmured Stewart, his attention mostly on Dr Shiny Teeth and his boring speech. 'And how they live.'

'This isn't the other half,' I scoffed. 'This is the point one percent. And they should be able to afford better caterers. Maybe I'll leave my card.' I hardly knew anyone here. This was not my Hobart.

'Did ye hear that?' Stewart said in astonishment as the crowd reacted to something Dr Shiny had said, muttering and gossiping together.

'No, I was bitching about the clothes and food. What did I miss?'

'See there.'

A woman stepped up beside Dr Shiny. She wore a simple dress—the kind of simple that costs thousands of Chanel dollars. Her apricot hair was pulled back in a clasp and she wore expensive 'I'm not wearing any makeup' makeup.

The crowd stilled.

'Natasha Pembroke,' Stewart whispered. 'Otherwise known as the Jiggle It archer herself.'

'I barely recognised her out of harem pants, but I did get that,' I whispered back. 'Are they going to turn on her like sharks?'

'Possibly.'

'Bits of designer frock everywhere?'

'Tabitha, it's no' always about the frocks.'

I glared at him. Was he calling me shallow? This is what happens when you go around snogging people—they get ideas above their station.

Natasha Pembroke was speaking, quiet and uncomfortable.

'I think most of you know that I had a very busy weekend.'

A few titters. Dr Shiny stood beside his wife, looking so pleased with himself that I wanted to hit him with a plate of chilli prawns. How could he put her through this?

'I have no excuse for my behaviour,' Natasha continued. Her shoulders looked … defeated. 'Except for the one explanation that really is no excuse at all. I was high on prescription medication when I shot that policeman. Prescription medication that I had obtained illegally.'

The whispers exploded through the room.

'I have been living a secret life for some time now,' she continued. 'And I am so grateful to my husband for supporting me after … the rather devastating shock he had upon my arrest on Saturday.'

'Aye,' Stewart muttered, eyes on Dr Shiny. 'I'm sure it came as a massive shock tae the man.'

'So cynical,' I whispered back. Stewart had his phone out, and was recording the speech.

Natasha Pembroke spilled her guts before the crowd of her peers. High stress lifestyle … easy access to medication … no excuse. She was in a day release treatment program now, was falling on her sword as far as the police investigation went, there were no excuses for her actions … and oh yes, she was taking the opportunity to make something good out of all this by sponsoring an awareness campaign, and she urged all her friends to contribute.

'Addiction is not just about the unfortunate, the down and out, the young and the immigrants,' she said finally. 'It can happen to anyone. I am very lucky to have a family who will support me through this hard time.'

The crowd lapped it up, applauding and smiling and oh so proud of her. No sharks here, we love you Natasha, isn't she brave?

I left Stewart to it, and nipped to the loo. 'I miss anything?' I asked when I came back.

'No, I think I'm done here.' He eyed the crowd. 'Is it wrong tae think their public support of her is somewhat insincere?'

'When I was in the stall I heard various women call Natasha Pembroke a silly bitch, a slut, a drug-addled whore and a lying hypocrite. Several of them emphasised that they were friends of hers, which was why it was totally fine for them say that.'

'Oh, nice.'

'Two of them were snorting cocaine at the time.'

'I should blog that.'

'Best not. I don't want some mad rich women hunting us down with their Versace fingernails. Let's go.' I looked around the room, shuddering a little. 'I feel dirty. You know what we need?'

'Coffee?'

'Down, boy. We need to dry you out.'

When I was a little girl, Dad used to take me out to his favourite milk bar near the station (probably the last place in Hobart that called itself a 'milk bar') and order me lime spiders in glasses so tall I had to stand up to drink them through the straw. It's basically lime syrup, ice cream and lemonade, thoroughly disgusting, and they never fail to cheer me up.

It wasn't working. I sat on the café counter, poking my own homemade concoction with a straw while Stewart worked on the mural.

It was killing me to keep Café La Femme closed. Not to mention that it wasn't the best financial decision I'd ever made.

I didn't have any specific reason to suspect that Darrow was involved with these odd crimes, but there was a horrible feeling in the pit of my stomach, and my stomach was usually reliable. Even when filled with sickly sweet bubbles, battling each other for the championship.

Instead of playing with shot glass trifles again, or preparing for tomorrow's cake crowd, I left a still-jittery Stewart in possession of my café, under strict instructions to a) leave the coffee machine alone, thank you very much and b) not host any gatherings of redheaded women unless I was there to chaperone and c) not invite me to any more shiny-toothed dentist parties, as they are bad for the soul.

I went home to an empty house. Ceege had written 'Staying the Night at Katie's' on the fridge in carmine lipstick, so my first order of business was cleaning that off. Arse.

The thought of that ping pong ball in my handbag was creeping the hell out of me. I didn't know whether it was some practical joke or an actual warning … but it was icky. The house was very quiet without Ceege thumping around, swearing about elves and flamewars and how hard it was to buy size twelve stiletto heels that were remotely cute.

The one thing I was not going to do was call someone to keep me company. Especially since the first person who came to mind was Stewart. I'd only known him a week, how had he become the most reliable person in my life?

An independent and feisty young woman with awesome hair and a wardrobe of glorious vintage clothes does not need a pet Scotsman to keep an eye on her at all times. Even if he does have nice eyes, and artistic hands.

Blah. None of this was getting me anywhere. What I needed was a repetitive task to keep busy, and shut off my traitorous brain. Cleaning out the fridge would do it. Followed by baking. Much baking.

I flung open the fridge door, and a wave of white ping pong balls cascaded out of the fridge and over my feet.

I screamed and jumped backwards, flailing so violently that I slipped and crashed to the floor, cracking the back of my head on the lino. Shit! Through the panic, I managed to process that many of the balls had touched my feet and legs, but I had felt no electric shocks.

Shock, yes. Electric, no. My head felt like someone had whacked it with a skillet. Or, you know, a floor.

I sat up and prodded a finger at one of the ping pong balls that flooded my kitchen floor. Still no shock. I grasped it firmly and pulled myself to my feet, then put the ball on a chopping board, grabbed my best bread knife and sliced the damn thing in half.

It was a ping pong ball. No circuitry inside, just air. Bloody hell!

I had gone way past scared and was furious now. I shook a garbage bag out of one of my kitchen drawers and started stuffing the balls in, as fast as I could. I was about halfway through when I grabbed hold of the one ping pong ball in the lot of them that actually was electrified.

I screamed and swore, dropping the garbage bag. More of the little sods spilled across the floor.

My house. Whoever was doing this had been inside my house.

It wasn't a joke any more.

16

It was getting dark by the time I parked my car in the usual spot outside the café. I sat there for a few minutes, enjoying the illusion of safety. A woman in a parked car in the middle of town at night wasn't especially safe, but it felt better than my own house right now.

After those few indulgent minutes, I got out and headed inside, around the front rather than through the kitchen. The lights were on, and Stewart was painting.

Many of the figures were fully finished, now. I really did adore that mural—the mashing together of my favourite pop culture characters, the chaotic scene of tables and gorgeous food and beautiful people. It was everything I wanted in a wall, and it absolutely made Café La Femme.

I pushed open the door. 'That's it. I'm opening tomorrow. Screw Darrow. Let him keep his secrets. I'm done.'

Stewart literally jumped in the air, and barely stopped himself from crashing to the floor. 'Bloody hell, Tabitha. Are ye trying tae kill me?'

'I won't have Bev's cakes and bikkies, because I was stupid enough to cancel this week's order, but I can whip up some caramel tarts now, maybe do a special on scones.' I could think of nothing better than spending my whole day tomorrow bringing trays of hot scones out of the oven, and serving them to customers. 'I've still got the good jam from the Berry Farm … a few calls will get the usual meats and salad stuff delivered.'

'Tabitha,' Stewart said, staring at me. 'I thought ye were off home.'

I looked him straight in the eye, and lied. 'I'm fine. Just decided to stop letting a missing landlord rule my life. If you need me, I'll be burning sugar in the kitchen. With style.'

I made two gorgeous caramel tarts, with flaky pastry and gooey innards. I made three kinds of biscuits—Anzac, cranberry shortbread and Monte Carlos with real raspberry jam. I was cooking apples for a pie when Stewart came in to the kitchen, and sat at the table.

'It's almost done,' he said. 'Maybe a few more bits to glue on, a wee finishing touch or four. I've pinned up a sheet until the grand unveiling.'

I smiled without looking up from the stove top. 'Excellent. You must get some business cards run up so I can recommend you when people ask who painted it. And I know we haven't talked about money yet, but…'

'I didnae do it for money. Tabitha, what's wrong?'

'Nothing's wrong, I've got a lot to get done before tomorrow.'

'Tabitha.' Stewart had to be the only person I knew who didn't shorten my name in some way once they felt comfortable around me. He never called me Tabs, or Tabby or babe or cutes—and we won't even get started on Tish. Even Darrow never called me Tabitha—he preferred the double meaning of Darling, drawling it at me with a smirk every time.

Damn, I missed Darrow.

'Stewart, I'm busy.'

He reached over my shoulder and turned off the hot plate, then drew me away from the simmering pan of apples. 'Ye won't even look at me. What's going on here?'

'You're very alpha male tonight,' I grumbled. 'It doesn't suit you. Remember who's the sidekick around here.'

Stewart lifted my chin, and made me meet his eyes. 'Tell me. Why are ye no' at home?' His voice and that accent. So warm I wanted to cry.

'It's full of ping pong balls,' I muttered.

Stewart sucked in a breath. 'Aye, is tha' so?'

'They were in my fridge. And now they're all over my kitchen floor. So I am here, and I am cooking, and you are not going to stop me.'

'Have ye told Bishop?'

'No.'

'Why the hell not?' I flinched away at his tone, and he calmed down a little when he saw my reaction. 'Sorry, Tabitha, but this is not someone sticking something in yer handbag in a public place. This is someone breaking into yer home. Ye have to tell him.'

'If I tell Bishop about this, he will never let me out of his sight again. And if you say that I subconsciously want him to become my permanent stalker, I will *hit you*.'

Stewart folded his arms. 'Better stalked by Bishop than by an alleged murderer with a trap fetish. The police need tae know about this. They think the Trapper's our dead busker.'

I knew when to give up. 'I'll tell him in the morning. Promise.'

'Ceege home yet?'

'Staying the night at Katie's,' I mumbled. I wasn't going to ask, I just *wasn't*.

'D'ye have anyone brave who can stay with ye tonight?'

I lifted my eyes, and gave him a hopeful smile.

Stewart groaned. 'So what yer saying is, ye *want* Bishop to shoot me.'

'Two kisses does not give him ownership of my affections,' I sniffed. 'And by the way, you'd be sleeping on the couch.'

'Thank Christ for tha'. No offence, Tabitha, but I get the feeling ye'd be a high maintenance girlfriend.'

Well, obviously.

My fridge at home should still have been full of leftover *hors d'oeuvres* from the Oscars party, but the bastard with the ping pong balls had stolen my leftovers before perpetrating the crime.

Stewart and I ate pizza on the couch instead.

I put on a Doris Day movie for comfort, but Stewart started twitching in a manly fashion every time she burst into song or moved in for a blurry close up, so I hit the mute button. The living room was dark around us, with just Doris and her cheerful cast for illumination.

'D'ye think it's someone ye know?' Stewart asked.

Darrow, Xanthippe, my treacherous brain came up with as an instant response. 'I hope not,' I said. 'But then—I know everyone, don't I? So, chances are.' I picked a loose bit of cheese and pineapple off the cardboard box. 'I wish I knew what was going on with Xanthippe. She's acting stranger than usual—even for someone who is arranging eccentric PR for a rock band, and hunting my landlord down for God-knows-what purpose.'

'Do ye think she's the Trapper?'

'No,' I said automatically, then let my brain catch up to my mouth. 'No,' I said again after a moment's serious thought. 'This whole setting traps thing is completely stupid. If she was doing it, it would be stylish.'

'Attacking a rock band with a knife kind of stylish?'

'Exactly. Wait, were you being sarcastic?'

'I don't know. I've lost track.'

I thought about it for a minute. 'Natasha Pembroke. She talked about the case when she made that phone call to the police.'

Stewart nodded. 'She said nothing she couldnae have read in the papers. Might have chosen that story randomly.'

'It makes more sense if the stories are connected. Despite what *Sandstone City* like to claim, Hobart doesn't usually have this much weird all at once.' I jumped suddenly, smacking my greasy hand down on Stewart's leg. 'Did you see that? Outside.'

'What?' He went to the window.

'Not too close. I saw a light. Someone has a torch out there.'

He peered out. 'I don't see anything.'

'Right.' I reached under the couch, and came up with a cricket bat and a fishing net, both heirlooms from Dad. Ceege likes to keep them handy for the zombie apocalypse. 'Choose your weapon. I am not going to let some trap-obsessed creep besiege me in my own house.'

Stewart looked weary as he took the cricket bat off me. 'Ye say it's Hobart tha's suddenly got weird. From where I stand, these things are only happening around Tabitha Darling.'

That was uncalled for. Surely everyone has a stockpile of possible zombie weapons under their couch.

There's something surreal about creeping around your own back garden after dark. I couldn't help but feel like I was the intruder. 'Do you see anything?' I whispered as we made our way around.

'I didnae see anything the first time,' Stewart whispered back.

My ears went hot. 'Are you suggesting that I made it up?'

'Did I say so?'

'You're thinking it, though.'

'How can I possibly respond to tha'?'

'Aha, you admit it.'

'Let's do one circuit, then back inside.'

'Proving that Tabitha was imagining things after all, the silly girl.'

'Shush.'

'You shush! Don't you shush me!'

'You know,' broke in a cynical female voice. 'You two? Not stealthy.' A shadowy figure stepped out from behind my back door, and I caught a whiff of banana conditioner.

Of course, by the time I recognised her, I had already *died of shock*. 'Zee, what the everloving *fuck*?'

Xanthippe switched on her torch, pointing it at the grass so that it didn't blind either of us. 'You were expecting maybe Humphrey Bogart?'

'He wasn't my first suspect, no,' I muttered. 'What are you doing here?'

'In case you haven't noticed,' she said. 'You're the latest target in the game that our mutual friend is playing. I figured someone had to look out for you—and if it means catching him in the act, all the better.'

I led the way back into the kitchen, where the ping pong balls were still scattered across half the floor, and switched the lights on. 'You knew about this?'

'I heard about the one in your handbag,' Xanthippe said, looking around. 'This doesn't surprise me. I intercepted a package on your doorstep this morning.'

I stared at her. 'A package. What package?'

'A love token from your imaginary friend,' she said. 'A pretty pink box with a ribbon, full of mouse traps. Ever so subtle.'

'And ye didn't think Tabitha should know about tha' earlier?' demanded Stewart. 'Or tha' the police might want tae know?'

'I can protect Tabitha better than her darling Leo,' Xanthippe shot back. 'He has to follow rules, and go home when his shift is over.'

I put the kettle on. To hell with preserving the crime scene, I needed chamomile. 'This is all very nice, Zee, but you're working from a false premise. The Trapper is not Darrow.'

'Come on,' Xanthippe said incredulously. 'It's got his manicured fingernails all over it. Who else would be this bloody dramatic for no evident gain? He's been messing with everyone's heads, Tish. Now he's messing with yours.'

'Did you see him deliver the package?' I asked. 'Did you see him put anything in my handbag? Have you actually seen him at all since you came back to Tassie?'

'*You* have,' Stewart said, looking at me.

I glared at them both. 'He's driving a taxi. But he's not the Trapper, and he's not my stalker, and he's not a murderer. I won't believe it.'

'That man's capable of anything,' Xanthippe insisted stubbornly.

I lost my patience. 'Okay, tell me! I told you about the taxi—that's the biggest clue yet on how to find him. So you tell me what Darrow did to inspire this obsessive little vendetta of yours, right now, because this is way more than post-breakup mania.'

Xanthippe blew out a breath, looking furious at me, and then threw herself into one of my kitchen chairs. It wobbled under the shock, but stayed upright. 'My car,' she muttered. 'He crashed my car into the Richmond Bridge.'

'Oh, *Zee*,' I said, feeling the need for a sit down myself. 'Not the Lotus.' I wanted to hug her. Only we didn't do that. I hated how awkward things were. Ten years ago I would have hugged her and she would have pushed me off, and I would have said something stupid to make her laugh and it would have been okay.

I missed my friend.

'My personally-restored 1967 Lotus Super Seven Roadster,' she said miserably.

'I'll kill him for you,' I breathed. 'Oh, your pretty car...' Back when we were starting uni and the Lotus was up on bricks in her mum's garage, Xanthippe and I had planned to go on a road trip around the state, wearing 1960s outfits and playing cheesy nostalgia music. We'd never got around to it, and now we never would.

She shrugged it off, speaking to Stewart rather than me. 'It was supposed to be safe in storage while I was on the mainland, but he begged me to let him take it for a tune up and a run to keep the engine purring. Like a complete moron, I agreed. Two days later I got a text message—Crashed Lotus into Richmond Bridge, sorry, write off, will make it up to you.' She growled under her breath. 'They don't *make* cars like that any more.'

'How did I never hear about this?' I said. 'Come to that, how did he walk away from a crash like that?'

Stewart snapped his fingers. 'I remember this. Near Miss for Heritage Landmark. Simon covered the story for *Sandstone City*—not quite a Hobart story, but we do love a sandstone connection. Some idiot left the handbrake off a sports car and it ran down a grassy slope intae the river—technically it only dinged the bridge supports, but the water did the most damage, o' course...' He stopped, realising he was being far too enthusiastic while Xanthippe's face got grimmer and grimmer.

'Nice car,' he added weakly. 'Ye want his head on a plate. Understandable. It was insured, aye?'

'Insured for its value on paper,' Xanthippe muttered. 'Which doesn't come anywhere near what it actually cost me, in time as well as money. Also, I don't get the insurance money until he signs the statement about what happened to the damn car. Hence me trying to track him down with my supreme ninja skills. Meanwhile, he's screwing with my band, because apparently he hasn't messed my life up enough.' She kicked the table leg.

'If he is the Trapper, which he's not,' I put in. Now was not the time to mention that her 'supreme ninja skills' had yielded zero results.

'Whatever,' Xanthippe said, getting back to her feet. 'It wasn't an insulin overdose that killed Julian Morris in the net. It was a particularly nasty grade of heroin. He wasn't the only one, either—there have been more overdoses in the emergency room of the Royal this fortnight than there have been all year. It's all linked to some new dealer that people are calling The Vampire.'

Stewart dug a battered notebook out of his jeans, and took notes. 'How do ye know this?'

'I have my sources,' Xanthippe drawled. 'Tabitha isn't the only one who knows a lot of people in this town. Plus, I listen at keyholes.'

'And you're going to be hanging around protecting me on a regular basis, are you?' I said, very suspicious of the whole thing.

'When I don't have anything better to do. I don't know if you've noticed, Tish, but you're a magnet for weird lately. If I stay close, maybe I've got a better chance of figuring out what's going on.'

I hesitated. Xanthippe was scary, and I was pretty sure we weren't friends any more, but she was a good person to have in your corner. She also wasn't the first to notice that the madness seemed to be orbiting me specifically. 'We have a spare room now that Kelly's moved out,' I offered.

Xanthippe laughed. 'I think that might be a little too close, don't you? I'll see you two around.'

She strolled out of the kitchen, and I deadlocked the door behind her. 'Okay,' I said, for no particular reason. Apparently I didn't have anything to follow it up.

Stewart had that slightly glazed look that straight men got after talking to Xanthippe, fruit-flavoured femme fatale that she was. 'Is she in the Mob, or something?'

'No,' I said. 'She's just Xanthippe.'

'Right.' He recovered a little, and bumped his shoulder deliberately against mine. 'Ye never offered *me* the spare room. Ye offered me the couch.'

'Well? She'd be a live-in bodyguard. What are you going to do if a serial killer bursts in to attack me? Flip your kilt up at him?'

'If I'm not manly enough to keep ye feeling safe and secure, ye know exactly what to do.' He mimed a phone call. 'Hello, police? Aye, this is Superintendent Darling's wee girl, can ye send around five panda cars and a gun squad? I'm making gnocchi…'

I smacked him. 'I will call them tomorrow.'

'Promise?'

'I already promised. Sheesh.'

'So what do we do tonight?'

As for that, I did have a plan. 'We barricade ourselves in the living room, and watch Doris Day movies until we lose consciousness.'

Stewart nodded, respecting my fine taste in classic movies. 'Or ye could just hit me repeatedly with the cricket bat?'

The morning brought many things. A sore neck. The odd sensation of Stewart squashed behind me on the couch, one arm slung around my waist as he snored into my shoulder blades. The sight of Ceege, grinning down at us like a maniac. 'Geez, Tabs. We have three beds in this house. If you want to shag him, why not get on with it? Try to leave mine as a last resort…'

I unwrapped myself from Stewart and threw myself at Ceege. 'I missed you. Katie can't have you anymore. I need you here to protect me.'

'Aw, that's sweet. What's with the ping pong balls in the kitchen?' Ceege pushed me off him. 'I only care if it's something kinky.'

'I'm being stalked.'

'Nice. Only you could get stalked with ping pong balls.'

'If you see my stalker, maybe you could hint that I'd prefer flowers,' I said sarcastically.

Stewart started making mumbly noises from the couch. 'Wha' time is it?' he groaned.

'Eight,' said Ceege.

'What?' I howled. 'I was going to open the café today.'

'Did ye call Nin, or the girls?' Stewart asked.

That stumped me. 'Um, no. But I made cakes.'

'Without Nin, yer not going to open today,' said Stewart, which showed how much he had been paying attention.

'Bloody Lotus-smashing Darrow,' I muttered. 'I've lost my getting-up-early superpower, and I blame him.'

Stewart sat up on the couch and pushed his hand through his hair. 'To be fair, we were up until about 3AM. Will ye now—'

'Yes, *Mum*. I'm calling them.' I flounced to the kitchen. 'Have a shower. You look like something died on your head.'

'Oh, yer so charming to wake up to,' Stewart yawned.

'Welcome to my life, mate,' said Ceege with sympathy.

17

Bishop turned up within fifteen minutes of my phone call, in uniform but alone. Presumably so he could shout at me without any official witnesses. It was wrong of me to enjoy the moment when Stewart came out of the bathroom with wet hair, shirtless in yesterday's jeans, but I did.

If Bishop didn't have such a lousy temper, I wouldn't be tempted to provoke it all the time. It's hardly my fault.

'So,' Bishop said, working hard to pretend that Stewart had not just appeared all damp and rumpled. 'You're in trouble?'

'Amazing deductive reasoning,' I said brightly, dipping a fork into my plate of scrambled omelette. 'I can tell they're going to promote you any day now.'

'Be nice,' Stewart muttered, heading for my coffee percolator. I'd put some of the good stuff on to drip already, out of the kindness of my slightly grateful heart.

I closed my mouth, and smiled politely at Bishop. He gave Stewart a startled look, then drew his attention back to me.

'Tabitha Darling, what exactly makes you think that the Trapper—who is dead—is stalking you?'

'Well—'

'Because Inspector Clayton closed the case this morning. He's making a statement to the press in about an hour.'

'Where's the press conference?' Stewart asked quickly. 'I dinnae suppose *Sandstone City* got an invite.'

Bishop gave him a dirty look. 'They certainly did not.'

'Ahem,' I said, waving my fork to get their attention back to me. 'The case is closed? Already? The flatmate changed her story, then.'

Bishop continued looking at Stewart. 'If the Press could give us some privacy?'

Stewart headed to the living room, pretending he didn't care. 'Fine. Ceege had better have some clothes without sequins, so I can borrow a clean shirt.'

When he was gone, Bishop looked at me. I looked back at him. 'Tea?' I suggested.

Bishop unwound about a centimetre. 'God, yes.' Obviously the prospect of tea was alluring enough that he was prepared to remember, for a minute or two, that we were friends. Or maybe it was just the relief of having this case done and dusted.

'Changed is a pretty mild word for what the flatmate did to her story,' he admitted, sitting down at my kitchen table. 'Now she says Morris was injecting, sniffing and snorting everything he could get his hands on, and there was nothing out of the ordinary about him keeping heroin in old insulin containers. Clayton and the team are convinced that the traps were down to Morris being a lunatic prankster. He got caught in the last one when all the shit he'd been shoving into his veins caught up with him. We still suspect the band put him up to building the damn thing in their spare room for some PR stunt, but we can't pin anything on them. So, that's it. Tabitha goes back to her kitchen, Bishop makes inroads on his paperwork, life returns to normal.'

Even without knowing what I knew, this sounded dodgy. Bishop didn't really believe this story Inspector Des was pushing, did he? Dad would have worked at a case like this until it was watertight, and I'd always thought Bishop was the same kind of police officer. Dogged and cynical, and never going for the easy solution unless he was absolutely certain.

'It wasn't the last trap,' I said, putting a strong cup of tea in front of him.

Bishop leaned over and picked up my fork, helping himself to the last of my eggs. 'What are you talking about? You didn't make much sense on the phone.'

I took a deep breath, knowing how dumb this was going to sound. 'At the coffee fair, yesterday. I found an—an electrified ping pong ball in my handbag.'

Bishop coughed on a mouthful of egg. 'I'm sorry, you found a what?'

'Don't laugh, this is serious. It zapped me. And—' I gestured towards the garbage bag in the corner of my kitchen. 'When I came home, the fridge was full of them. They spilled out everywhere.'

'Sure it wasn't leftovers from one of Ceege's gamer parties?'

I glared at him. 'Have you even thought about how difficult it would be for someone to fill a fridge with ping pong balls? The physics alone is bewildering.'

'I've got to say, Tish, I've never been asked that question before.' Bishop shook his head. 'Were they all electrified?'

'Just one of them. But someone had to break into my house to do it.'

Bishop reacted to that, at least. 'Any sign of forced entry?'

'No,' I had to admit. 'The window in the front room is dodgy, they could have come in that way. Potentially.'

His eyes darkened. 'A policeman's daughter with crappy security? Marvellous.'

I handed him a Tupperware container with the second electrified ping pong ball inside.

Bishop picked the ball out of the container, and dropped it as the thing stung him. 'Tabitha,' he said, in a tone of voice usually reserved for swear words.

'I did tell you it was electrified! There was a parcel, too—a creepy stalker parcel, with mouse traps inside.' I had a horrible feeling that I was sounding like someone who had been watching too many B-grade horror movies.

'And where is that?'

I felt myself going red, damn it. 'I didn't actually see it. It was … intercepted by a friend.'

'Which friend?' he asked in a voice that remained professional but had a little extra growl in it. 'McTavish?'

'No.' This was going to be bad. 'Xanthippe,' I admitted.

There was a small choking sound in the back of his throat. 'Xanthippe is back in town. Brilliant. Why don't the two of you just kill me now?'

'Leo,' I said, to show him I was serious. 'I wouldn't call you over some prank. I know the evidence is ropey, but someone is trying to freak me out here. And I think it's the Trapper.'

'Someone with a sick sense of humour,' Bishop agreed. 'Maybe someone who knows you've been poking your nose around this case, for God-knows-what reason—'

'I have not!'

'But the guy who made those traps is dead. And even if he's not—the death was accidental.'

'Are you really sure about that?' I said in a small voice.

Bishop gave me one of his patented big brother looks. 'I'll put you down in the register as a person of concern. If you get any more strange packages, let me know. Some officers will swing by every now and then, to check you're okay. Plenty of the lads will volunteer, to make you feel better.'

'Fine,' I said, knowing I sounded like the brat he always said I was. I couldn't help it. It was all I could do not to cross my arms and pout.

He looked frustrated. 'I do care about you, Tabitha.'

'But you don't care about my opinion. You're better than this, Bishop. You can't give up on everything Dad taught you because he's not around any more and some inspector is trying to play politics with your case.'

'Tish—'

'Don't call me that,' I snapped. 'Stop calling me Tish. You've always called me that because he did, but I doubt you even know what it means.' I had tears in my eyes now, and I really hated myself for it. One rolled down the side of my nose, and I swatted it away. '*Xanthippe* knows what it means,' I added. 'Ask her, if you're interested. She always knew me better than you did.'

Bishop had that frantic expression that some men get around crying women. 'Tabitha, if you need to talk…'

'Thanks,' I said, getting control of myself. 'I have friends for that.'

He nodded, putting his professional face back on. 'You should maybe keep your head down for a while.'

'Until when?' I said. 'Until you've caught my imaginary stalker?' He turned to go, and I darted forward, grabbing at his sleeve. 'No, Bishop, wait. I know this sounds mad, believe me, I know. I haven't had much sleep, which isn't helping. But the café, and Amy and Danny, and Margarita's place is just around the corner, and I went out with Julian at college—I can't help thinking that maybe this whole mess is connected to me. Somehow.' Yep. That really did sound stupid.

Bishop looked at me for a long time, as if trying to figure out a tactful way to tell me I was nuts. Then, of course, he remembered that he was *Bishop*. 'You're nuts. I know you miss your dad—'

'Don't. It's not about that.'

'Isn't it?' He looked tired—tired of me, maybe. I didn't entirely blame him. 'The world doesn't revolve around you, Tabitha. Maybe it's time you learned that.' And then he left.

A few minutes later, Stewart came back in to refill his coffee cup. He was wearing one of Ceege's band t-shirts, a grey thing with something obscene scrawled across it. 'How long has it been?' he asked after a long quiet moment.

'How long what?'

'Since yer dad passed away.'

'Oh,' I said. He'd figured it out, then. Good, I suppose. I hated telling people. Hated talking about it. Pretending it wasn't a thing was easier. 'About three months ago. Before Christmas. But he wasn't here for a couple of years before that—retired to Queensland. Died there. I'm okay,' I added fiercely. 'I'm fine.'

'But you and Bishop—are not normally like this.'

I wiped my face with the back of my hand. 'Not as bad as this, usually, no.'

'A whole lot of things are starting to make sense.' Stewart put down his coffee and put his hand on the back of my neck, drawing me into him.

I put my arms around his back, and hugged. 'You smell like Ceege,' I said into his shoulder. It was bony.

'Is that a bad thing?'

'I can live with it. Almond soap. The boy knows how to moisturise.'

The phone rang, and I answered it without de-hugging Stewart. 'Hello? Yep, he's right here.' I handed it over. 'Simon for you.'

Stewart took it from me. I washed up my omelette plate as he talked. 'How do ye even have this number? Oh, really, yer a reporter? First I've heard of it.' Ooh, Stewart was sarcastic in the mornings. I kind of liked it. 'Aye, I heard about the press conference. Planning to crash it? Don't need me, surely—hardly worth taking decent photos. Oh. Cheers, I'll call her. See you later.' He hung up.

'Do you have to go to Inspector Clayton's little shindig?' I asked.

'No, but I'm away to the office now. Have to return a phone call to Melbourne.'

'You can do that from here,' I told him. 'We have like a dozen free interstate calls on our plan, and I'm—well, I'm not calling Queensland much, these days.' Before he got his serious face back, I batted my eyelashes at him. 'Plus, Ceege is paying the phone bill this month. Really, it's fine.'

'Cheers,' said Stewart. 'I'll take ye up on that.'

'No problem. I'm going to have a bath.'

Baths are the best thing in the world. If you get the perfect combination of water temperature, steam, bubbles and oils, then you can entirely forget your troubles. Even if your troubles include a ping pong ball stalker and a police officer who keeps snogging you out of misplaced loyalty to your dead father, but doesn't actually think you have two IQ points to rub together.

Well, maybe not all your troubles.

Like most old rental houses, our bathroom was pretty grim. Exposed pipes lined the walls, the cracks in the lino had reached epic proportions and the mirror only barely showed a reflection. The state of the bathroom was actually top of the List of Reasons Why Kelly Didn't Feel Guilty About Moving Out Despite Sticking Ceege and Tabs with the Extra Rent.

There was a pot of teal paint in the corner that I had bought with every intention of brightening up the little room, but it had never even been opened. Who has time for home improvements when there are soups and salads to perfect?

The bath was our crowning glory, the one thing which made up for stubbed toes, peeling paint and pipes which bounced noises all the way from one end of the house to the other. It was a fabulous tub, huge and deep. It also stood up from the floor, raised on four claws of solid, greenish metal.

I pinned my hair up, and stepped into the hot water, immersing myself in glittery foam. The scents of tea tree and peppermint washed up through my skin, flooding my senses. One long mmmmmmmmm.

I sighed, closed my eyes, and tilted my head against the water pipe. It was an interesting feature of our otherwise horrible bathroom that anything spoken on the stairs, immediately outside the back door or anywhere near the kitchen sink could be heard perfectly from this particular vantage point.

Not that I intended to eavesdrop on Stewart and his phone call. Because that would be wrong.

'Di,' he said in a low burr.

For one shocking moment I thought he'd said "Die", but I blame the bath bubbles and a misspent youth watching Hitchcock movies. Then I remembered Diana Glass, and rolled my eyes at myself. Of course she was the person in Melbourne he would call.

'What are ye doing back home?' Stewart asked. 'I thought ye'd be in the States for … is Col there?'

There was a very long pause, during which I scrubbed my toes with a pink flannel, and wondered what the legal ramifications were of tapping one's own phone. It was no fun just hearing half the conversation.

'How did tha' happen?' Stewart said suddenly. 'Di, what the hell—'

My toenails were in a state—definitely time to make a triple mud cake for Sara at the salon, to swap for a pedicure.

'No, no, I'm no'—I know I shouldnae have got ye into this.

I never thought … what do ye need me tae do about it now?'

So frustrating. I resisted the urge to run naked and soapy into the kitchen, demanding to know all the details. Instead, I dipped my head under the water, blowing bubbles. Not my business, not my business, not my business… But I resurfaced, of course, and kept listening.

'Christ,' said Stewart, so quietly I barely heard him. 'I like this job, Di. I've only just started. This is no' the best timing.'

A long, long pause.

'I love you, I love you! Yer the best.'

I washed my knees very thoroughly, and tried not to be depressed. Stewart's personal life was none of my business. Really, truly.

'Ow—Kinky Boots, gerroff!' He laughed, and I let the sound wash over me. 'No, it's a cat, trying tae kill me. I'm staying at a mate's place. No, no' a girlfriend, shut up. Aye, me too. Talk tae ye later. Bye.'

I stepped out of the bath, and dried myself off while the water gurgled and splurted its way down the plug hole. Then I wrapped up in my green kimono and padded out to the kitchen.

Stewart was on his third cup of coffee. 'I was going tae track down Claudina today, for the follow up on the "Morris isn't a drug user" story. Want tae come with?'

I thought about ping pong balls, and how annoyed Bishop would be. 'You bet. Since I'm apparently not running a café today.'

Stewart passed the phone over. 'Call Nin. If ye really want to get back tae normal tomorrow, let her know. No going back. Ye'll feel better.'

I stared at the phone as if it might bite me.

'Or you could tell her in person,' Stewart suggested.

Okay, phone it was.

Nin was short with me, but agreed to come in for her Thursday shift. She muttered something about being glad I had come to my senses, and then offered to call Lara and Yui for me, to tell them it was business as usual. I felt better when I hung up.

'No choice now,' said Stewart. 'Holiday's over.'

'Holiday,' I said grumpily. 'Half a week of insanity, more like. I'm going to murder Darrow when I see him again. No, worse. I will bake a peach meringue roulade and refuse to let him have any.'

'D'ye think,' said Stewart, and then cleared his throat. 'Ye like Darrow a lot, don't ye? He's a mate.'

'Yes. Not a cuddly on the couch, watching Doris Day movies when I feel bad kind of mate. But I'm used to having him around. He comes into the café a few times a week, when he's not mysteriously disappearing. Hangs out, chatting to my customers. I make fancy French gateaux for him, and we have stupid conversations.' I kicked the table leg. 'I miss him and his laptop and his annoyingly beautiful coats.'

'And yer not prepared to lose any more men in yer life,' Stewart said pointedly.

I gave him my patented death stare. 'You'll save me a fortune on therapy.'

'I'm only saying—it explains a lot.'

I got up and poured myself the last of the drip coffee, so Stewart couldn't have it. He looked sad as I added milk and sugar. 'Have I been acting completely off the show?' I asked.

'It's hard to tell. I've only known ye a week. I don't know what's normal.'

'I didn't even start worrying until I found out Xanthippe was looking for him. Darrow, I mean. He often does vanish for weeks at a time, and it's not like he owes me an explanation. He's never been a hands-on business partner—he leaves the café stuff to me. But my rent isn't transferred automatically. He always collects it in person. And he hasn't missed this many fortnights before. He can't be that scared of Xanthippe … well. Maybe he is. It was a very pretty car and no one knows better than him how long her vengeful streak can be.' That didn't explain why he had refused to sign the insurance papers, but I had my own theory about that one. Men are stupid.

'Still,' said Stewart. 'There's only so much ye can do until he comes back of his own accord.' He looked more closely at me. 'Tabitha, are ye glittering?'

'New bubble bath. I tried to resist, but the call of the sparkly bubbles overpowered my senses.'

Stewart reached out, and touched my cheek. Glitter came off on his fingers. 'I'm pretty sure most people would rinse this off.'

'You must know some strange people. Are we going to call Claudina, or just turn up?'

'We don't want tae give her the chance to dodge us. Get dressed.'

'Good plan.' I got up, managing not to fall out of my kimono as I headed out of the kitchen.

'Oh, and Tabitha?'

'Yes?'

'Why *did* yer dad call you Tish?'

I smirked at him, and bolted for the stairs. 'Eavesdropper.'

18

For interviewing suspicious characters, I had chosen today's outfit very carefully. It was what I liked to call my anti-goth ensemble—shoes, stockings, skirt, top, jacket, choker, handbag, nail polish, and three locks of false hair in my ponytail, all the same shade of powder blue.

Okay, possibly I just chose the whole outfit to match the nail polish I was already wearing.

We had to go through town to get to Claudina's place, and that meant driving past the café. As we got close, I clenched the steering wheel a little harder than I should have, every inch of me screaming to run inside and wrap pesto bagels for the lunch crowd.

What had I been thinking? I didn't stop trading when Dad died, and yet I'd done it for three days in the (misguided) hope of luring my missing landlord out of hiding? Very stupid, Tabitha.

Of course, I looked at the café as we passed. Something caught my eye. I flung the car into a bus zone on the next block, and parked messily.

LIVIA DAY

'Tabitha, we cannae stop here,' Stewart said in alarm.

'I'll only be a sec.'

I ran back across the lights in my wedge-heels, past the café and around to the yard behind. 'Locks!'

Lockwood the drug dealer was sitting himself down on my back steps when I called his name. He gave me a reproachful look and started levering himself up again. 'I'm just hanging out for a bit, no funny business. I'll move on...'

'No,' I said, out of breath. 'I mean—I wanted to talk to you.'

He lit a cigarette, not meeting my eyes. 'Café's closed. You don't have anything to bribe me with. Unless you're going to give me cash for pills?'

'I'm re-opening tomorrow. I'll bring you coffee and a sandwich out here, every day for a week.'

He didn't look tempted. 'I'd rather have marshmallows. Or, hey. Some of those melty biscuits. Those are good. Are you and that cop on together?'

I blinked at the quick change of subject from sweets to my love life. 'I'm not talking to you about Bishop.'

'Fair enough, thought I'd check for facts before spreading the goss.'

'Don't,' I said flatly. 'I want to talk to you about The Vampire.'

That amused him. 'So you're not fucking a cop, you're collecting evidence for him...'

'Don't laugh.'

'Dangerous territory, cutes. I find it pretty funny stuff.

"Vampire." Too much to hope for a more specific reference like Nosferatu? Would be classier.'

'Do you have much to do with him?'

'Nah. You know me, I'm small time. Limited supply and demand, special parties, enough to keep me in Cocoa Pops and Nintendo. But this Vampire bloke—he's a corporation, near enough. A real professional, here six months and looking to expand, if you know what I mean.'

'Do the police know about him?'

'The police always know. But what are they going to do? They don't know what his real name is. No one's ever nabbed one of his couriers. He doesn't pick innocent faces, he's smart enough to know that the real innocents are too noticeable. He finds the people that no one ever notices—man's an artist when it comes to delegation.'

'You sound impressed,' I accused.

'Got to respect the fellers at the top of the food chain, babe.'

'Do you know his name?'

Lock's eyes were wary behind his glasses. 'No one knows.'

'You're not going to tell me?'

'Nuh.'

'Anything you *can* tell me?'

'It's always the people you least suspect.'

'That will be a real help. Was Julian Morris working for The Vampire?'

Now Locks looked at me as if I really had said some- thing

funny. 'Tabitha Dah-ling. Such a nasty suspicious mind. I'll want my coffee tomorrow. Don't bother about the sandwich.'

I glared at him. He was too damn thin, that much was obvious even under the stupid moth-eaten coat that covered everything. Every time I saw him, I wanted to sit him at my kitchen table and give him a good square meal. 'Take care of yourself,' I said as I walked away.

'Always do,' Locks drawled, and lit another cigarette.

'Is this it?' I said a while later, when I pulled the car up outside Claudina's place. It was a grey concrete slab that apparently passed for a block of flats, standing out in the centre of an otherwise attractive suburb of weatherboard houses and European trees. 'I was expecting something more bohemian.'

'Could be nice inside,' said Stewart.

'Only cos you can't see the outside from in there.' There was a mountain view from the car park, at least, which made me feel better. It always does. 'Exactly how many redheads are we likely to find in this hovel?'

'Only the one, unless we're very lucky.' We got out of the car, and surveyed the building. 'So,' said Stewart, after a while. 'How are we gonnae play this?'

'You're the plucky ace reporter. I drove the car.'

'Psychological warfare?'

'At the very least.'

Someone had beaten us to the psychological warfare. Claudina opened the door in a tatty old dressing gown and an oversized t-shirt nightie with a giant teddy bear on it. People who design women's nighties these days should be beaten with a big stick.

'What do you want?' Claudina asked. She was a mess, her eyes too bright above dark circles. Whoever had convinced her to change her story for the police had done a real number on her.

I immediately changed my mind on how to tackle this. This woman didn't need to be pushed any further. A cup of tea and a sympathetic smile would just about break her.

So I broke her.

My mother is one of those natural hostesses. Even in other people's houses, she's the one who takes over the kitchen, makes a cuppa, and ensures that everyone is comfortable and looked after. It's a sneaky tactic, which leaves its victims befuddled and utterly vulnerable. I only channel Mum in dire emergencies.

'I was hoping to talk to ye about the story ye gave me a few days ago,' Stewart started. 'It seems ye might hae changed—'

I cut him off. 'Don't bother her with that now, Stewart. The poor girl looks awful. Are you sick, sweetie? A good cup of tea, that's what you need.'

Claudina stepped back in bafflement, and I took the opportunity to bustle right past her and into the flat.

It was exactly as grim inside as out, with mismatched share house furniture, coupled with lousy housekeeping skills.

The carpet was actually that awful bristly stuff that they used to put in school corridors to stop the students making out on the floor.

'You sit down,' I said to Claudina. 'When did you last get a decent night's sleep?'

She moved slowly, as if she needed to be told what to do. 'Sunday, I think.'

'Three days?' said Stewart. 'Is something wrong?'

I made a face at him to shut up. *Let me do the mothering.* 'Right, then. We need to pour a cup of something soothing down you. Do you have anything with chamomile in it? Sleepytime is my favourite.' I headed for the kitchenette in a corner of the living room.

'Please don't bother,' Claudina said weakly, but she did at least drop on to the couch.

'We're somewhat obliged!' I called out while I inspected her inadequate tea-making supplies. 'Stewart can't interrogate you about changing your story for the police while you're in this state, now can he?'

Stewart shrugged at Claudina and leaned against the wall, knowing when to leave me to my work. Good boy.

I emerged from the kitchen to inspect Claudina's DVD collection. 'What we need is a nice relaxing old movie. Aha!' I snatched up *The Philadelphia Story*. 'Perfect.'

Claudina tucked her feet up under her as I fiddled with the remotes, and got the movie going.

'Uh, Tabitha…' said Stewart, nonplussed by my brilliant interview tactics.

I threw my keys at him. 'Given that there is nothing remotely non-caffeinated in that kitchen, I need you to fetch me some supplies. There's a pink shoebox above the stove at my place, with my special tea stash in it. Also, we're going to need biscuits.'

'Anything else?' he said sarcastically. 'Maybe a Doris Day movie in case Cary Grant doesnae cut it?'

'That's a brilliant idea,' I said, blowing him a kiss. 'You're getting the hang of this.'

Stewart went out, muttering something. It was probably for the best that I didn't hear the actual words.

Claudina and I were immersed in the angry banter between a bad-tempered socialite (Katharine Hepburn) and her wisecracking ex-husband (Cary Grant). We both jumped when there was a knock at the door, and Claudina looked afraid. I filed that away for future reference, even as I patted her reassuringly on the arm and went to let Stewart in.

'I found the shoe box, but no biscuits,' he said, handing over the box and (what a sweetie!) my Doris Day box set. I like a man who isn't prepared to assume that I'm joking about stuff like that.

'Not to worry,' I said. 'Scones will be ready in a couple of minutes.'

'You baked *scones*?' He really hadn't known me very long. No one else of my acquaintance would be remotely surprised.

'No, the scone fairy left some under the lampshade. Of course I baked scones.' I rummaged through my box and came up triumphantly with my favourite teabags. 'Claudina, I'm going to make you a cup of this, and get those scones out of the oven, and then maybe you can tell us what's got you so worked up that you haven't slept all week.'

Stewart dropped into an armchair, beaming. 'Tabitha, I'm taking ye on all my interviews from now on.'

'Still no coffee,' I told him.

'I think ye fail to appreciate how excited I get about homemade scones.'

I made the tea—Irish Breakfast for Stewart and me, and Sleepytime for Claudina. I found butter and half a jar of jam, and brought the hot scones out of the oven.

As I carried the makeshift tea tray into the living room, I saw something that made my whole body tense up. Stewart saw my distress, and leaped up to take the tray out of my hands. By all means, let's save the scones first. 'Tabitha, what's wrong?'

I marched across the room, and found a ping pong ball, wedged in the crack between the carpet and the wall. I poked it with a finger gently to check it, then pulled it out and flourished it at Claudina. She stared at me as if I were pointing a gun at her. 'I think you'd better tell me what's been going on,' I said. 'Really, truly.'

'I can't,' Claudina said in a whisper, barely even a sound.

I started pulling at drawers and cupboards, panicking. 'Where are the rest of them? Where did—' The words choked up in my throat as I pulled on one of the desk drawers, and saw that it was piled edge to edge with ping pong balls. I poked at them one at a time, and eventually found one that zapped my finger. 'Bloody hell.'

Stewart came and took my arm, and led me over to sit beside Claudina on the couch. I let him. 'Right,' he said, in that gentle, lovely voice that certainly made *me* want to spill all my secrets. 'Claudina, do ye no' think it's time tae start talking? Yer not the only one this has happened tae.'

Claudina took a deep breath, and finally spilled.

I don't know why it felt worse to know I wasn't the only one being stalked by ping pong balls, but it did. It made it real.

'They were in a bucket, balanced on top of my bedroom door,' said Claudina. 'You know, like a practical joke—something kids might do with water or confetti.' She smiled weakly. 'I got the shock of my life—literally. About half of them have an electric charge, but the worst it did was frizz up my hair. I wasn't hurt, but shaken and scared.' She pressed her hand to her mouth. 'It was when I read the note that I really started freaking out.'

'What did it say?' asked Stewart, and I was glad he had taken over the interview. The sight of those ping pong balls had made it impossible to channel my mother any further—I don't think she's ever been afraid of anything in her life.

No, I wasn't afraid of ping pong balls. That was silly. The rush of my stomach into my throat every time I saw them was … well possibly I could come up with an excuse for it if I had the time.

Claudina spoke in a flat voice. 'The note said that he could get in any time, that nowhere was safe from him, that he knew my routine, that I should expect him to come calling again if I didn't tell the police that Julian was into drugs, a total junkie, into everything. And—also that he was a practical joker, to make them think *he* was the one who set those stupid traps.' She looked suddenly very fierce. 'He wasn't, though. He wouldn't. It's all wrong…'

'Ye told the police he was a drug addict, and probably the Trapper,' Stewart said, making notes.

Claudina hesitated, and nodded. 'If there was heroin in his insulin container, he didn't put it there,' she said quietly. 'I mean—he's not that person. I shouldn't have said he was. But I got scared.'

'Where's the note now?' I asked.

'I burned it. It said I had to.'

'So much for evidence,' I sighed.

'I was scared,' she flared at me. 'Wouldn't you be? Whoever it was, got into my flat without me even knowing he'd done it. I'm alone now, with Julian gone. Wouldn't you be scared?'

I was, I admitted to myself. *And I have Ceege, when he's not gadding about. Stewart, too. Bishop … maybe.* Interesting that my favourite police officer came third on the list of reliable menfolk, and I should probably rank Xanthippe higher than all three of them. 'You're not alone now,' I said aloud. 'Trust me on this.'

Claudina gave me a sceptical look, flashing some hint of the kind of person she was when not grieving or frightened for her life. 'You're going to protect me, though, are you? Going to stay here every night to make sure I'm not raped and murdered and electrified and God-knows-what else?' She turned on Stewart. 'You are not going to put any of this in your damn blog.'

'No' yet,' he said, looking startled at her outburst. 'I'm thinking there's nae story here until it's all over. Don't wannae publish something stupid, or dangerous.'

'And no,' I put in. 'I'm not going to protect you, Claudina. But I know a woman who can. If I find someone to stay with you, keep you safe until the person who killed Julian is caught, will you come to me with the police at the end of it? Make a proper statement about the truth?'

Claudina didn't look comforted. 'What sort of woman?'

'Trust me,' I said again, heading for the door. 'You'll be as safe as houses. I'm going out to make a phone call—you two watch the movie. There's a good bit with Jimmy Stewart coming up. And eat those scones before they get cold.'

It was nice to be outside the flat for a few minutes, to breathe slightly fresher air and look at the mountain again. Always worth checking that it was still there. I dialled Darrow's number, and waited until the answering machine picked up. 'Zee? I know you're still sponging off my missing landlord. Answer the phone!'

Xanthippe picked up. 'Found him?'

'Not yet. Got some leads, though,' I lied shamelessly. 'I've got a job for you. Fancy being a bodyguard to a terrified witness?'

'Are you going to pay me?'

'With actual money? Of course not.' I hesitated, not entirely ready to sell my soul to the devil. But Xanthippe didn't eat cake, which was my usual currency of choice for bribery and corruption. There was only one choice. 'I'll find Darrow for you. This week.'

'Tish, you haven't exactly had much success at that so far…'

'I'm close.' Lies upon lies.

'Lies upon lies,' said Xanthippe. Whoa. She was good. 'Who am I supposed to be protecting, and from whom?'

'Julian Morris's former flatmate,' I said. 'From the Trapper, and possibly my stalker.'

'I'll be right over.'

I gave her the address, and hung up with a sense of accomplishment. Now all we had to do was hand custody of Claudina over to Xanthippe before she found out about the Doris Day movies.

19

Stewart was depressed as we left Claudina's. 'This has no' been a bloggable day. Next time I start pursuing an actual news story, remind me there's more hits to be had from coffee fairs and meringue porn.'

'You can take pictures of what's left of Darrow after Xanthippe catches up to him. Will that count as news?'

'Only if it gets really bloody.' He leaned against the car window. 'Better throw myself on Simon's mercy and see wha's going on at the office.'

'I should do some prep work for tomorrow—try to get back into Nin's good books.'

'Good luck wi' that.' Stewart didn't say much else until I parked the car in my usual spot, on the loading zone near Café La Femme. 'Coffee break first?' he said hopefully.

'You haven't done any work yet. Come back down in an hour.'

'Slave driver,' he said, and loped off towards the building.

I took my time, working my brain back into kitchen mode,

figuring out what I could do today to make less work for tomorrow. Yesterday's bakingfest would help somewhat, those cakes were still good.

The kitchen door was unlocked. I didn't even react to that until I was inside. It was normal for Nin to get to work before me. But she wasn't due in until the morning. 'Nin? Is that you?'

Silence from within. I know at that point I should have yelled up the stairs for Stewart, or called Bishop, but I had been relying on those two too much lately, so I didn't. Instead, I walked through the kitchen and pushed open the door to the main café.

Eight-year-old Kevin Darrow sat at one of my tables near Stewart's mural-in-progress, doing what looked like homework. 'Gah!' I said. 'What are you doing here?'

The boy glanced up, and past me. I turned to see a familiar, well-dressed man in a gorgeous coat standing at *my* café counter, drinking *my* coffee. 'Darling. Mind telling me why my café has been closed for the past three days?'

I looked at Darrow for a long moment, not entirely sure that he was real.

The thing about Darrow is—he's delicious. There's nothing pretty about him. He's built of strong features: wide hands, prominent nose, dirty gold hair, caramel eyes, confident mouth. He doesn't wear *clothes* like normal people, he wears Clothes with a capital Everything. Silk shirts, linen waistcoats, handmade suits, expensive shoes. He was once spotted in an eighteenth century cravat, and damned if it didn't suit him.

Not your average Aussie bloke.

'Well?' he asked, in his chocolate-melted-into-cream voice.

'It's not your café, it's my café. Where have you been?' I demanded.

'Hiding from Xanthippe, obviously. Do you *know* the mess I made of her car?' Darrow gave me one of those smiles he uses to get anything he wants.

I couldn't let him get away with it. I couldn't slip into our usual banter and pretend that everything was normal. 'Cut the crap. What's going on?'

Darrow's smile slipped a little, but only just. 'You know she's moved into my house? That woman's got persistence. Remind me why we broke up? Once she's got over trying to kill me, I may have to hire her. She'd make a kick-arse bailiff.'

I slapped my palms flat on the counter. 'Darrow, talk to me. You went missing, and someone got murdered, and the police have been asking questions about *you*.'

My landlord laughed at me. 'If you'd just screw Bishop and get it over with, maybe he'd stop trying to pin crimes on every bloke you talk to. Sexual repression is a sad, sad thing.'

I scowled at him. 'That's what Stewart keeps saying.'

'Who's Stewart?'

'New best friend.' I leaned over and smacked Darrow between the eyes. 'The old one dumped me.'

'Ow!' He batted my hand away. 'No violence, please.'

'I was worried about you, you complete tool.'

Darrow took my hand. 'Didn't mean to make you worry, Darling. I needed some time out. Went off to the mountains for a while. I would have been back a week ago if it wasn't for Xanthippe sniffing around.'

'And the taxi?'

'Research.' He hesitated, looking appealingly vulnerable for about five seconds before the old cocky Darrow reasserted himself. 'I'm writing a book,' he announced. Ridiculously pleased with himself. Bastard.

There was one question that had to be asked. 'Am I in it?'

'Obviously. All fourteen of the characters are based on you. Especially the murderous old ladies and cheeky Cockney schoolboys.'

I squeezed his hand, not wanting to give in and be friendly too soon, but I'm a soft touch, and we both knew it. 'So you haven't been sneaking around, building traps and administering heroin overdoses to random buskers, or stalking women with electrified ping pong balls?'

Darrow stared at me. 'Is that what the police think?'

'It's what Xanthippe thinks.'

'That bitch.' Heh, the 'why did we break up' talk hadn't lasted long. 'Listen, Darling. Kev told me about the ball in your handbag. Someone's targeting you personally. You know I wouldn't do that.'

'Of course not,' I said quickly. 'But you know something, don't you?'

My door banged open, in the kitchen. 'Tabitha?' Bishop's voice called out from there.

'Damn—I'll get rid of him,' I promised in a whisper. The last thing we needed was those two in a room together. I pushed my way through the door into the kitchen to greet the noble representatives of Tasmania Police. 'Café's still closed, boys.'

Constable Gary, leaning against the fridge, smiled at me in his usual friendly puppy dog way. 'Hi, Tabby.'

Bishop, by the door, didn't snap or glower. For a minute I wondered if he was an imposter. 'Tabitha. You all right?'

'I'm fine,' I said brightly. 'Action stations to re-open tomorrow. I might even toss a few steak pies in the oven for old time's sake. Don't tell Inspector Bobby, though, I don't want to be responsible for yet another police divorce…'

'Have you received any further strange parcels, or messages?' Bishop asked, very businesslike.

'No,' I said.

There was a pause, while we both waited for the other to say something snarky.

'Gary, wait outside, will you?' Bishop said.

I made Gary wait a moment while I hacked off a large piece of the apple pie to take with him. He went, cradling it in his hands like it was something precious. I love a man who knows how to appreciate my food.

'I'm sorry about this morning,' I said very fast, the second Gary was out of the door.

Bishop's reflexes were poor, for a police officer. He only got as far as 'I'm so—' in the same time. Which was cute, but I still totally won. 'I am taking this stalker threat of yours seriously,' he said, after we concluded our apology sprint. 'Just because I don't think it's related to the Trapper case…'

'I know. I should trust you to do your job.' And I mostly did. I was feeling guilty now, about keeping Claudina's evidence secret from him, but what could I do? She had to be the one to change her statement again. I couldn't do it for her.

'I—' Bishop ran his fingers through his hair. When it was longer, he would have tugged at the curls, but it was too short for that right now. A shame—I rather liked those curls of his. 'I don't know if Clayton is right,' he admitted. 'But I don't have the clout to go against him, not without any more evidence.'

I shouldn't have said what I did to him earlier. What did I know about solving crimes? I didn't have any evidence to help, not yet. I'd keep my mouth shut until I did. 'I've been horrible to you,' I admitted. 'Without Dad around—'

'You don't have him to push against any more,' Bishop said. 'It feels like—you've been trying to push against me, instead.'

I was horrified. 'I'm not looking for a replacement *Dad*.'

'Good! Because that would be—'

Unsettling, to say the least. 'Icky, and wrong. It explains all the shouting, though.'

'I used to wonder why he shouted at you all the time,'

Bishop said, sounding depressed. 'I thought maybe he didn't understand you…'

'He understood me.'

'But you've been acting like such a brat, and he wasn't here to do the job—'

'Hush, I get it.' I stepped a little closer, and tilted my head to one side. 'That explains the shouting, Senior Constable Bishop. It doesn't explain the snogging.'

He looked embarrassed. 'I wanted to remind you that I'm not … your dad. Or your big brother, or anyone remotely related to you—this is all pretty twisted, isn't it?'

'Hell yes,' I said, and leaned forward to take his lower lip between my teeth. He went very still, and I nibbled my way around to the side of his mouth. Then, just as he tried to kiss me properly, I slid away to press my teeth lightly against the side of his neck.

Bishop made a small noise, and stroked the base of my spine, his fingers creeping under the hem of my top.

I concentrated on his neck for a little while. Such a nice neck. I mapped it, all the way up to his ear.

'Tabitha?' he said, sounding a long way away.

'Mmm?'

'Will you have dinner with me, tomorrow night? Actual "eating and talking" dinner?'

I was a fraction away from nipping his earlobe when the question sank in. 'You mean, like a date?'

'Yes.'

I leaned back to look at him. His eyes were darker than I had ever seen them before, and he was still stroking my back. This was so much more pleasant than screaming at each other, but terrifying at the same time. 'That's crazy talk.'

'I know.'

'Okay, then.' I was about to go back for his ear when reality crashed back. Darrow was in the other room, and he had something important to tell me about my ping pong ball stalker. 'You'd better go now,' I said quickly. 'Um. Because otherwise I will have to ravish you on the kitchen table, and I'm far too busy for that sort of thing.'

Bishop laughed, and tugged my ponytail. 'Do you have someone to stay with you tonight?'

For a minute, I thought he was propositioning me, but then I remembered. Stalker. Right. 'Yep. Ceege. All good. Tomorrow, then?'

Bishop laughed again, and *oh* that was a gorgeous sound. As he left, I resisted the urge to lick the back of his neck.

I locked the door behind Bishop, and ran into the café to finish the conversation with Darrow. He, of course, had skipped out the front door with Kevin while I was distracted.

One of Kevin's exercise books still lay on the table where he had been working, with the words LATER scrawled across the cover.

'He knows something,' I howled at Stewart. 'Darrow knows, and he couldn't wait five minutes—' while I pashed a police officer in my kitchen '—to tell me about it.'

'Tabitha, I'm working,' Stewart protested, barely looking up from his computer.

I paused. 'Excuse me, what now?'

'Simon didnae care I was running around with ye as long as I brought in the stories, but I havenae written a single post since the coffee fair, and now there's a list o' people I need to call and make appointments with—'

'Oh. Actual work.'

'Ye didnae even bring me coffee,' he said sullenly.

'Fine. Make it all about you.'

Stewart leaned back in his chair. 'Ye cannae do anything about Darrow until he turns up again, right?'

'Right.'

He waved a hand airily at me. 'So cook something. It will make ye feel better. I'm going to be stuck here most of the afternoon. If Darrow wants to tell ye anything, at least he'll be able to find ye.'

Wow. He was actually telling me to go back to the kitchen. 'If you're going to be sensible, I don't think we can be friends any more.'

'Do ye want me tae stay over tonight?' he asked, when I was almost at the door. 'I mean—will Ceege be home?'

For a second I thought I had just received my second proposition of the day, then I remembered. Stalker. Funny how I kept forgetting that part. Apparently denial is the only way to get things done. 'He might be, but I'm never sure. I'd like it if you could stay. If it's not a bother…'

'S'fine, but I'll have to go by me place to pick up clothes first. Around six?'

'Okay.' I waved a finger at him. 'There won't be nearly as many snuggles on the couch, though. I don't want to make Bishop jealous.'

'You always want to make Bishop jealous.'

He did have a point. Sadly. 'That was before we were dating,' I said with a nod.

Stewart looked sceptical. 'Ye stopped bitching at each other long enough for Bishop to ask ye out?'

'For dinner,' I said, trying not to sound like I was still in high school.

'You've known him for how long?'

'Ten years.'

'And you started flirting with him how long ago?'

'Pretty much straight away.'

'With actual intent?'

'Six years.'

Stewart shook his head. 'And he still wants to buy ye dinner first. Man's a fucking saint.'

'You are simply jealous because you don't have a date with a hot policeman.'

'Oh, aye. Green with envy. Run away, Tabitha. Leave me be.'

He was hiding his extreme heartbreak suspiciously well, what with those shooing motions and everything.

I spent the afternoon catching up with my regular suppliers by phone, and cooking up a storm for tomorrow's reopening. I was in a Bavarian mood, and happily made herb soup, marinated vegetables for a salad, and constructed an epic pork and cabbage casserole.

The kitchen smelled amazing by the time I packed all the food away in the fridge, and I found myself thinking fondly of Bavarian Bruno, the third worst boyfriend in the world, and his gorgeous mother Hélène, who let me work at her restaurant and taught me everything I ever needed to know about sauerkraut.

I wondered about Bishop's mother Elena, and how many Greek recipes she had shared with me over the years. Damn it, he might not have anything but an Aussie accent, but he still fit the pattern. That thought was more depressing than it should have been.

By 6 PM, I had scrubbed the café spotless, and finished all the prep work for a nice, easy day tomorrow. I had checked that Nin, Lara and Yui were all clear on who was taking what shift for the rest of the week, and was feeling pretty cheerful by the time I closed up and headed over to pick up Stewart from his manky flat. I took Kevin Darrow's exercise book with me, in case Darrow and his kid sidekick turned up again.

Stewart's door was unlocked. 'Are you in?' I called as I let myself through. 'Also, did you not get the memo about stalkers? Your security's worse than mine.'

'Entertain yerself for a minute, can ye?' Stewart yelled through the bedroom door. 'I cannae find my shoe.'

'That's what they all say.' I stole a banana from his kitchen and peeked into a few of the more intriguing boxes still littered around the living room while I ate it.

'Anything exciting happen today?' Stewart asked finally, strolling out of his bedroom with shoes on both feet.

'Apart from the lust of my life finally getting off his arse and propositioning me?'

'Aye, apart from tha'. If ye want tae brag, get girl friends.'

'Also Darrow finally turning up and annoying the hell out of me as only he can?'

'I know that, too. Has nothing happened since?'

'It was a slow day. Mostly, I cooked.' I swallowed the last bite of banana. 'Stewart, you're not a fan of romance novels, are you?'

He gave me a shifty look. 'Why would ye ask?'

'It's an obvious assumption. You made something of an online pest of yourself when you went after Diana Glass. You slagged off the whole genre in *Vogue*.'

'Aye,' he said suspiciously. 'So?'

'I can't help wondering why someone who hates romance novels so very, very much, has a whole stack of them stashed behind his couch.'

'Tabitha!' he yelped. 'A man's couch is his castle. Keep the hell off me turrets.'

'I only peeked a bit. One turret.'

'Yer a menace tae society.'

'You say the sweetest things.' I checked the books off on my fingers. '*Heart Aflame*, by Diana Glass. Five copies. *Bodyguard's Choice*, by Diana Glass. Five copies. *Portrait of Desire*, by Diana Glass. Four copies. Multiple copies of the same book, all by the same author. Do you know what that says to me?'

Stewart crossed his arms defensively. 'Stalker?'

'Author copies,' I said with great relish. 'You're Diana Glass.'

'That's insane.'

'Actually, I think it's hilarious. Still doesn't explain who the woman on the phone was.' I grabbed at his portfolio and flipped it to the page of the gorgeous brunette woman. 'Or who this is, for that matter. Unless you're way better at drag than Ceege, and I don't think that's possible.'

Stewart pulled the portfolio away from me, looking mad as hell. Possibly I had overestimated how amusing this situation was. 'Have ye been listening in on me phone calls?'

'Not intentionally! My bathroom has mystical eavesdropping superpowers. How many super-sized long blacks will it take before you tell me who the woman in your author photo is?'

My mobile rang, saving Stewart from having to answer. It was a new number. 'Hello?'

'Not easy to have a conversation with you when you keep entertaining the police,' said Darrow in that warm and melty voice of his.

I switched the phone to speaker, and waggled my eyebrows at Stewart to indicate how open and sharing I was. 'You could have stayed. I got rid of Bishop as fast as I could.'

Darrow gave a throaty laugh. 'Yeah, I heard how hard you were trying to get rid of him.'

Okay, I was blushing. That was embarrassing. Regretting the speaker phone. Moving on. 'Anyway...'

'Did you get my present?'

I frowned. 'All you left me was some exercise book.' I wiggled my hand expectantly at Stewart, and he pulled it out of my handbag, thumbing through the pages.

'Thought a clever lady like you would have figured it out by now,' drawled Darrow.

Stewart held the book open to a page full of sketches. Line drawings of poles and traps and nets, and the inner workings of electrified ping pong balls, surrounded by scientific notations in a neat, childlike handwriting. 'What. The. Fuck,' I said aloud.

I could practically hear Darrow smirking, that beautifully dressed rat bastard. 'Thought this conversation might go better at a distance. I know what you're thinking now, and you're so very wrong.'

'Your baby cousin Kevin is the Trapper.'

'See, I *said* you were wrong. Kev came up with the designs, sure. I asked him to.'

Stewart pushed a chair at me, and I sat down in a hurry. '*You're* the Trapper?'

'Not even that, Darling. Keep up. I told ye: I'm writing a novel.'

'A lot of that going around,' I couldn't help snarking. Stewart rolled his eyes at me.

'I'm serious,' Darrow went on. 'A fabulous detective novel. It's going to revolutionise the genre. That's why I went AWOL, I was on a writing retreat.'

'To write a novel.' The universe kept making less sense.

'Sure, Darling. I got little Kev to come up with those traps months ago, to use in my book. He's a smart cookie, that one. But someone else has been using his traps for real.'

'Why should I believe you?' I demanded.

'Darling, it's me. Do you really believe I'd swan around building dodgy man-traps and stuffing ping pong balls in your handbag? Don't I have a bit more class than that? What would I even wear for such an enterprise?'

'Fine,' I muttered. 'But who built the traps, if not you?'

'My laptop was stolen a few months back—your nice cop friends got it back for me, which I never expected. But whoever took it had access to my manuscript and scans of Kev's notes from that book you're holding.'

I pressed my lips together. 'A laptop thief happened across your sketches and got inspired? Or someone knew about your work in progress and used it deliberately?'

'The latter's not unlikely,' Darrow admitted. 'Possibly I talked about my manuscript to a few people. Customers of your café, mostly. I'm very proud of it.'

'Possibly,' I repeated. 'Not helpful. Remember any specific people you told?'

'I talk to a lot of people. I'm friendly.' There was a long pause. 'I can think of one person I told about it,' Darrow said finally. 'Mocked me thoroughly, the wench. And she's had access to my house, where the contents of my laptop are backed up on my desktop computer. She didn't even need to steal the laptop, unless she did that to steer suspicion away from herself.'

'Xanthippe,' I said quietly. Zee, whose life I hardly knew anything about these days. Who was working for a band that needed serious publicity. Whom I had left in charge of Claudina, the only witness who might help the police learn the truth about the death of Julian Morris. 'I've got to go.' I ended the call, but made sure to save the number.

'Do ye really think—' said Stewart. He didn't finish the question, but I knew what he was worried about. He liked Xanthippe. Hell, I liked Xanthippe. I wanted us to get back something of the friendship we'd let slip through our fingers.

I still didn't trust her as far as I could throw that waterlogged Lotus of hers.

'Let's find out,' I said.

Stewart handed me my overstuffed handbag. 'Saw ye put those Diana Glass novels in yer handbag.'

'I have some reading to do.'

'*Really* wish ye wouldnae.'

'Tell me everything about the woman in the author photo on the way to Claudina's, and I might change my mind about reading all the juicy bits in your novels. Aloud. To Ceege. And all of our friends.'

'This would be why I write under a pen name,' Stewart groaned.

20

'It's not exactly a long drive,' I pointed out when we had driven three blocks, with Stewart yet to spill his guts even a little bit.

He gave me a weary look. 'I'm still working on the part where it's any of yer business.'

'Stewart,' I gasped. 'How can we have secrets? You know all about my love life.'

'Not by choice as I recall.'

I waved him off. 'Not important. I want to know who the "Di" on the phone is, if you're Diana Glass.'

'Dinah Leiber,' he said reluctantly. 'She was—is one of my best friends. We shared a flat for a while, in Melbourne.'

'Not a girlfriend?'

Stewart looked embarrassed. 'I wouldnae have minded, but she had other ideas. She got married a couple of years ago. Went off to be a theatre designer in San Francisco.'

'And she didn't mind you plastering her face all over the internet as the author of romance novels?'

'I didnae put her face on the internet,' he protested. 'Well, not exactly. I needed a female author photo for the press release of the first book, year before last, and she let me use one I'd taken of her. She figured it wouldnae affect her, since she was in another country.'

'Hmm,' I said. 'I hear they have bookshops in America.'

'The internet thing was an accident,' Stewart confessed. 'I did the *Vogue* article a couple of months back tae drum up some publicity for book sales, and then ... it went viral, and so did the bloody photo of her. Di only found out about it recently, when friends from Melbourne started emailing her tae ask about her secret life as a romance novelist...'

'You won't come out of the closet to let her off the hook?'

'Not if I can help it,' he said fervently. 'I have a reputation as a cynical reporter now. Fluffy bodice-rippers dinnae fit with tha'. Simon would think I was a complete wanker—I might lose the *Sandstone City* gig, and I like this job.'

'But you're happy for people to think you're an internet troll,' I sighed. 'Honestly, *boys*.'

'So that's it,' Stewart said, spreading his hands wide as I pulled into the little car park of Claudina's apartment block. 'All my secrets, laid bare before ye.'

'I believe you,' I said, though I didn't, really. Surely there was still more to be discovered about Stewart McTavish. 'Come on. Let's dig up some of Xanthippe's secrets for a while. It's definitely her turn.'

Xanthippe answered the door on the first knock. She glowered at me. 'Whose bright idea was it to feed Doris Day movies to this woman? I don't know if getting my hands on that bastard Darrow is actually worth all this—one more amusing misunderstanding with Rock Hudson and I will stab myself in the eye. Both eyes. Then I'm going to start on *other people's eyes*.'

'So glad I'm unqualified to be the bodyguard,' Stewart said in a low voice.

'We need to talk,' I said, ignoring their Doris Day hatefest. Savages. 'About this.' I flashed her a glimpse inside Kevin Darrow's exercise book.

Xanthippe rolled her eyes. 'That took you long enough. Come on in.'

Claudina, her bloodshot eyes fixed to *By the Light of the Silvery Moon*, didn't even look up from the couch.

'Bonus points for the insomnia cure,' said Xanthippe, giving me two very sarcastic thumbs up. 'I think you melted her brain. We can talk back here.' She led the way to an empty bedroom.

I assumed it had belonged to Julian. There was furniture here but someone—his mother or sister, perhaps—had cleared out everything remotely personal.

Xanthippe had an overnight bag stashed in one corner, and a pile of face and hair products in a box on the otherwise empty bookshelf. Making herself at home. She had also brought some furnishings that I had last seen in Darrow's house.

'So,' I said. 'You're stealing stuff now? How many lamps and doonas does it take to balance out a trashed Lotus?'

'More than he owns,' Xanthippe said grimly. 'Let's get on with this. What do you think you know?'

I kicked off my powder blue boots and sat on the bed, bouncing experimentally. I picked a nail polish out of Zee's collection and started painting my big toenail in Ocean Aqua. 'Well, I found Darrow. The closed café finally got his attention. He says he's writing a novel, and he got young Kev to devise some theoretical traps for him to use.'

Xanthippe snorted. 'And I'm Calamity Jane. You believed him?'

I capped the bottle and reached for another, *Peppermint Pink*, for the second toe. 'No reason why I shouldn't.'

'Well, I know *I* didn't chuck a postman in a cage or snare a cat in a net,' Xanthippe said, crossing her arms.

I raised my eyebrows and said nothing as I started on the third toenail with *Iceberg Cobalt*. Stewart said it for me: 'No mention of the trap in Crash Velvet's flat. Does that mean ye did that one?'

Xanthippe glared at us both. 'Darrow is the one who set the Trapper loose. I found the plans on his computer.'

'But when did you find them?' I asked, sorting through the remaining nail polish options. I found a lovely bright scarlet called *Lurve* and set it aside for later. 'Before Julian Morris built the trap in Crash Velvet's spare room, or afterwards?'

'If you know Morris built it, why are you hassling me?' Xanthippe huffed.

'Because he doesn't have any motive for doing it,' I replied. 'The most logical reason is if someone paid him. Musicians. Always broke. Who do we know who might want to get Crash Velvet a bit of extra publicity, and capitalise on the "Trapper" story that had already featured on the *Sandstone City* blog?'

'Their new PR advisor,' Stewart said helpfully.

I lined up several nail polish bottles on the bedside table— a blue, a green and a brown, all strangely matte with metallic flecks through them. 'I see you've been collecting the new Gee Bee range. It's crap, apparently. But here's the funny thing—when Julian's body was taken into Forensics, they found traces of a Gee Bee nail polish on his fingertips, as if he'd been painting someone's nails with it.'

'That's your evidence?' Xanthippe said. 'Substandard nail polish? It's not overly sound as detective work goes, Tish.'

I just looked at her. 'This range of polish comes in a four pack. Where's your *Poison Flesh*, Zee?'

Xanthippe fidgeted impatiently. 'What are you going to do, dob me in to Leo? Last I heard, *not* being in possession of a bottle of nail polish was not a hanging offence.'

'She has a point,' agreed Stewart.

I pointed a bottle of *Mermaid Foam* at Xanthippe. 'This

isn't about Bishop, or evidence. The point is, I know you're involved. Darrow is involved. Apparently I'm involved. So tell me what the hell is going on before *Leo* starts arresting us all.'

Xanthippe flopped on the foot of the bed. 'You don't honestly think I've been sneaking around putting ping pong balls into handbags?'

'I don't know what to think!' After a moment, I gave in. 'No. But Darrow thinks you're the Trapper, and you think he is. If you weren't both so obsessed with this little cat and mouse game over the Lotus—yes, I know, beautiful car, destroyed, tragedy of epic proportions, put it back in your pants—then you would have pooled your information by now and you would have realised that someone has used *both* of you.'

Xanthippe blew out the breath. 'What do you want from me?'

'A timeline of events. A confession about everything you were directly involved with.' I raised a hand to ward off her protests. 'I'm not telling Bishop anything right now. As if he'd believe me. But I have to know what you did, and what Darrow did, so we can get together and figure out what *someone else* did.'

'Fine,' said Xanthippe. 'For the record, I don't think Darrow is the Trapper. I think Morris was the Trapper, and Darrow paid him.'

'What makes you think that?'

'Because I paid him too.'

I threw the bottle of nail varnish at her. She ducked, and it hit the wall in a crunch of glossy-green-on-cream. Oops. Good thing this wasn't my house.

'Right,' said Xanthippe, straightening up. 'Timeline. I found out about my car via text a couple of weeks ago—can you believe Darrow didn't have the balls to at least call me in person?'

'Bravery is not one of his superpowers,' I agreed, managing to stay calm.

'So I decided to take the job with Crash Velvet—kCeera's an old friend, and they'd been asking me to sort out their PR for months, but I didn't fancy coming back here.'

'Until you needed an excuse to come and whip Darrow's arse,' I put in.

'As if I need an excuse. Yeah, so I got here, what, a week and a half ago? Sunday before last. Started looking for Darrow, and working with the band. I read up on *Sandstone City*, which seemed the local media most likely to play ball.' She nodded in Stewart's direction. 'Saw his stories on the Trapper, and wondered if it was something we could use, but didn't think much of it. But I needed somewhere to crash that night, and I broke into Darrow's place. And I found the plans.'

'You assumed he was the Trapper?' I said, shaking my head with disbelief.

'You don't know half the dodgy stuff he gets up to, Tish. It wasn't unreasonable.'

'Not to an ex-girlfriend with a grudge, no.'

'Anyway,' Xanthippe grunted. 'I figured it was poetic justice, using Darrow's freakishness to help me out in my job. So I set up one of his traps myself.'

I went cold. 'Just how important is promoting this band to you?'

Xanthippe looked furious. 'What the hell do you think of me? I'm going to run around killing buskers for fame and profit? Believe me, if I was prepared to *murder* people to promote Crash Velvet, we wouldn't be relying on some pissy little blog to get the news out. No offence,' she added, to Stewart.

'None taken,' he said, bemused.

'I asked around some pubs last week. Found out some busker had been boasting about being paid to set stupid traps around the streets of Sandy Bay. Morris was easy enough to find. You're not the only one who knows people around here, Tabitha. He had a copy of the same plans I did—never admitted who paid him for the first traps, though I dropped enough hints that I already knew. I paid him to do one for me. That was the Monday and Tuesday before he was killed.'

Damn, she is good. 'So you already knew Morris?' I asked.

Xanthippe gave me another of those 'are you high' looks that she was so very good at. 'Tish, you went out with him at college. We all knew him.'

'Huh.' Maybe I should be keeping some kind of diary.

Now Xanthippe was shifting uncomfortably. 'Morris was supposed to put a dummy in the net, done up in freaky bondage gear. I got a shop mannequin for him, and the clothes, and even gave him the damn nail polish. Imagine the look on my face the next morning when the band told me that instead of a dummy, it was Morris hanging in the net, with a needle sticking out of him. I don't know what happened. But if Darrow is responsible, this is serious shit, Tabitha. He can't get away with this.'

I couldn't quite believe what I was hearing. 'Why did *none* of you tell the police that you had hired Morris to build the trap?'

'Crash Velvet don't know,' Xanthippe said. 'I mean—they know not to mention my name or my involvement with them to anyone. They're good like that. But I let Morris into the flat when they were all out—the band don't know what I did.'

'And you,' I said in a hard voice. 'Why haven't you told Bishop about your role in all this?'

'Are you kidding me? I can't put him in this position, Tish. You know how bad it's going to look.'

'It will be worse if it comes out now. Or later—if the case is compromised because of it? You can't do this to him, Zee.'

'I've already done it.' Xanthippe's voice was on edge—this was the most freaked out I had ever seen her. 'I can't tell him now. He'll kill me.'

'He loves you, he won't—'

'Hang on a minute,' Stewart broke in. 'Am I missing something here, about Bishop and Xanthippe?'

I had forgotten that he hadn't been here our whole lives. 'She's his sister.'

'Oh, right.' It apparently required a bit of mental readjustment to add that detail into the mix. 'Different last names?' Stewart asked after a moment.

'Halves,' said Xanthippe. 'Different dads. We're not that close. But it's not exactly going to help out his career if I admit I commissioned the Crash Velvet trap.'

'Or if you're arrested for murder,' I pointed out.

'Yes, thanks for that.' Xanthippe sighed. 'The police have decided it was an accidental overdose. Maybe it really was.'

'Maybe,' I said, knowing how much she needed to believe that. 'But if that's the case—what happened to the mannequin?'

'We're missing something,' said Stewart, the only one left in the room who wasn't sitting on the bed. 'Some detail that will make the rest of this make sense.'

'Just the one?' Xanthippe said sarcastically. 'Shall I check my handbag?'

'Don't mind him, he reads crime novels,' I said.

'Oh, one of those.' She gave him a pointed look. 'This is *off* the record, by the way, Mr Bloggy McBlogger.'

'Don't worry,' said Stewart. 'It's my policy not tae publish anything that will make Bishop want to hurt me.'

'Amazing how much ground that policy covers,' I said, wanting to smile despite everything.

'Ye were right the first time, Tabitha,' said Stewart. 'None of this will make sense until we get Xanthippe and Darrow in a room together, and figure out which bits of this the two of them are no' responsible for.'

I nodded. 'You grab Claudina and the Doris Day stash. I'll make some calls. Let's get this done tonight. My place. I have a café to open tomorrow.'

Gateaux. Panini. Bagels. Gluten-free friands. I wanted my old life back.

I also wanted Stewart to stick around, and Darrow to stop disappearing, and Xanthippe to be my friend again, and Bishop to kiss me like he did in the stairwell that time, only more.

I wanted my dad back, while we were at it, but that wasn't going to happen. I'd settle for the rest.

'Ceege!' I yelled as soon as my key turned in the door. 'You home?'

'No need to yell,' said my housemate, strolling out of the kitchen in his grubbiest Nirvana t-shirt and a pair of half-dead jeans that I swear I have binned twice for his own good. 'Didn't tell me about the dinner party.' Ceege shared a very male nod with Stewart, cast a startled look over the mess that was a sleep-deprived Claudina, and eyed up Xanthippe with interest. 'Long time no see. I keep telling Tabs she needs more lady friends. Come around any time.'

'Eyes back in your head, or I'm telling Katie,' I told him. 'What's this about dinner?'

Ceege jerked a thumb towards the back of the house. 'Darrow. In the kitchen. With a wooden spoon. He wasn't expected?'

'In a manner of speaking.' I'd been calling all of Darrow's numbers, including the new one, but had received no reply. Apparently, that was because he had spent the afternoon camped out in my kitchen.

I knew what he was cooking before I reached the kitchen door. Bouillabaisse. My bouillabaisse, to be exact—well, my recipe by way of Jean-Michel's mother in the Dordogne, that angel on earth who taught me how to make melt-in-the-mouth croissants and heavenly pie crusts.

'Should I have brought bread?' I asked as I stepped into my kitchen, but several baguettes were already lined up on the counter.

'Sent Ceege out for some,' Darrow said.

Xanthippe was already moving forward, with the momentum of a freight train. 'You stupid, selfish, careless, bastard *arsehole*.'

He turned as she reached him, and stuck out the wooden spoon to ward her off. She hesitated, caught in a mesmerising haze of tomato and seafood and *mmmmm*. 'Try it,' said Darrow in his smoothest voice.

Suspiciously, Xanthippe blew on the contents of the spoon, and then took it into her mouth, tasting the soup.

'Does it need pepper?' Darrow asked.

'It's fine,' she said, strangely calm as she licked the spoon. 'It's good.' She pulled a document out of her hand-bag and smacked him in the chest with it. 'Sign this. Now. Dickhead.'

'You only had to ask,' he said, eyes innocent. Even I would

have smacked him for that, but apparently bouillabaisse is the universal currency of forgiveness, or at least of temporary cease-fires. Xanthippe stood there glaring while Darrow signed the insurance forms with a flourish. She took them back and checked every signature.

'I've been working on a way to make it up to you,' Darrow added, his caramel eyes all warm in the soup haze.

Oh, yeah. I'd called it. The only reason he hadn't signed those papers at a distance was because he wanted her to hunt him down. These two were so damaged for each other.

'Don't,' Xanthippe muttered. 'You making things up to me is always more hazardous than the original disaster.'

Darrow grinned that wicked 'oh I'm off the hook' grin of his, and fetched bowls.

We ate the soup with piles of French bread, the six of us. Ceege slurped his down in a hurry, then beat a retreat to *World of Warcraft*. We were being way too weird for him, and he needed a dose of reality that could only be provided by metrosexual elves. Claudina kept nodding off in her chair.

Darrow and Xanthippe watched each other in ways that made me think I should either offer them pistols at dawn, or a bedroom for the night.

'So,' I said finally. 'Someone stole Darrow's laptop and gave copies of the trap designs to Julian Morris, before Xanthippe came back to town, paying him to build the first two traps. Someone stalked me with electrified ping pong balls, and did the same to Claudina, to freak her into changing the story she told the police. I'm assuming that none of those things were done by people in this room?'

Xanthippe and Darrow shrugged at each other.

'It never occurred to me anyone would actually build the traps,' said Darrow, raising his eyebrows at Xanthippe. He had already been brought up to speed on her side project. 'Let alone *pay* people to build them. They were purely designed for fictional mischief.'

'Better be a bloody good book,' said Xanthippe.

'Lots of violence and smut,' he shot back.

'Sounds trashy. And my car…?'

'I was researching a scene,' Darrow admitted, appropriately shamefaced.

'A scene in which the protagonist is dumb enough to leave off the handbrake when he gets out of a vintage sports car?'

He gave her a genuine expression of sorrow and guilt. 'I have been looking for a replacement.'

Xanthippe folded her arms. 'You've been avoiding me while you look for a replacement?'

'No, I've been avoiding you so we wouldn't have to have this conversation until you lose the urge to strangle me with a computer cord.'

'I'm not sure that day will ever come,' Xanthippe told him.

Darrow smiled warmly. 'I promise to make it up to you. Many times over, if I have to.'

'Hmmm.'

I opened my mouth to point out that the best way Darrow could have avoided Xanthippe and her strangling urges was to sign those insurance forms when her lawyer first sent them to him. Then I shut my mouth. Interfering in other people's love lives is always a bad idea.

'Anyway,' Stewart interrupted. 'We dinnae know who, or why. After all tha', the only thing we've achieved this evening is our tea.'

'You're welcome,' said Darrow.

Claudina yawned, blinking her eyes rapidly. 'Was I asleep? What did I miss?'

'Not much,' said Stewart. 'Is there anything you havenae told us, Claudina? Morris was killed by a heroin overdose. If he was no drug user, where did he get it?'

Claudina rubbed her eyes, looking miserable. 'Oh, I know where he got it.'

'Now it gets interesting,' Xanthippe said under her breath.

'Well?' I demanded.

'It's not exactly easy, to make rent on what Centrelink gives you, and busking,' said Claudina. 'Julian was broke all the time, and he kept needing more money—there was a woman or something. I think she was married and he wanted her to run off on her husband with him. I didn't even know what he'd got into until he already … and he never used the stuff himself, I *told* you that.'

273

Stewart stemmed the flow of panicky explanation with a steady hand on her wrist—and I for one was grateful for the brief pause. 'What exactly are ye telling us, now?' he asked.

Claudina looked around the table. 'Julian was a drug courier,' she admitted, with a sigh. 'He didn't—he only did it every now and then, when he needed the money. He was trying to stop, really, he would have stopped as soon as he got Nat away from her husband…'

Xanthippe blew out a breath. Stewart shook his head. Darrow looked entirely unsurprised.

'One precious detail,' I said quietly. 'Bloody freaking brilliant.'

This one we couldn't keep from Bishop.

21

'Tell us everything you know,' I said, not actually wanting to hear it.

'I knew Julian was getting money from somewhere,' Claudina said. 'I never thought of drugs at first—he really was completely against using them.'

'But not selling them,' said Stewart.

'His family don't know,' Claudina said quickly. 'All that stuff Ange and the others told you, for your blog, that was true.'

'Not the whole truth, though,' he said.

'He needed the money,' she said, staring at my kitchen floor. 'And there was a new guy in town who was throwing money at people Julian knew, to sell or to courier. Nat—Julian's girlfriend—I think she was involved, somehow. He never told me all the details. I didn't want to know.'

That was the second mention that Julian's honey was called Nat. I exchanged a look with Stewart. Nat could be short for Natalie, or Natalia, or even Nathan. There was no reason why this Nat had to be Natasha Pembroke, who had called the police when high on prescription meds, promised to tell them something important about Julian's death and then shot one of them with a bow and arrow instead. Oh, except she had that apricot hair. Julian did like his redheads. Predictable to the end.

Be a hell of a coincidence if it wasn't her. But Hobart was Coincidence City.

'That wouldn't be The Vampire, would it?' Xanthippe asked. 'The man in charge of the drugs operation?'

'That's what they called him,' said Claudina. 'I don't think it was his real name—'

'No shit.'

Darrow raised his eyebrows at me. 'Hate to say it, Darling, but it's time to let your uptight cop boyfriend know what's going on. Like now.'

'Easy for you to say,' Xanthippe said. 'For once, *you* haven't done anything dodgy.'

'Comes as a shock to me, too,' admitted Darrow. 'Still, the night is young.'

They all looked at me. 'You want *me* to be the one to tell Bishop about all this?' I squeaked.

'It has to be you,' Xanthippe said as if this was the most obvious fact in the universe. 'Between you, me, Darrow and McTavish, you are the person he is least likely to throw in a holding cell.'

'Hmph,' I said, pulling out my mobile. 'Obviously you don't

understand anything about how our relationship works.'

Voicemail. Fantastic. 'Bishop, it's me, Tabitha. I'm at my place, and—well, I have some new evidence about the Morris case. You're not going to like it. But I need to talk to you. As soon as you can?'

'Mm,' said Xanthippe after I disconnected. 'You didn't mention the rest of us. Good call.'

'I'd prefer he not turn up with a gun squad,' I sighed. 'Or, you know. Multiple pairs of handcuffs.' I waved them all out of my kitchen. 'You can all go to the living room and watch Doris Day movies. I'm going to make a blueberry syrup cake to lull a police officer into a false sense of security before I make him wish he'd never been born.'

Claudina was the last to leave the kitchen. 'Tabitha—are you sure this man of yours is trustworthy? It's just—there was a police officer hassling Julian, before he died. He was really freaked by it.'

'Bishop's one of the good guys,' I assured her. 'Pretty much the definitive good guy.' I didn't mention his habit of being insanely suspicious of the men in my life—if I barely remembered dating Julian, he didn't count, right? 'If I can anaesthetise him with enough cake, he will —' probably '— listen to us, and make sure the information goes to the right place. You're safe here. Promise.'

Claudina smiled suddenly, the expression looking odd on her pale and drawn face. 'I feel safe around Xanthippe. I reckon she could hold her own against an army of police or drug dealers, or anything.'

'You have no idea,' I muttered.

There was always the possibility that Bishop wouldn't hear my message until morning, but I kept finding more excuses to stay awake. First, the blueberry syrup cake had to bake, and then I made hot drinks for everyone, and then I did the washing up. I would regret it at 5AM when it was time to drag myself out of bed and meet Nin at the café, but it wasn't the first time I'd pulled an all nighter and gone on to bake for ten hours straight.

It was after midnight when I made one last check on my living room full of people.

Ceege had gone to bed. Claudina was asleep on the couch, her head on Xanthippe's lap and her feet on Stewart's. They were both asleep, too. Darrow sat in my favourite armchair, his feet up on the coffee table, snoring lightly.

The end of *Die Hard* was flickering on the screen—after Claudina went to sleep, the others had taken a quick vote for anything but Doris Day, and I had been too busy baking to put up a fight about it.

I switched off the TV, and left them all to their sleep. They would be moaning about cricks in their necks tomorrow, but it made me feel safe to have them around.

Just as I turned the key to lock the back door, there was a knock on it that scared me out of my skin. 'Tabby?' said a voice on the other side.

I practiced some deep breathing for a second and then unlocked it again. 'Constable Gary! What are you doing here?'

My favourite constable eased himself in the door, cheerful as ever. 'Smells like blueberry syrup cake. Expecting Bishop, are you?'

'You know me well.' I locked the door after him. 'Want a piece? He seems to have stood me up.'

'Thought you'd never ask. I'm just checking up on you,' he added. 'Bishop said something about a possible stalker? We wanted you to know there are people around, looking out for you. A few of the blokes volunteered to help out.'

'I didn't think he was taking it that seriously,' I said, a little surprised.

'You know we wouldn't take any risks when it comes to you, Tabby.'

Aww, sweet. I wasn't going to bitch about them being overprotective after the week I'd had, anyway. I cut Gary a piece of cake, and gave it to him on a saucer. 'I left Bishop a voice message earlier, but I don't think he's checked his mobile.'

'Probably not.' He ate a bite of cake, licked his fingers, then pulled a familiar mobile phone out of his pocket. 'He left this at the station. I was going to drop it into him on the way home, but it's pretty late. Might wait until the morning.'

'Oh,' I said, checking the temperature of the cake before I popped it away in a Tupperware container and into the fridge to chill. I flinched like I did every time I opened the fridge door now, and I could feel Gary looking at me strangely so did my best to hide my reaction. 'It can wait until tomorrow, I guess.' Part of me wanted to confess everything that was going on, but I stopped myself. Bishop was going to be annoyed enough already without me going to a constable before I talked to him.

'Is it true you two are going out now?' Gary asked, through another mouthful of sticky crumbs.

'In a manner of speaking,' I admitted. 'If he doesn't change his mind between now and tomorrow night.' Which he could well do, once I confronted him with Darrow and Xanthippe's evidence, not to mention Claudina's little bombshell.

'Thought it was the Scotsman you fancied,' observed Gary.

'No,' I said firmly. 'It's always been Bishop.' Well, mostly.

I was distracted by a strange twist on Gary's face, and had a horrible thought. He wasn't seriously interested in me, was he? The girls at the café always teased me about his crush, but they say that about everyone. Two complete strangers walk through the doors, they start planning how the two of them should hook up.

And besides, if he did have a crush on me, that didn't have to mean anything. I get crushes on people all the time, and it barely slows me down.

Gary smiled again quite normally as he finished his cake and rinsed the plate in the sink. 'Should cheer him up, anyway. He hasn't been the same since … well, you know.'

I was getting to be an expert in avoiding references to my

dad, spoken or otherwise. 'We're all fine here,' I said brightly, hoping to hurry him on out of there. 'I've got...' *a living room full of outlaws and desperadoes*, '...people looking out for me. You know, with the whole stalker thing. So, I'm fine. Good.'

'Fair enough,' said Gary. 'Give us a call if you hear anything suspicious.' He paused by the kitchen door, flashing me another one of those cheerful, freckled smiles that took over his whole face. 'It wasn't urgent, was it? The message you left Bishop?'

'Oh, it was nothing,' I said. 'Just—date stuff.' Gary had worked with Bishop for ages, and I'd known him since he was a new recruit. I don't know why I suddenly felt like there was something wrong going on here.

'You're not still poking your nose in about the Trapper, are you?' asked Gary, and he sounded genuinely concerned. 'The case is closed.'

I managed a laugh. 'I never was poking my nose in, thank you very much. That was Bishop's delusion. Between you and me, I think he has a Nancy Drew fetish.'

Okay, that was the wrong thing to say. Gary's smile froze off his face, making him look empty and just *not* the cheerful lad who rocked up to my café for lunch four or five times a week. A stab of worry went right through me, like I had missed something really important. 'You shouldn't lie, Tabby. Not to me.'

Even then, with the warning signals blaring, I didn't quite believe what was going on here. Gary: harmless. It was built into me to not take him seriously. But there was weight to his words, and a whole lot of what sounded like threat.

I stepped back, opening my mouth to call out to Xanthippe and the others, but Gary came at me, slamming my side into the kitchen cupboards. We both went down in a tangle on the floor, and I got in a closed-fist thump on his ear before he smacked me hard in the mouth. 'You can't tell me you didn't notice,' he said in an ugly tone. 'Not after all this.'

He pinched his hand hard over my nose and mouth, and my brain flared with red panic as I saw him pull a roll of industrial tape out of his jacket pocket. I bucked under him, but he had the better position, and pinned me to the floor with his body. I drummed my heels on the floor, desperate to make some kind of noise.

The lack of breathing was a problem.

Here I was, struggling under him while he taped up my mouth, dealing with a whole bunch of thoughts that were really coming in far too late. The police had got Darrow's laptop back—and I had never thought to ask which police officer actually did the bringing back. You didn't expect stolen laptops to find their way home, police or no police. Gary hung around the café a lot. He could have been one of the customers that Darrow discussed his novel with.

But that was an entirely stupid train of thought, because that suggested that Gary might actually be…

Well, yes.

Gary was friends with Amy and Danny. He had access to their house. Which would explain how a cage was constructed in their basement long before Danny fell into it. There had been a police officer hassling Julian, too, but I couldn't remember who had told me that, because my lungs were burning now, and my head had gone all black and woozy.

Gary had Bishop's mobile, and if he listened to the messages, he knew I had evidence about the Trapper case.

Gary always ate his side salad. Damn it, I was never going to hassle anyone about side salads ever again.

Gary regularly asked me advice on his love life, but never followed through on my suggestions. He had also regularly chatted to me about the Trapper, passing on the gossip, trying to impress me with it.

Gary must have stuffed my fridge full of ping pong balls. Someday, I would have to ask him how he did that. Because, you know. Fridge full of ping pong balls. If you think about it, that's a bloody hard thing to do.

Gary was the one who threatened Claudina.

Gary was trying to kill me.

Sleepy now. Lungs hurting. Between his hand and his tape, I still couldn't breathe. And everything went black…

22

I woke up, which was a plus.

My first thought was that it was getting late (or rather, early) and Nin was going to kill me if I didn't make it to the café on time, for our re-opening. The prep work filling the fridge might placate her, but nothing short of actual attendance would be good enough for those eyebrows of hers. She would judge me so hard, and there was a serious possibility that she might bake me in the oven for dessert.

My second thought was that I wasn't wearing shoes. Given that the shoes I had been wearing were my powder blue Prada wedge-heeled boots that I had bought in *Italy*, this was cause for some distress.

Not quite ready to open my eyes, I reached out with my bare feet in case my boots were somewhere nearby. My toes came into contact with the crisp, cold metal bars of a cage.

That was when I remembered the whole bit about nearly

dying on my kitchen floor, and realised how lucky I was to be alive right this second.

Except that I was in a cage. Gary had tried to kill me, and he had left me barefoot in a cage.

Son of a bitch.

I sat up so fast that the cage floor rocked under me. Not just a cage. A hanging cage. Like Tweety Bird.

My throat hurt, and my chest as well. Panic lurched through me as I remembered the details. Gary had held me down and stopped me breathing.

And I used to give him extra marshmallows in his hot chocolate.

Holy everloving fuck.

'How are you feeling?' he asked now, and the sound of his voice made my whole body clench up in fear. I could hear him, but not see him.

'Oh, just fine, Gary,' I said after a moment, tucking my bare feet under me. In my cage. I had a cage now. 'You know, kidnapped. And it's a bit chilly in here. But otherwise…'

'Sorry I had to do that,' he said. I could see him now, folded back in a corner of the room, sitting on a rickety stool beside a workbench. There was no electricity down here—the dim light came from an old-fashioned kero lamp. The place was full of old, broken furniture, and boxes of junk.

'Yes, well I can see why you had to,' I said sarcastically. 'What with me being all relaxed and joking in my kitchen. Obviously I deserved this.' I clamped my lips down, as I could see the sharp tone was affecting him. Pissing him off was not the best plan right now, even if sarcasm was my automatic reaction to feeling afraid and angry. 'So,' I went on, brightly. 'If you wanted to put me in a gilded cage, you might have scraped the rust off first.'

Long silence.

'That was a joke,' I added. 'Am I not supposed to joke with my kidnapper? Maybe you should let me know the rules. The management requests that abductees not enjoy moments of levity in the presence of their captor.' More silence. Except, you know, from me. Because I don't do silence. 'Have I been kidnapped, Gary? Wouldn't want me to get the wrong end of the stick about this one.'

'Mostly,' he said, sounding a bit embarrassed.

'Mostly kidnapped. I suppose I can work with that.' I took a deep breath, willing myself to keep up the bantering tone. Light-hearted, frivolous. Like, it's totally normal to be locked in a cage by a police officer and former friend. 'Are we thinking ransom, Gary?'

For a minute, I pictured a Mel Gibson movie style scenario, with Stewart dropping a package of money into a rubbish bin, Bishop hiding on a rooftop with a covert gun squad, Xanthippe and Darrow as the loose cannon vigilantes, and Ceege in a cocktail frock leading an army of beautifully dressed elves as they came to my rescue.

With my brain, I'm never bored.

'No,' said Gary, and I had to reel back my thoughts to figure out the question I had asked.

So, not ransomed. 'What do you want from me?'

'You,' he said, and he tilted his head up so he was finally looking at me. 'I want you, Tabby.'

It was a lot harder to pretend that this situation was in any way funny. Breathing calmly and evenly had also become more difficult.

We were in the space under someone's house. It was musty and dark, and not properly sealed. There were a couple of yellowed slits of windows on the far wall, which suggested the house was (like most houses in Hobart) built on a slope. My eyes were getting used to the dim light, and I could see various shapes hanging from the ceiling. Models of Kevin Darrow's traps, made from paper and sticky tape and icy pole sticks. There were a few ping pong balls littered around the place. And there, jammed up between a chest of drawers and an old wardrobe, was a shape that looked like another person.

'Who's that?' I asked, straining to see.

Gary laughed, and leaned over to give the figure a push. It lolled out like a corpse, and I screamed before realising that it wasn't a person, alive or dead.

It was a mannequin. It wore some of Crash Velvet's costume items, and had a mad wig of blue hair. Lurid makeup had been scraped over its face. I knew without looking that its nails would be sparkly matte purple—*Poison Flesh*. 'Julian Morris's masterpiece.'

'Nice job, don't you reckon?' said Gary. 'Of course, your mate Xanthippe put him up to it.' He shook his head in disgust. 'A police officer's sister. She should know better than to mess around with people like Morris.'

'You didn't like someone else stealing your idea, did you?' I said. 'Julian Morris was your errand boy, building those traps around Sandy Bay. First the one in the street, then the one under Amy and Danny's house. You must have given him access.' Near my house, hell, one of them in my stepsister's cellar, so when I heard about it, I'd feel *involved*. 'But then Xanthippe stole him from under your nose, and he started building a trap for her instead. Tell me, what did happen to Julian?'

As soon as I'd asked the question, I wished that I hadn't. I suddenly wanted nothing more than to stay in blissful ignorance of how Julian had died. Accidental overdose? Worked for me.

'He was a drug courier,' said Gary. 'Just like dealers, scum of the earth. Even when you get them into the prison system, they always reoffend.'

'Right,' I said. 'So, you're like Batman. You're out to punish the criminals.' Except Batman never kills anyone. People forget that bit, but I had it drummed into my head from the time Ceege got into a flamewar about it on Tumblr.

Gary obviously liked the analogy. His freckled face creased into a delighted grin. 'Yeah. Like Batman. Got to get them off the streets, Tabby. Risdon's too good for that sort.' Yes, our local prison was renowned for being a comfy place for drug dealers, all sunshine and Nintendo. 'Too easy. Got to make an example of them.'

'So,' I said, going out on a limb. 'Why am I in a cage, Gary? What are you punishing me for?'

Gary looked at me for a moment, and I half thought I might have won this round. But then he moved to a shuttered wicker basket, opening it up. A cat emerged, purring and cooing.

For one mad moment I thought he'd got hold of Kinky Boots, but when Gary turned toward me I saw a scraggy and toothless old Siamese, who wound her limbs lovingly around Gary's neck and shoulders.

I'd seen that cat before, in a basket of elderly lace accessories. It was Margarita's Moonshine.

'She likes me,' said Gary, with wonder in his voice. 'I trapped her in a net, and she still likes me. I'm going to try it with you.'

Not liking the sound of this *at all*. 'Bondage and incarceration might be a turn on for some people,' I said sharply. 'I'm not one of them.'

Gary's face fell a little, as he realised I wasn't going to swoon with gratitude. He put the cat down on the ground, and she wound around his ankles. Huh. She really was a fan.

I moved in for the kill. 'Why don't you let me go? No one has to know about all this … silliness. It can be our secret.' *For three minutes until I get to a phone, you utter maniac.*

'If I let you leave,' said Gary. 'You'll just go back to ignoring me. Like before. I did it all for you, Tabby, and you still didn't notice me.'

'Of course I noticed,' I said. 'I gave you lasagne and your favourite biscuits. Wasn't I always nice to you?'

'You're like that with everyone,' Gary said. 'You feed everyone, you smile at everyone. I was special.'

Now I had to to stroke his ego? I wasn't sure I had the patience to make nice with somebody whose idea of wooing was to lock me in a homemade cage. On the other hand, my life depended on it. Ick. Ick. Ick. 'I've always thought you were special, Gary. But if we're going to explore this —' Gah '— thing between us, then can't we find somewhere nicer? I mean, we're under some old house. It doesn't scream "romance" to me.'

'No!' Gary yelled. 'This is our place. I made it for you.'

'Oh,' I said faintly. Lovely. Just what I've always wanted.

'I did everything for you,' he added.

It wasn't the first time that Gary had said something like that, and I didn't like the sound of it any better. 'Define "everything", please?'

Gary smiled, and if it weren't for the fact that he was a raving lunatic, he would have looked sort of cute. He'd always had that schoolboy Jimmy Olsen thing going for him. Even as my brain screamed 'Keep back, fiend,' the rest of me (which hadn't caught up to recent events) still wanted to give him coffee and cake and ask him about his day.

He *was* special—he'd always been one of my favourites. In a puppy dog kind of way.

'I wasn't hurting anyone,' said Gary, sounding delighted

with himself. 'I just wanted to get your attention. It would have worked, too—but then Xanthippe had to go and interfere. I should have known that a loser like Morris couldn't be trusted to keep my secrets. I should never have trusted him with my plans.'

Kevin Darrow's plans, I thought about reminding him. I managed to restrain myself, though. See, Bishop? In dire circumstances, Tabitha Darling can actually keep her big mouth shut.

'If Bishop's sister could find out who built the traps, anyone could,' said Gary. 'Paying him to be discreet wasn't enough. I had to make sure he stayed quiet forever, didn't I?'

Put like that, it sounded perfectly reasonable... No, hang on a minute. 'So you found out that he was cheating on you with Xanthippe. Building a trap for her.'

'Exactly,' said Gary, as if he genuinely thought he was explaining something sensible and normal. 'When I spotted him sneaking around your building with his tools, I knew what he was up to. Couldn't trust him after that.'

'Right,' I said. 'So, you didn't trust Morris after Xanthippe corrupted him. And you decided to ... teach him a lesson?' I stopped short of accusing him of murder. We were having this civilised conversation and everything. I didn't actually know for certain that Gary had...

Gary laughed out loud. 'You think I was scuttling around, switching insulin for heroin? I'm a police officer, Tabby.'

'Okay,' I said, breathing just a little easier. 'So you didn't kill Julian Morris?' Things might not be as bad as I was imagining.

'No,' said Gary with a soft smile. 'But I let The Vampire know that Morris was screwing his wife. Within twenty-four hours, Morris mysteriously died of an accidental overdose, injecting pure heroin instead of insulin into his own veins.' He paused. 'I suppose he could have done it himself, but it doesn't seem likely, does it?'

Huh. That actually made sense. It didn't make me feel a whole lot better about being kidnapped by Gary, but at least he wasn't technically a killer. I might still talk my way out of this, if I kept my cool. 'If you knew who The Vampire is, why didn't you simply arrest him?'

'No evidence,' Gary said, sounding almost normal. 'Most of the cops in Hobart know who he is. Keeps his nose pretty clean, though, and we've never had an opportunity to bust him. He's a dentist,' he added with a sneer. 'Respectable as you like.'

Dentist. So Julian's Nat was apricot-haired Natasha Pembroke, and … her husband Dr Shiny Teeth was The Vampire. It was vaguely reassuring to find out he was a villain. Those blinding teeth were way too disturbing to belong to an innocent person. 'So she knew what she was doing when she shot you with the bow and arrow.' Not a random drug-related freak out after all.

'Natasha Pembroke,' said Gary in a biting voice. 'That woman. Completely flipped out after Morris was found dead. Like she couldn't find some other deadbeat toyboy to replace him.'

'Weren't you worried she would tell the police about your deal with Morris?' I asked.

'She did. After we arrested her for the siege. She told Bishop and half a dozen other police officers that she shot me because I arranged for her lover to be killed. And you know what? They laughed at her. Bishop said it was the funniest thing he'd ever heard.' Gary's mouth twisted a little. 'They never believed I could do anything like that—not good old Gary, the one everyone can trust. Mrs Pembroke changed her mind about accusing me when it came to making a formal statement. She couldn't prove it, and she's not stupid, so she claimed to be acting irrationally under the influence. It would have been her word against mine.'

Why was he was telling me this now? I couldn't help but worry about that. If I knew all his dodgy secrets, what was he planning to do to me?

I clung desperately to the idea that he wasn't a murderer. Maybe this was semantics, but since I was going to be caged by a raving madman with a crush on me anyway, I would prefer it to be one who didn't go around spiking people's insulin with heroin.

'They didn't take me seriously,' said Gary, and it occurred to me that he wasn't all that happy that Bishop and the others had so easily dismissed the idea that the Trapper was a criminal mastermind. 'They didn't think I was capable of killing one scummy little dealer.'

'But that's a good thing,' I said. 'You're a hero, remember? A police officer. Not a bad guy.'

'Oh,' said Gary, sounding a little far away. 'But you don't know what I've done.'

I tried not to look worried about that ominous comment. Delaying tactics were called for. 'Gary, I'm starving. What time is it?'

'Nearly lunchtime. You slept most of the morning.'

'Well, I had a late night. Plus, chloroform.' I tried not to think of Nin working away in the café without me. If I survived this, she was going to kill me. Or worse—she might quit.

Yes, I was still thinking about ordinary, everyday things. It was the only way to keep from screaming.

Gary left the cellar. He came back a while later with a doorstop dark rye sandwich on a plate, looking pleased with himself. 'I know you like pesto, and smoked salmon, and semi-dried tomatoes, not sun-dried. There's some baby spinach in there, too.'

Hipster food. My stomach gurgled anyway. Talking about murder raises an appetite.

The sandwich was so big that I had to turn it on its side to get it through the bars. I managed to eat some of it, my brain spinning away at top speed. Lunchtime. That meant I'd been in Gary's custody for about ten or eleven hours. Holy hell. Where was my rescue team?

I had never suspected Gary. Had anyone else? Would Stewart

and the others go to Bishop when they found me missing?

Dad always joked that he should use a tracking system, so he could locate me when I was running around giving him grey hairs during my teen years. I suppose it was too much to hope that Bishop's paranoia had led him to secretly microchip me?

Yeah, that probably was too much to hope.

I was on my own. I was going to have to use all my skills to get out of this cage, out of this cellar and out of this house, to safety.

Most of my skills involved cooking and accessorising, and it was hard to see how that would be helpful, unless Gary suddenly got an insatiable craving for cannelloni, or needed to choose the perfect pair of earrings.

So, cross off all of Tabitha's skills that require a kitchen or her handbag collection, and what are we left with?

Feminine wiles. Fuck.

'Wonderful sandwich,' I said, swallowing hard. 'Best I've had in ages. Really hit the spot. How did you know just what I would like?' Best not mention that I hate the combination of smoked salmon and semi-dried tomato. Could have been worse. Could have been capers.

'I know you, Tabby,' said Gary. 'I watch you all the time. Haven't you figured that out yet?'

I sighed, and leaned my head against the bars. 'I think I'm starting to. Any chance of a cup of tea?'

'Wouldn't fit through the bars,' he said.

I looked down, as if surprised that I was still in the cage. 'Oh. Do we still need this? It's not like I'm going anywhere.'

'I'll put the kettle on,' Gary agreed, and sidled away. Moonshine gave me a dirty look and stalked after her new master.

Out of the cage. That would be a damn good start. A cuppa wouldn't hurt, either. And then—freedom.

All I had to do was figure out how to get from A to B.

When Gary returned with the cup of tea, he unlocked the cage. I unwound myself from the confined space, carefully not thinking things like 'I could hit him over the head right now and run away.'

For a start, I had nothing to hit him over the head with except for a warm (but not hot) cup of tea. Also, despite his casual clothes, I could see his police issue handgun holstered under his jacket.

I sat on a wobbly stool and drank my tea. He had put sugar in it, which annoyed me. I only take sugar in coffee. For a stalker, he sure hadn't been paying much attention to my actual likes and dislikes.

'Right,' I said finally. 'You've got my attention. What do you want now?'

'I want you to respect me,' said Gary. He hadn't brought a cup of tea for himself, probably because he wanted to keep his Glock within easy reach.

'Okay,' I said. 'Respect. Well, I'm pleased to hear you haven't been running around killing dealers and dumping them in my building, net or no net. But how exactly are you going to make up for all this? Because I've got to tell you, most successful romances do not start out with one of the participants locking the other in a cage.'

'I know,' said Gary. 'I'm sorry about that. But I needed to talk to you. Properly. Without any of those—people around you.'

'You mean my friends?'

'They're no good for you. I mean, who have you been hanging around with lately? That Xanthippe—she has trouble written all over her. An internet hack. That cross dressing freak you live with.'

Now was not the time to give him a lecture about respecting the gender identity of individuals, and that men should be able to wear the occasional frock without being labelled by close-minded arseholes. I was really good at that speech, and it was painful to swallow it down. 'You brought me here and locked me in a cage—making me miss half a day of work, by the way—to tell me you don't like my friends?'

'That café,' said Gary. 'It's no good for you, either. It's made you forget about us—the ones who look after you. You changed your menu to try to get rid of us all, but we'll never walk away. It's time to clean up your life, Tabby. I can help you.'

Now he was speaking for the whole police force? As if. Dad would smack him silly for that arrogance. I almost forgot about the gun. 'What the hell am I supposed to do? Go back to working in the police canteen like a good little girl? You want me to waft around in a *Mad Men* frock with a tray of pies, playing the perfect housewife? That's not me, Gary.' Okay, the frock part does sound like me, but I was on a roll. 'I don't think you know me at all. The café is my dream—my true love. And thanks to you, I've been screwing my staff and customers over for nearly a week. Well, that's it. I'm done. I want my Prada boots right now, and I'm going home.'

I slammed down the cup, marched across the room and searched a beaten-up chest of drawers, opening and closing each drawer with a bang. Then I went under the work bench, scrabbling through boxes of crap.

Gary sat there, and let me do it. He let me walk to the wardrobe as well, and sat unmoving when I flung open the doors.

There was something in there. Not my boots. A large, bulky shape, wrapped in garbage bags. I backed up a few steps. 'Gary, that had better be another mannequin.'

'I told you it was time to start cleaning up your life, Tabby,' he said bitterly. 'I've made a start for you. You're bloody welcome.'

I hyperventilated, and my vision went black around the edges. 'I've already seen one dead body this week, and I'm still a little bit freaked out by it. Please *tell me* that there isn't another one right there in that wardrobe.'

'See,' said Gary, walking towards me slowly and steadily. 'You have to understand the lengths I'm prepared to go to, to save you from yourself. You're too nice to everyone. You allow the wrong people to stay in your life, even when they've used up all their chances. It's important that you see how much I care about you.'

I backed up so far that I hit the cage, and hung on to the metal bars to keep myself upright. My brain ran through a list of horrors, as I considered who might be dead in that wardrobe.

Gary dragged the bags out of the way, and for a moment I just saw a mess of a dead person. And then I knew who it was. Numbness set in. Crying would have been nice, but I couldn't get there yet.

'I bet you gave him lasagne too,' said Gary, with something like triumph in his voice.

'Coffee,' I said quietly. 'Too much sugar.'

It was Locks. And sure, I'd known for a long time that he wasn't going to live to a ripe old age. Too damn thin, too much sampling his own dodgy merchandise. But that was different to seeing him slumped in a wardrobe, cold and stiff in that stupid old coat of his.

My legs went from under me. I found a grubby wall to press against, and closed my eyes for a minute. 'What are you going to do now?' I asked when I could breathe well enough to speak.

'I've got a couple of weeks personal leave,' said Gary. 'They were pushing me to take it after the siege and everything, and I finally agreed. Thought we could go away for a while, just the two of us. Somewhere nice, away from all the —'

'Bad influences in my life?' I was so damned tired.

'That's right,' he said, as if it was obvious. 'I've got your phone. I can send texts to your Mum, and Nin, and Bishop. Anyone who might come looking for you.'

'You've still got Bishop's mobile,' I said.

Gary shook his head. 'Dropped it off at his place this morning. After I erased your message.'

'Okay.'

'What do you mean?'

I lifted my eyes and stared at him from under my eyelashes. 'Okay. I'll go away with you. Might be nice.'

His face lit up in a genuine grin. 'That's great. I knew I could convince you.'

My stomach felt like there was something hard and spiky living in it. 'Sure. I'm going to need my boots, though.'

'Of course. I'll go get them.' Gary was already on the stairs when the doorbell rang, pealing loudly through the house.

I stared at my feet, determined not to let anything like hope show on my face.

'Be quiet,' Gary warned me, and went upstairs. I heard him lock the cellar door behind him.

I stood up as soon as he was gone, and padded over to Locks. I didn't even know how Gary had killed him. 'I'm sorry,' I whispered. God, of all the dumb things Locks did in his life—I wouldn't have thought accepting the occasional cup of coffee from me would be the riskiest.

Doorbell. That meant there was someone here. Time to make some noise. I grabbed the stool I had been sitting on earlier, and made for one of the tiny yellow windows. I wasn't even sure if I could fit through one of them—not unless I lost a couple of inches off my hips. Probably shouldn't have eaten that sandwich.

Then again, I didn't have to fit through. I could smash them.

The first swing of the stool thudded pain through my shoulders as it connected with the glass, and didn't make a dent. Sometimes it sucks to be a girl. Okay, a girl who doesn't go to the gym. I swung again, and managed to break one of the windows. 'Help!' I yelled through the hole.

'HEY,' roared Gary, returning much faster than I'd expected.

I swung around, the stool held up like a weapon. Cool as you like, he drew his Glock and pointed it at me.

Don't point a firearm at someone unless you intend to shoot them. A memory of my dad's placid voice filled my mind. I couldn't move. My hands were shaking as I held the stool, but I didn't dare lower it. I just stared into Gary's bright blue eyes and his freckled face. 'Okay,' I said finally, hardly above a whisper. 'I'm going to put this down now.'

'Good idea,' he said.

I placed the stool carefully on the ground. 'Someone will have heard me. You may as well…'

'No one heard you,' he said, sounding almost sympathetic. 'The front door's at the other end of the house. It was Bishop and Constable Heather. But I didn't answer the door.' He cocked his head slightly, and I heard the distant sound of car doors slamming, and an engine starting up. 'And now they're leaving.'

'How did they find me?' I asked.

'They didn't find you, Tabby.'

'How did they even know to look here?' I didn't know where here was, but it was a good sign that Bishop had been so close, even if he had totally failed on the white knight front.

Gary smiled. 'I heard them talking together, on the doorstep. Turns out your friends have raised the alarm about you missing. They told Bishop you left him a voice message last night. He knows I had his phone, so I guess he wants to ask me about why the message isn't there. That's all, Tabby. He can't have been very suspicious, or he would have looked around the place, even without a warrant.'

'And he didn't find me,' I said, trying not to give away how gutted I was. What was the point of having a police officer as a not-quite-boyfriend if he couldn't be appropriately obsessive about searching for my kidnapped self?

'He might be back,' Gary admitted. 'And those friends of yours don't necessarily care about search warrants. It's time to go.' In one quick, professional move, he holstered the Glock.

I breathed a bit more comfortably than when it had been pointing at me. Guns, they suck all the air out of a room. 'Boots?'

'Here.' Gary grabbed my Prada wedge-heels from where he had dropped them, and passed them to me. I pulled them on. It felt good to have them back. Not to have a matching ensemble, though. This was survival. *Footwear means I can walk. Maybe run, if I have to.*

Mind you, if physical fitness was going to be an essential element in surviving this situation, I was stuffed. I had plenty of stamina from long days on my feet, but I wasn't exactly a jogger.

'So,' said Gary. 'Let's get out of here.' He sounded excited, like we were going on a date. For all I knew, this was the best time he'd had in ages. He stepped close to me, and I tried not to flinch as he took my arm.

He moved his hand to my neck, and something clicked against the pale blue leather collar that I still wore around my throat. 'What the hell?' It was a leash. A freaking leash. 'You have to be kidding me. Why do you even have a dog leash? You don't have a dog!'

'Cat leash,' he corrected. 'I can keep you close this way. Take your jacket off.'

Glaring at him, I shrugged the powder blue jacket off. Gary threaded the leash down one sleeve and then gave it back for me to awkwardly put back on. I wondered if this was one of Kev Darrow's little innovations, and hoped not. The boy was too young to be displaying S&M tendencies.

When the jacket was back in place, Gary looped the end of the leash around his wrist, and then jammed his hand, my hand and the end of the leash into his own jacket pocket.

'If you really want to put some distance between yourself

and Bishop, you'd be better off leaving me here,' I said. 'I'm going to be useless in these heels. And I'm very slow. Also chatty and annoying. You'll make your getaway much more efficiently without me hanging around your neck.'

Gary smiled like he was still trying to impress me, or flirt with me, leaving aside the fact that he had recently stuck a gun in my face. 'I like you close.' He tugged on the leash, and I felt a hard pressure on the collar at my throat.

'Great,' I muttered. 'This is what I get for trying to revamp a tired fashion trend.'

I was never going to look at collars the same way again.

23

We walked through the house, Gary holding my hand and the end of the damned leash in his right hand. The holstered firearm would be easy enough for him to reach with his left. From a distance, we might look like a smoochy couple, the girl holding her boyfriend's hand in his pocket.

The thought of us being a smoochy couple made me see black and white spots in front of my eyes, but I could cope with this, I could, I could.

When we stepped out the side door of Gary's ordinary weatherboard house, I finally got my bearings. I could see the Tasman Bridge below us, and the River Derwent. We were on the east-facing side of the hill, with the Domain above and behind us, and the Botanical Gardens below. Nice spot. Moonshine sat in a patch of sun, and gave me the same haughty look she had before. Obviously she didn't approve of Gary's taste in kidnap victims. Couldn't say that I did, either.

I couldn't quite see Mt Wellington, as we had the peak of

the hill between us and it, but I knew roughly what direction it was in. That was some comfort, at least.

Gary pulled me around the side of his house and down to the street by way of his sloping lawn, and not the actual driveway. We stopped behind some large native bushes, and he squeezed my hand very tight in warning.

I peered around the shrubbery, and saw why he was taking such precautions. Bishop and Constable Heather had only made it a couple of houses up the road. They were parked a little way along, fenced in by a large yellow taxi and my blue Renault. Bishop and Heather stood in the middle of the street, arguing loudly with a group I mentally dubbed Tabitha's Cavalry.

I could see Xanthippe, the loudest of all, waving her arms as she shouted at her brother. She was wearing a long leather coat that I had last seen hanging in my wardrobe (sure, it was hers originally, but she'd abandoned it for five years and I had squatter's rights). I felt an overall sensation of warmth. Zee wouldn't stop looking for me. That was the kind of friend she was. No matter what. Bishop might let his ego and his sense of reality get in the way, but not my girl.

Stewart and Ceege and Claudina were there, too. Darrow hung back, looking amused as hell by the whole proceedings. Xanthippe kept gesturing back towards Gary's house, and I guessed she was trying to bully Bishop into returning to snoop around the place more effectively.

To scream or not to scream?

Gary's fingernails grazed my palm. 'If you attract their attention,' he said casually. 'I'll start shooting. Not great at this range, but they're all grouped together like that. I'd almost have to hit someone.'

'Okay,' I said. 'We'll do it your way.' As I spoke, I dropped the contents of my right jacket pocket on the grass behind us. A lip gloss, one of Xanthippe's nail polish bottles, and a couple of crumpled tissues. Here was hoping that one of my cavalry stopped arguing with the forces of law and order long enough to notice a fabulous clue when they saw one. If they saw it at all.

'Good girl,' Gary said, failing to notice my stealthy move. He led me back around the bushes, and across his neighbour's front yard. Their property curved around, down the hill, and it was only a few seconds before we were out of sight of my deeply ineffective rescue party.

'So,' I said, a few minutes later, as we continued down the road away from Gary's place. 'Not escaping in a car or anything? That's so environmentally sound of you. Got to think about your carbon footprint.'

Gary laughed. 'I've got something better than a car. I told you, we're going on a real holiday.'

'What's your long term plan?' *Don't ask these things, Tabitha, do you really want the answer?* 'The longer we're both missing at the same time, the more suspicious you'll look. And, you know. There is a dead body under your house.'

'Won't be a problem,' said Gary.

'Uh-huh.' Who was I to challenge his delusion? 'What about me? What's your long term plan for me?'

'Once we're a good long way away, you'll text all your friends and family to say we've gone on a holiday together. Spur of the moment thing. I'm afraid they'll think you're very irresponsible, but given your behaviour lately, it won't be unbelievable.'

Nin would flay me with an egg beater if she thought for one minute I'd skipped town on her without warning. Except she wouldn't. None of them would believe that. Possibly it wasn't the best idea to point out this fatal flaw in his plan. 'What happens in two weeks time?'

'That depends on how things go with us.'

I couldn't stop myself shuddering at that one. Ew.

We turned down towards the Botanical Gardens car park, still walking in that odd joined-at-the-hip lope together. Gary's jacket smelled like liquorice chews, and that reminded me of Locks, which made me want to cry. 'Are we going to the Gardens?'

'Passing through,' said Gary. 'It's a good place not to be noticed.'

Okay, I thought to myself as we passed through the big iron gates of the Botanical Gardens. *Time to get serious about this, Tabitha. How exactly are you planning to escape?* I had to assume that there was some kind of vehicle waiting for us on the far side of the Gardens. So this was my best chance to break away from him, while there were still people around.

How unhinged was he? Would he start shooting people at random?

The leash was the problem. Maybe I could wrench it away from his fingers, but that would slow me down long enough for him to get the damned gun pointed at my head again, and I was willing to do pretty much anything to prevent that.

'Hey, Tabby,' called out a familiar face as we passed the snacks kiosk.

'Hey,' I called back in a weak voice.

Gary tugged sharply on my leash. 'Who was that?' he demanded.

'I don't know. Melinda something, I think. I know her brother.' Melinda something had a baby jogger with her, and I willed her not to come over to chat. 'If you wanted to walk through a major tourist attraction without being noticed, you should probably have kidnapped someone who doesn't know everyone in Hobart.' I wiggled my right fingers in a half-hearted wave to one of my old college teachers, who had an arm around some goth girl half his age.

By the time we reached the floral clock, I'd also been greeted by two regular café customers, my favourite bank clerk, and a couple of Ceege's gamer friends. Also, I didn't get any of them shot. Go me.

Leaving aside my evident popularity, Gary hadn't chosen a good day for this. It was March, and sunny. The last almost-guaranteed good weather before Hobart turned into its usual frosty-rain-and-wind five month winter. Not only were the Gardens full of picnics, primary school excursions and general merrymakers, they were also packed to the gills with bridal parties and photographers.

Chances were, if Bishop failed to rescue me today, he'd be able to spot me in the background of several wedding snaps in tomorrow's paper.

Gary was getting nervous. He twitched every time someone said hello to us. Instead of heading straight down to the exit at the foot of the hill, he dragged me into the Japanese Garden by my leash and jacket sleeve.

There was a wedding here too, the bridal party gathered for photographs with the miniature Mt. Fuji in the background of their shots.

Gary hissed between his teeth, and moved me sideways into a little pool area with a bridge and some elaborate bamboo sculptures. The spot was sheltered by high bushes, and reasonably private. 'We'll wait here a while,' he said, trying to conceal his panic. 'Until there aren't so many people around. Then we can cross the highway, and get to the boat.'

'Okay,' I agreed, and we both sat down on the little wooden bridge. It was a relief—my boots were pretty, but not designed for endless hill walking. Boat. We were going by boat. Was now the time to mention that I get seasick on fairground rides, or should I wait to throw up on him at the most opportune moment?

Gary checked his watch. A minute later, he did it again.

'Are we really waiting for the crowds to thin?' I asked.

'Not just that,' he admitted, and gave me one of those happy freckled smiles. No longer charming at all.

'They're going to find Locks, you know,' I said. And, hey. I managed to say his name without blubbing. 'Bishop might have to wait for a warrant, but Xanthippe's not backward when it comes to break and enter.'

'All the better if she is there. With all those perverted friends of yours.' Gary looked pleased. 'That would be excellent.'

'You've lost me.' In so many ways.

'It's simple enough,' said Gary. 'The story will be that Lockwood was working with Morris. They were both the Trapper. Lockwood was brought into the station once, for questioning about Morris's death, and the traps, and that will support the new theory. Bishop even had him on the suspect list as your stalker. Today, Bishop's going to find evidence that Lockwood tried to plant a trap at my house. But tragically, the dealer stuffed up and got himself killed. Boo hoo, case closed again.'

'Because, what?' I asked flatly. 'He hit himself over the head and wrapped his own body up in garbage bags?'

'Nah,' said Gary, giving the leash what he probably thought was an affectionate tug. 'He tried to set a bomb. But he wasn't very good at it, so it blew up in his face.'

I don't care how sunny the afternoon was, it was cold where

I was sitting. 'When will it happen?' *How long, in other words, do I have to get the hell away from you, and warn Bishop and Xanthippe and the others not to go anywhere near that house of yours?*

There was a deep sound in the distance, a rumble high on the hill above the Botanical Gardens. I looked up, and fixed upon a slow-moving billow of black smoke beyond the trees. Oh.

'With any luck, that got your rescue party,' said Gary. The smugness in his voice was unbearable. For a few precious seconds, I was angry enough to not be scared of guns. I grabbed the leash in my left hand and wrenched hard on it, shoving him aside with my hip.

He came up on his feet after me, but I slammed him again with my hip. I wouldn't have gotten away with it if the bridge wasn't so slippery, but he lost his balance and fell, half into the pond, almost dragging me with him.

I snapped the press-stud at my throat, and released the collar. It and the leash whooshed down my sleeve as I ran for it.

The Japanese garden was like a maze, so I was out of his sight in an instant, tearing my way around corners, along pebbled paths, and past the startled bridal party.

Somewhere behind me, I heard the cracking sound of a single gunshot.

I exploded out of the Japanese Garden, running hard across the soft lawn in my deeply impractical wedge-heels. It was exposed out here, not enough hiding places. I ducked and weaved around the English trees and hedges. There had to be a good place to hide. With walls. Walls would be really good right now.

The path loomed up before me, hard and unwelcoming to my poor tortured feet (next time I get kidnapped, I want my sneakers!) but mercifully equipped with direction signs. I veered to the left, running up the hill. I didn't dare turn around, to see how near he was, or even if he was in sight. Maybe he wouldn't shoot me. He wanted me alive, right?

Then again, without the illusion of the lovely, romantic brainwashing holiday Gary had planned, I was just some chick on the loose with information that could destroy him. I couldn't bet my life on him being sentimental.

I hate running. My lungs felt like they were about to collapse. My head hurt, and my hair was a mess. I'd lost my hair tie in the struggle, and my ponytail was a thing of the past.

I almost cried as the cactus house came into view. More of a cottage really; a small shed with opaque white glass walls. I scrambled towards it. Walls. I am so *not* an outdoors person.

Where were all the people? The park, which had been so full of picnics, lovey-dovey couples and weddings only a little while earlier, was now deserted. Possibly the explosion had drawn them all off to see what the commotion was? In any case, the crowds had most definitely thinned. I reached the cactus house and looked around wildly to check Gary was nowhere in sight before I hurled myself through the doors.

The warm, greenhousey atmosphere overwhelmed me and my sore lungs as I made my way inside. It was mercifully quiet in here. I circled the rows of tall, spiky desert succulents, and made my way to the back. Once I was tucked away behind by a display of cacti, I allowed myself to drop to the grubby stone floor and have a proper panic attack.

Gary was the Trapper. Gary was a murderer. Gary had blown up his own house, and could well have taken several people I loved with it.

Gary had a big fat police issue firearm.

I concentrated on breathing in the steamy air, and the panic gradually bled away. Everything was going to be all right. We used to come to the Gardens on school trips a lot, when I was little. This place was my favourite. There was something about it—the heat, the silence. The sharp, pointy plants.

What it didn't have, of course, was a back door.

Of all the stupid things I'd ever done, this was the stupidest. Okay, running uphill across open grassland hadn't been a great survival technique, but trapping myself in a hothouse shed with only one door took a special brand of moronitude.

I had to get out of here.

Even as I began to unkink my legs, I heard the door swing open. I huddled down behind the cacti, trying to keep as quiet as possible. Maybe it wasn't him. Maybe it *was* him, but he didn't actually know I was here…

A gunshot cracked through the air, blasting the top off a large

Echinocactus platyacanthus right by my shoulder. I squeaked, and kept my head down.

'Tabby,' Gary said in a friendly voice, his feet treading quietly across the floor.

Caught.

The fallen top of the *Echinocactus* caught my eye. I reached out to it, pushing my fingers through the squidgy vegetable matter inside the cactus's core. I thought about medieval movies from the 1950s. I thought about spiked gloves. I drew the fallen piece of cactus into my lap, letting my hair fall forward to hide it.

Gary's steps slowed, and halted right behind me. I didn't look up. He wouldn't shoot me in the back, would he?

Unless, you know, he would.

The tip of the Glock slid along my shoulder. He had to know that I'd always been freaked out by guns, that Dad's determination to teach me to use the things safely when I was seventeen had resulted in something close to an actual phobia. Everyone knew it, all the cops who had worked with Dad back then. Looking at them scared me. Touching them made me completely lose my shit.

That's me, the police superintendent's daughter.

I could see the gun, hovering so close to my face, and it was almost enough to undo me. But there was Dad's voice again, clearly in my mind. Not a memory this time, but a barked complaint. *For God's sake, Tish, pull yourself together. It's not aimed at you.*

Fair point, Dad. The gun was pointing past me. Intimidating, but that was all.

My hand moved up, in an arc usually reserved for erratic pancake flipping. I threw the piece of spiky cactus up over my head, as fast as I could, and I heard it connect with his face.

Gary yelled, his gun lifted in reflex, and I ran. I skidded around the succulents and crashed back out through the door. I wasn't up to the mental challenge of figuring out how to trap him inside. I ran like a rabbit.

Up more grass, veering sharply to the left. I was on autopilot now, thinking only about getting up and away. I didn't want to be near people who could be at risk, but I didn't want to be here by myself either...

I'd been thinking and running too much, and somehow ended up in a part of the Gardens I didn't know. That was stupid. I spent half my childhood here, at birthday parties and picnics and school trips. I knew the damn place inside out—the only problem was that I remembered it as bigger than it was.

I had made it as far as a paved courtyard, with banked earth in neat little rows, supported by red bricks. Completely alien. But then I saw a notice on a signpost and realised what this was. It was the *Gardening Australia* organic garden left over from the old days when they filmed actual TV shows in Tasmania. Someone had been looking after it.

There was a veggie patch with a shed, and a nice stone wall. I looked around to check for any sight of Gary, and then pressed myself into the gap between shed and wall, hiding myself from view.

For a few minutes, I could breathe again. Well, wheeze, to be honest. Damn, I was unfit. The stone was cool against my head. It took a minute or two, but my brain finally started to calm down.

I'd done it again. I could kick myself. What the hell kind of survival instincts did I have, anyway? I had found myself yet another nice hiding place with no escape route if he actually caught me.

The main difference this time was the brick.

It was a loose one, a good size, red. Right by my foot. I picked it up, weighing it thoughtfully in my hands. A comforting brick.

'Okay, Gary,' I whispered to myself, nestling my prize close. 'We're even. You have your gun, and I have my brick.'

Stop talking to yourself, woman! I heard footsteps nearby, quiet on the paving stones. What the hell had I been thinking? A brick was no match for a gun. It wasn't even a projectile weapon. Well. Unless I threw it?

As a shadow fell across my hiding place, I straightened up and threw the brick as hard as I could, preparing myself for the nasty meat-squish sound as it hit Gary square in the nose.

Stewart McTavish stared at me in shock as the brick sailed harmlessly over his head. 'Bloody hell, Tabitha. Good thing ye throw like a girl.'

Stewart. Not Gary. Stewart. Good old not-here-to-kill-me Stewart. I stumbled out of my hiding place and threw myself at him. Not blown up Stewart.

Now there was crying.

Stewart hugged me, and let me snuffle into his neck. His hands squeezed my hair. Everything he wore smelled like coffee. 'Ye all right in there?'

I wasn't sure that I was ever going to detach myself from his neck. It was such a nice neck, warm and reassuring against my face. Almost as good as my brick, possibly better. 'How did you find me?'

'Yer skirt was sticking out. Also, I could see ye from the path above. So rubbish at hiding.'

'How did you find me *here*?' I asked, tightening my hold on his wonderful, wonderful neck.

'We spread out tae search. Bishop's called half the local police force out. Witnesses placed ye in the area—and there were gunshots reported.'

I wiped my eyes on his shoulder. 'Yep, those were definitely in my vicinity.'

'Tabitha, could ye loosen up yer grip a bit?'

I relaxed my hold, but only slightly. Police. Bishop. So many presents, and it wasn't even Christmas. 'Have they caught him yet? Have they arrested him?'

'I don't know. We all sort o' got separated.'

I stared at him in worry. Neck or no neck, Stewart wasn't

going to be much good against an armed and dangerous rogue police officer, if the uniforms didn't find us before Gary did. 'We have to get *out* of here.'

'Might have known,' said a steady voice. Gary. Of course it was Gary.

Slowly, Stewart and I both turned around to face him.

Gary was a mess. His face was badly scratched, and there was a long dollop of blood streaking down from his eyebrow. The cactus had done a fair job, but not good enough. The hand that held the gun was steady, and this time it was aimed directly at me. 'I was hoping to get through this without having to shoot people,' he said.

'You still could,' I said, eyeing the wrong end of the barrel for the second time that day. Didn't get any easier.

'No' doing so well with the blowing people up skills either,' said Stewart slowly, squeezing my hand. 'Didnae even get the cat. Why no' call it a day, and give yerself up?'

Gary shifted his gaze from me to Stewart, and I shivered. Maybe I could have talked him out of it if I was by myself, but I couldn't for the life of me think of anything to say that would stop him shooting Stewart.

The fact that we were holding hands probably didn't help, to be honest.

A tree came out of nowhere, swinging over the wall and cracking Gary's gun to the paving stones. Another tree smacked him over the head, knocking him to the ground. A third tree came around the other side of the wall, slamming Gary flat on the paving stones.

When my eyes uncrossed enough to separate the trees from actual bodies, I saw a dishevelled Xanthippe sitting on Constable Gary's back, a large uprooted sapling in either hand. Darrow was there too, sitting on Gary's feet with a third sapling flourished high above his head. His shirt was rumpled, and his eyes were sparkling as if he had done something wonderful.

I went a bit wobbly, and felt Stewart's hand in the small of my back, not quite holding me upright, but ready to do so if he was needed. Good to know that someone was on the ball.

Claudina and Ceege came whooping into the courtyard, brandishing more saplings. Bits of earth flew everywhere.

'Job's done, mates,' Xanthippe informed them. 'Too slow.'

I gazed at her. 'You *are* wearing my coat. Give it back.'

She arched her eyebrows. 'Say thank you, Tish.'

'You tore up actual trees?'

'They were convenient. And don't lecture me about environmentalism, sweetheart. I saw what you did to the cactus house.'

I looked down at Gary. His face was pressed into the grass, as if he didn't want any of us to look at him. I was mad as hell. If he hadn't shown his true colours, I might still be smiling with him and flirting occasionally and making his coffee just the way he liked it. I had considered him a friend.

Apparently you could know just about anything about a person, including how many sugars they took in their favourite kind of coffee, and not know something really essential, like whether or not they were capable of murder.

I stooped, and picked up my brick.

'None o' that,' Stewart said, deftly taking it away from me.

'Give it to me,' I said stubbornly. 'It's my brick.'

'Leave it, Darling,' said Darrow. 'We've got your back. Everything's fine now. Consider yourself rescued!'

'Tell that to Julian's mother,' I said furiously. 'Tell it to Locks.'

There were sirens everywhere, above and below us. The police were coming—pulling out all the stops for Superintendent Darling's baby girl, even against one of their own.

Especially against one of their own.

I wasn't in any state to greet them. Before the first wave of police officers arrived, even before Bishop got to us, my knees had buckled under me. I hoped that someone would catch me as I fell. That's what friends are for, right?

24

t was Sunday, and Café La Femme was inundated with police officers. For once, I had invited them. Officially it was a thank you barbecue for everyone who'd run to my rescue during the whole Botanical Gardens abduction fiasco.

Unofficially it was the wake I'd never got around to throwing for Dad.

It was a brilliant, lazy afternoon. My party crowd had taken over the courtyard at the back. Bishop and Inspector Bobby fought over who got to be in charge of the grill. Darrow made sinfully strong daiquiris in my kitchen, and flirted shamelessly with Xanthippe. She treated him like dirt. He seemed to like that. Even Nin loosened up, arriving with three dozen death-by-lemon-icing cupcakes and a banana lounge.

While all the fun happened outside, the café itself was strangely deserted. I had one tray already loaded up with perfect raspberry shot glass parfaits, and hummed to myself as I filled a second tray with espresso cup mocha trifles. Damn if they didn't look cute as buttons.

Chocolate jelly. Coffee custard. A dash of sour cherry curd, for contrast. Tiny specks of tiramisu sponge dotted throughout, and whole marinated cherries sitting fat and juicy on top of the cups. Perfect.

'All for me? Ye shouldnae have,' said Stewart in the doorway. 'I'm sure I couldnae manage more than eight or ten of those.'

I pointed a teaspoon at him. 'The Trapper's *Muse*? That's how history will remember me?'

He looked uncomfortable. 'Sorry about that.'

'I get kidnapped, and you blog about it?'

'Be fair. Even the mainland papers went with Botanical Gardens Terror Run headlines. Ye cannae blame a lad for making the most of being on the scene.'

'Can't I?'

'Anyway,' Stewart said with a sideway grin. 'Turns out our readers were far more interested in the story of Moonshine, the cat that survived the bomb blast. At least the cat turned up for a proper photo session. She's the true internet celebrity tae emerge from all this.'

'Not doing yourself any favours here,' I said, and slapped his hand when he got close enough to try for a cup. 'I don't think so.'

Stewart gave me puppy dog eyes. 'Ye wouldnae deny a man caffeine, would ye? No' after I stopped a bullet for ye, and beat off yer attacker with a small but effective trowel?'

I laughed at that. A lot of wrong details had appeared in the news, both the print and online media. Xanthippe and Darrow both managed to slink off before people started taking photos, but neither Stewart nor I had dodged the paparazzi. Which made it even more annoying when he turned the tables on me and reported the story himself.

We won't discuss the fact that I'm pretty sure Ceege set up at least three anonymous Twitter accounts pretending to be me, Constable Gary and the bloody cat, reliving the whole event in gory and completely fake detail. I live in hope that Bishop doesn't know what Twitter actually is.

The Morris case was re-opened, and Bishop was in charge of putting the pieces together. They were still untangling the incidents where Gary had tampered with evidence, and the charges against him were mounting. He, meanwhile, was making a very good case for being institutionalised and medicated long before the justice system got a chance with him. Dr Pembroke was in custody as well, and far more likely to serve jail time than Gary.

Bishop hadn't told me any of these things, but I had my sources.

Stewart nodded towards the brick that currently had pride of place on the shelf above my cash register. 'Keeping that, are ye?'

'It's a damn fine brick. I plan on framing it.' I smiled sweetly. 'You could add it to the mural.'

Stewart made a sceptical noise and stole one of my espresso mini-trifles off the tray, inhaling the coffee smell. 'And here was me thinking it was perfect the way it was.' He ate the cherry thoughtfully, and spit the pip into his hand. 'Ye do like it?'

What with police interviews and ducking journalists and trying to make it up to Nin in the kitchen, Stewart and I hadn't spent much time together for the past few days. I'd missed the moment when the mural was finished.

I had, however, spent all of today gazing with joy at my gorgeous, gorgeous wall. Stewart had added several cheeky finishing touches to the mural. There was a leather clad Xanthippe behind Mrs Peel, eyeing her up competitively. There was a Ceege in frock and war-paint sharing a cappuccino with Doris Day. At the very edge of the piece, in the far background, there were three tiny figures that looked a lot like a uniformed and disapproving Bishop, a smug and well-dressed Darrow, and Stewart himself with his camera concealing his face.

At an extra table in the bottom right of the wall, there were four squabbling, giggling women who just had to be me and Nin and Lara and Yui having a hell of a time with cherries, chocolate dipping sauce and a catapult.

I knew for a fact that Stewart had already received appreciative snogs from my two art student waitresses, who both adored their portraits. I also knew that Nin now kept an extra-strong pot of espresso in the kitchen just for him.

Stewart McTavish was insidious. No getting rid of him now.

He painted a pretty picture.

'I love it,' I said, and got a very nice grin in return. 'Don't let it go to your head.'

He knocked back the contents of the espresso cup as if it was actual liquid coffee. 'I can always scrub it off and stick up some trendy wallpaper instead…'

'Don't you dare! It's my wall, and I'm keeping it. Thank you.' I leaned forward to give him a friendly smack on the lips.

At least, that was the plan. But somehow the friendly kiss lingered longer than I meant it to. Stewart was warm, and tasted of mocha trifle and cherries, and if the counter hadn't been between us, I do believe I would have wrapped myself around him like a boa constrictor.

I hadn't expected it. Did that make me stupid? All I can say is that it felt good, and I didn't want it to stop.

'Ahem,' said a voice that was all smirk, and we leaped apart. 'Those trifles you promised?' said Xanthippe. 'I'd offer to help with the tray, but I see you have your hands full.'

The best barbecues are the ones that start at lunch, but keep going past dinner. I wasn't sure where the beer and steaks kept arriving from, but I wasn't complaining.

It was close to dark. We'd emptied the entire building of furniture, and stacked it around the courtyard for seating. Crash Velvet were playing from their top apartment with the windows open, so we could all hear the music. Every now and then, they sent down a basket on a long string, and we piled it up with cold tinnies and cooked sausages.

The espresso cups were empty, every single one of them, and I had a new recipe to add to my menu.

There were a few drunken, cheerful speeches about how great Dad was, and some nostalgic sniffles about the good old days when my mum ran the police canteen, before she ran away to live in rural paradise with her hippie mates. I drank to all the toasts and refused to make any of my own.

No one mentioned Gary, or the fact that I had almost been killed by one of their own. But if some of the lads and lasses of local law enforcement were a touch more protective or solicitous than usual ... well, I let them. It was the only way they could demonstrate how rotten they felt about it all. We had that in common.

I'd always thought you could read a person by the type of coffee they drank, but now I was sure I knew absolutely nothing. That feeling would pass, I hoped. As long as I didn't have to deal with any more surprises this week.

I sat on a *Sandstone City* desk in the courtyard, squeezed up between Xanthippe and Ceege, sharing a bottle of champagne. Across the yard, I could see Stewart hemmed in by Lara, Yui and Claudina, and I was working up the energy to go and rescue him. Right now, I was making the most of the fact that Zee and I were on good terms again. Not best friends yet, not nearly, but the awkwardness was going, piece by piece. I'd missed her so much, without even realising it, and when I'd needed her, she'd been there for me.

With saplings.

I was capable of getting into a whole lot of trouble without even trying, so I would probably need a girl like Xanthippe around.

'Ladies and gentlemen and valued members of Tasmania Police, Hobart division!' said Darrow, balancing dramatically on one of my Pop Art chairs. 'I have an announcement to make. Some of you may know that I was recently involved in a certain accident, with a certain car, belonging to a certain woman…'

Xanthippe snorted. 'Fully-restored 1967 Lotus Super Seven Roadster…'

'Yes, yes,' Darrow said with a wave. 'I have been racking my brains as to how to make it up to said woman.'

'Get on with it!' I yelled, and threw a cream bun at him.

'If there are no further interjections from the crowd,' said Darrow grandly. 'I would like to announce a compensation package—' and he waved some documents from inside his jacket '—which is to say, the ownership papers for a slightly used (I know you like a challenge) 1972 Alfa Romeo Spider, ready for restoration, and to fund said exciting new project, we have here a contract signing over forty percent of the business of Café La Femme to Xanthippe Anastasia Demetria Carides, long may she reign.'

'*What?*' Zee and I shrieked simultaneously.

A car. I understood the car part. But he was giving her my café. Suddenly my unobtrusive, policy-of-no-interference silent partner had dumped me and handed the power to a woman who thought sandwiches didn't need butter.

Xanthippe recovered faster than I did. 'Tish, some thoughts on changing the menu. How do you feel about Buddhist cuisine? Ethiopian-Caribbean fusion? Also, here's a novel idea, plastic cutlery that saves on washing up!'

I pushed her off the desk. She scrambled to her feet with good humour and ran across the courtyard to pounce on Darrow, asking questions about her new car. Obviously that was the prize she was really interested in, and he beamed at the attention she was giving him.

Maybe she hadn't realised yet that the café shares were designed to make her stay in Hobart. He didn't want to lose her again. Sneaky, but not subtle. She should know that. Maybe she did know that. Maybe she wanted the excuse to stay…

And I was caught in the middle of their courting dance, yippee.

'You know,' said Ceege thoughtfully. 'If Xanthippe's sticking around Hobart and needs a place to live, I reckon she could be the third housemate we need to take over Kelly's room.'

I rescued the bottle of champagne from him, and then pushed him off the desk too.

''Scuse me,' said Bishop, grabbing me from behind and hauling me off the desk. 'Let's remove you from further temptation to do violence to your friends, shall we?'

He drew me into the kitchen, and as soon as I was away from the crowd, all my objections spilled out in one crazy lump: 'Xanthippe in my café, we'll murder each other, Darrow never interferes but I know she will, he's only doing this to get in her knickers again and Nin *hates* her, it's going to be flat out war, and how can we be friends again if she's in my face twenty-four hours a day...' I couldn't cope, I really couldn't cope with this; I needed no more surprises.

'Morticia,' said Bishop.

I blinked at him. 'What did you say?'

'I know what Tish means. Before I met you, there was an embarrassing goth phase, yes? So your dad called you Tish after Morticia, from *The Addams Family*.

Xanthippe picked it up, because it annoyed the hell out of you. And I picked it up off them both without knowing what it actually meant.' He crossed his arms, and looked almost as smug as Darrow on a bad day.

'Xanthippe told you,' I accused.

'Nope. I figured it out all by myself. Well, I found the old picture your dad used to keep on his desk, at the station. And it clicked.'

'Oh,' I said. 'Well, good thinking. Well done, there.'

'I won't,' Bishop said, and hesitated. 'I won't call you it any more, if you don't want me to. I know it was your dad's thing.'

Of all the horrible things I've ever said to him, this is the one he remembers?

'I don't mind. Well, obviously I do mind, it's a nickname designed to humiliate me by reminding me what a complete try-hard I was at high school, but you've been calling me Tish for a while. It would be weird if you stopped now.'

'Well,' Bishop said with a smirk that reminded me that he was, after all, related to Xanthippe. 'We wouldn't want things to get weird.' He swept his arm towards the open kitchen door, and the raging party beyond. 'This was a good idea.'

'I owed it to them,' I said softly. 'I haven't been very nice to Dad's mates this year.'

'You were grieving. Trying to push us away.'

'Not successfully.' And how.

He gave me a friendly hug, patting me cheerfully on the back as he did so. All mates here. 'It's not something you want to get good at.'

I breathed him in, enjoying the rare moment of not shouting at each other. Then I tensed up. Only a couple of hours ago, I'd been molesting Stewart in the café with kissing and trifles. Now this—what the hell was I doing?

I shifted with a vague plan of putting some distance between us, but Bishop spoke against my hair, making me not want to move away at all. 'All the arguing this year wasn't completely about me trying to protect you now your dad's gone,' he muttered. 'Actually, most of it was not about that.'

'I know,' I said as his breath tickled my ear. 'Hey, wait. What?'

Then he was kissing me, and I was letting him, and my hands were all—well, busy—and my brain had temporarily left my head, obviously, and still neither of us had closed the damn door behind us.

What was it I had decided I wanted, in that aeon before Gary came to my kitchen door and everything went to hell? *I want my café back, and Stewart to stick around, and Darrow to stop disappearing, and Xanthippe to be my friend again, and Bishop to kiss me like he did in the stairwell that time, only more.*

Now I was *never* going to get uniformed patrols out of my café, there was going to have to be meat back on the menu all over again, and I had Xanthippe as a business partner who was going to drive me up the wall, moving into my house and stealing my clothes on a regular basis. All that and I had pashed two different boys on the same afternoon. Just like bloody high school all over again.

I mumbled something against Bishop's mouth.

'What?' he said, drawing back a little to look at me with those drop-dead dark and gorgeous eyes of his.

'Be careful what you wish for if you don't know what you really want,' I said, more clearly.

It was one of those things Dad used to say, when he suspected I was about to do something profoundly stupid.

Kissing now. Thinking later. Priorities, Tabitha!

Livia Day fell in love with crime fiction at an early age. Her first heroes were Miss Jane Marple and Mrs Emma Peel, and not a lot has changed since then! She has lived in Hobart, Tasmania for most of her life, and now spends far too much time planning which picturesque tourist spot will get the next fictional corpse.

You can find her online at www.liviaday.com

ACKNOWLEDGEMENTS

My dad introduced me to crime fiction, to so many authors and characters who are still among my favourites: Robert B Parker's Spenser, Sara Paretsky's VI Warshawski, and Dick Francis' Kit Fielding, among others. It is a great joy to me that later, as an adult, I have introduced him to some new favourites I discovered myself, such as Janet Evanovich's Stephanie Plum, and Kerry Greenwood's Phryne Fisher and Corinna Chapman.

Surely the whole point of having children is so they can grow up to recommend awesome books to you? And maybe write a couple...

My friend Isabel continued my crime fiction education, and still occasionally throws books (and detectives) at my head to this day. Someday I hope to see her awesome murder mystery series on the shelves alongside mine.

A Trifle Dead began many, many years ago. I wrote a version that is almost entirely different (only the names remain the same) back in college for a writing class (we were only supposed to write 5000 words, I wrote a novel) and then I wrote it again, the following year, with a plot that showed how much I still had to learn about murder mysteries.

With the financial assistance of Arts Tasmania, for which I am very grateful, I wrote the book a third time, from scratch, and it started to look a lot closer to the one you are holding in your hands right now.

Thanks go to Ron Serdiuk, who attempted to give this book a home some years ago, and to Diane Waters and Angela Slatter, for their editorial work on the manuscript.

A billion thanks to Alisa Krasnostein, who gave the book its last (and lasting) title as well as bringing it to publication. If publishers were muses, she would be mine. Thanks also to her team at Twelfth Planet, especially the magnificent Amanda Rainey, who makes us all look good, even when there are bloodstains in the trifle.

Three cheers for the writers of the recipes and those who took part in the Great Trifle Test Kitchen, eating quantities of custard that were above and beyond the call of duty. Your sacrifice was not in vain.

As always, I am grateful for my family that keeps me sane and forgives me for being cranky and distracted when it's proofreading time.

Livia Day
Hobart, Tasmania

CHOCOLATE LIME SHOT TRIFLES

KATHRYN LINCE

This trifle differs from most in that it uses biscuits (cookies) for the cake base instead of, well, cake! Biscuits are particularly good to use in a shot glass trifle, such as this, because they will normally soak up surrounding flavours faster than cake, without going overly mushy.

This trifle will work well with any plain dark chocolate biscuit—nothing too sweet. Arnott's Choc Ripple Biscuits are ideal if you are pressed for time and want to make this trifle as simple as possible. However, if you want to get a bit fancy, you can also make your own chocolate biscuits, and use them instead. One recipe that works well in this trifle is Garret McCord's Chocolate Cookies with Cocoa Nibs and Lime (see: http://www.simplyrecipes.com/recipes/chocolate_cookies_with_cocoa_nibs_and_lime/).

Making your own biscuits has the added advantage giving you the option to make both normal size biscuits, to chop and use in the trifle, plus tiny, half-sized, biscuits to decorate the top. They make a nice alternative to either kiwi fruit, candied cacao beans—and tiny biscuits are so cute!!

Makes 5 individual trifles, or around 15 shotglasses

Preamble

Ingredients

One packet (approximately 250g) of shop bought plain chocolate biscuits or cookies, or an equivalent amount of homemade chocolate biscuits.

3 kiwi fruit

Juice of 1 lime

2 teaspoons caster sugar

300 mL (10 oz) thickened cream

Candied coca nibs for decoration (optional, see recipe below)

Method

Mix lime juice and sugar.

Slice all three kiwi fruit into 5mm slices, and chop all except three or four slices very finely. Marinate in the lime sugar mixture for an hour or more. For the remaining slices, quarter each slice, then half each quarter into a triangle and reserve for decoration.

Chop two or three biscuits into 5mm chunks to use as the biscuits base, chopping additional biscuits as needed during assembly.

To assemble, alternate layers of biscuits, kiwi fruit, and cream, using approximately 1 teaspoon of each per layer (vary as desired or required by the size of your shot glass).

Decorate each trifle with candied cocoa nibs, a small cookie, or kiwi fruit as desired.

Candied Cocoa Nibs

Adapted from
http://candy.about.com/od/chocolate/r/candiedcacaonib.htm

Ingredients

50 grams (2 oz) cocoa nibs

30 grams (1 oz) sugar

1/2 teaspoon butter, softened

Preparation

Line a baking tray with baking paper.

Place the butter in a dish within easy reach of the stove.

Put the nibs and the sugar in a small saucepan over a medium heat.

As the sugar begins to dissolve and stick together continually stir the mixture.

Cook until the sugar becomes a liquid. Remove from the heat and stir the butter in thoroughly.

Scrape the coated nibs onto the prepared baking sheet, separating them as much as possible. Allow them to cool at room temperature before breaking them apart by hand.

Store in an airtight container. Do not refrigerate.

DEATH BY TRIFLE CHERRY AND MARZIPAN TRIFLE

LOUISE WILLIAMS

Cherries and almonds both have cyanide in them, but you would explode from the sheer volume of this trifle before you consumed enough cyanide to kill you. To make this trifle extra deadly, substitute ground cherry or apricot pits for some of the ground almonds.

Make sure the sponge cake you use is dry (not buttery) and if possible slightly stale. I use a bought sponge but if you want to make your own any plain sponge recipe will work as long as you make it in advance.

Makes 6 individual trifles, or around 18 shotglasses

Ingredients

Cherry Jelly

2 cups apple juice

250g (9oz) whole cherries (fresh or frozen)

Sugar if required

2 leaves of titanium gelatine

Marzipan

80g (3oz) ground almonds

½ cup caster sugar

½ cup water

¼ teaspoon almond essence

Custard

1 cup cream

1 cup milk

½ cup sugar

1 vanilla pod or 1 tablespoon of vanilla essence

2 tablespoons cornflour

1 sponge cake

Prepare the layers beforehand. When assembling the trifle the custard, marzipan, and cherry jelly should be cool but not completely set.

Cherry Jelly

Put the gelatine leaves in cold water to soak.

Place the juice and cherries in a saucepan and bring to the boil. Lower the heat to a simmer and cook, covered, for around 20 minutes until the fruit is soft.

Press the fruit and juice though a fine sieve, then discard the seeds and skin.

Taste the cherries and add a small amount of sugar if necessary to make the cherry pulp slightly sweet.

Return the sieved cherry pulp and juice to the pan and warm until slightly higher than blood temperature.

Squeeze excess water from the gelatine leaves and stir into the cherry pulp; they should dissolve quickly.

Marzipan

Combine the almonds, sugar and water in a saucepan.

Stir on low heat until the sugar is dissolved, then bring to the boil and cook until the mixture until thickens to the consistency.

Take it off the heat and let it cool slightly, then stir in the almond essence.

Taste and add more almond essence if desired.

Custard

Mix the cornflour with a bit of the cold milk to form a smooth liquid.

Combine the milk, cornflour mixture and cream with the sugar in a saucepan.

Split the vanilla bean in half lengthways and scrape out the seeds; add the pod and seeds to the pan.

Stirring continuously, bring the mixture to a low simmer and cook until the mixture is thick enough to coat the back of a spoon.

Taste and add more sugar if desired.

Strain to remove the vanilla pod and any stray lumps that may have formed.

To assemble

When assembling the trifle, allow each layer to set slightly before adding the next layer.

Crumble sponge cake into the bottom of each glass—for individual trifles you need about ½ of a cup of cake each, for shot glasses about 1 tablespoon—and sprinkle with some of the cherry pulp (around ¼ cup for individual trifles, about ½ a tablespoon for shot glasses). The cake should be wet but not soaking; add more cake or cherry liquid as required.

Press the cake and jelly mixture down with the back of a spoon to even the surface, and put the glasses in the fridge to firm up a little.

Spoon about half the custard over the cake, then top the custard with the remainder of the cherry jelly, followed by the marzipan, then finally with the last of the custard on top.

Refrigerate until firm, at least a couple of hours but preferably overnight.

Twelve Planets

aurealis awards FINALIST

Nightsiders

Sue Isle

In a future world of extreme climate change, the western coast of Australia has been abandoned. A few thousand obstinate, independent souls cling to the southern towns and cities, living mostly by night to endure the fierce temperatures and creating a new culture in defiance of official expectations.

A teenage girl stolen from her family as a child, a troupe of street actors who affects the new with memories of the old, a boy born into the wrong body, and a teacher pushed into the role of guide, all tell the story of The Nightside.

'... [Isle's] writing is uniquely hers, direct and honest and crowned by a deft ear for dialogue.' —Marianne de Pierres

2012 Tiptree Long List Finalist

Twelve Planets

Locus Recommended Reading List for Best Collection in 2011

aurealis awards
FINALIST

Love and Romanpunk

Tansy Rayner Roberts

Thousands of years ago, Julia Agrippina wrote the true history of her family, the Caesars. The document was lost, or destroyed, almost immediately. *(It included more monsters than you might think.)*

Hundreds of years ago, Fanny and Mary ran away from London with a debauched poet and his sister. *(If it was the poet you are thinking of, the story would have ended far more happily, and with fewer people having their throats bitten out.)*

Sometime in the near future, a community will live in a replica Roman city built in the Australian bush. It's a sight to behold. *(Shame about the manticores.)*

Further in the future, the last man who guards the secret history of the world will discover that the past has a way of coming around to bite you. *(He didn't even know she had a thing for pointy teeth.)*

History is not what you think it is.

'Connie Willis meets Gail Carriger over much more than a cup of tea.' —*Helen Merrick*

Winner of the WSFA Small Press Short Story Award

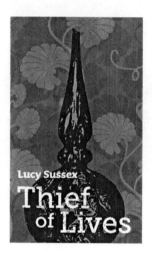
Thief of Lives

Lucy Sussex

Why are certain subjects so difficult to talk about? What is justice? Why do writers think that other people's lives are fair game? And what do we really know about the first chemist?

A story about history, women, science (and also the demonic); a crime story, based upon a true crime; a realist satire of the supposedly sex-savvy; and a story exploring lies, and the space between the real and the unreal.

Welcome to the worlds of Lucy Sussex, and to her many varied modes.

'Pay attention to this woman! Turn these pages! Here be monsters and mysteries and marvels.' —*Karen Joy Fowler*

Twelve Planets

aurealis
awards
FINALIST

Bad Power

Deborah Biancotti

Hate superheroes? Yeah. They probably hate you, too.

'There are two kinds of people with lawyers on tap, Mr Grey. The powerful and the corrupt.'

'Thank you.'

'For implying you're powerful?'

'For imagining those are two different groups.'

From Crawford Award nominee Deborah Biancotti comes this sinister short story suite, a pocketbook police procedural set in a world where the victories are relative and the defeats are absolute. Bad Power celebrates the worst kind of powers both supernatural and otherwise, in the interlinked tales of five people—and how far they'll go.

If you like Haven and Heroes, you'll love Bad Power.

'These appetisingly wicked stories give you the perfect taste of Biancotti's talents.' —*Ann VanderMeer*

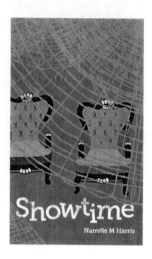

Showtime

Narrelle M. Harris

Family drama can be found anywhere: in kitchens, in cafes. Derelict hotels, showground rides. Even dungeons far below ruined Hungarian cahles.

(Okay, especially in Hungarian dungeons.)

Old family fights can go on forever, especially if you're undead. If an opportunity came to save someone else's family, the way you couldn't save your own, would you take it?

Your family might include ghosts, or zombies, or vampires. Maybe they just have allergies.

Nobody's perfect.

Family history can weigh on the present like a stone. But the thing about families is, you can't escape them. Not ever. And mostly, you don't want to. There's a horror story for you.

'Narrelle Harris represents the new generation of Australian speculative fiction writers, with a sharp wit, a clear vision, and a language entirely of her own.' —*Seanan McGuire*

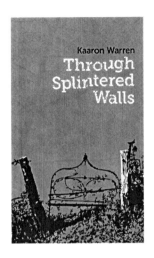

Locus Recommended Reading List for Best Collection in 2012

Through Splintered Walls

Kaaron Warren

From Bram Stoker Award nominated author Kaaron Warren, comes Book 6 in the Twelve Planets collection series.

Country road, city street, mountain, creek.

These are stories inspired by the beauty, the danger, the cruelty, emptiness, loneliness and perfection of the Australian landscape.

'Kaaron Warren is a powerful, take-no-prisoners author with an uncanny talent, a deliciously depraved flair for black comedy and a twisted nerve.' —*Alan Kelly*

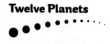
Twelve Planets

Locus Recommended Reading List for Best Collection in 2012

Cracklescape

Margo Lanagan

A presence haunts an old dresser in an inner-city share house. Shining sun-people lure children from their carefree beachside lives. Sheela-na-gigs colonise a middle-aged man's outer and inner worlds. And a girl with a heavy conscience seeks relief in exile on the Treeless Plain.

These stories from four-time World Fantasy Award winner Margo Lanagan are all set in Australia, a myth-soaked landscape both stubbornly inscrutable and crisscrossed by interlopers' dreamings. Explore four littoral and liminal worlds, a-crackle with fears and possibilities.

'Her new collection…may come as something of a revelation even to devoted Lanagan readers.' —*Gary K. Wolfe*

'Margo Lanagan's *Cracklescape* and Kaaron Warren's *Through Splintered Walls* collect four stories apiece, but have more heart and head than many longer books, and feature several of the very best stories of the year.' —*Jonathan Strahan*

Caution: Contains Small Parts

Kirstyn McDermott

An intimate, unsettling collection from award-winning author Kirstyn McDermott.

A creepy wooden dog that refuses to play dead.

A gifted crisis counsellor and the mysterious, melancholy girl she cannot seem to reach.

A once-successful fantasy author whose life has become a horror story – now with added unicorns.

An isolated woman whose obsession with sex dolls takes a harrowing, unexpected turn.

Four stories that will haunt you long after their final pages are turned.

'Kirstyn McDermott's prose is darkly magical, insidious and insistent. Once her words get under your skin, they are there to stay.' —*Angela Slatter*

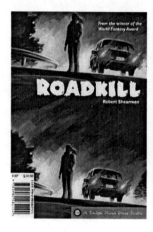

Roadkill *Robert Shearman*

Siren Beat *Tansy Rayner Roberts*

A Twelfth Planet Press Double

Two novelettes—*Roadkill* by Robert Shearman and *Siren Beat* by Tansy Rayner Roberts—published in tête-bêche format form the first Twelfth Planet Press Double.

Roadkill is a squeamishly uncomfortable story with the kind of illicit weekend away that you never want to have.

Siren Beat is a paranormal romance sans vampires or werewolves but featuring a very sexy sea pony. A minor group of man-eating sirens on the docks of Hobart would not normally pose much of a challenge for Nancy, but she is distracted by the reappearance of Nick Cadmus, the man she blames for her sister's death.

Siren Beat
Winner of the WSFA Small Press Short Story Award
Roadkill
Shortlisted for British Fantasy Award for Best Novella

Horn *Peter M. Ball*

There's a dead girl in a dumpster and a unicorn on the loose. No-one knows how bad that combination can get better than Miriam Aster. What starts as a consulting job for city homicide quickly becomes a tangled knot of unexpected questions, and working out the link between the dead girl and the unicorn will draw Aster back into the world of the exiled fey she thought she'd left behind ten years ago.

Dead girls and unicorns? How warped can this get?

Locus Recommended Reading List

Shortlisted for Best Fantasy Novel and Best Horror Novel, Aurealis Awards

Bleed *Peter M. Ball*

For ten years ex-cop Miriam Aster has been living with her one big mistake—agreeing to kill three men for the exiled Queen of Faerie. But when an old case comes back to haunt her it brings a spectre of the past with it, forcing Aster to ally herself with a stuntwoman and a magic cat in order to rescue a kidnapped TV star from the land of Faerie and stop the half-breed sorcerer who needs Aster's blood.

Shortlisted for the Australian Shadow Award for Best Long Work

The Company Articles Of Edward Teach
Thoraiya Dyer

Angælien Apocalypse
Matthew Chrulew

A Twelfth Planet Press Double

The Company Articles Of Edward Teach

Learning to live inside your own skin is hard enough, but what if you were thrown back in time, to another body; a different world…?

Angaelien Apocalypse

Reports had come in as the revolution erupted: myriad rotating discs approached Earth at speed. Panic and joy spread around the planet in viral waves. Few needed any help to identify these flying objects. They were the angælic vehicles.

And at the helm of the lead saucer was the Man himself. Jesus Christ.

The Angaelien Apocalypse
Shortlisted for Best SF Short Story, Aurealis Award 2011

The Company Articles of Edward Teach
Winner, Best Novella/Novelette Ditmar 2011

Above *Stephanie Campisi*

Below *Ben Peek*

A Twelfth Planet Press Double

A city has fallen from the sky.

In the wreckage, two men—Devian Lell, a window cleaner in the floating cities of Loft, and Eli Kurran, a security guard in one of the polluted, ground-based cities of Dirt—will find their lives changed.

Devian, who has done what few in the floating landscape have by stepping outside the sanctuary of his home, will be drawn into the politics of Loft, as he is recruited to be the assistant for Dirt's political representative. On the ground, Kurran, still mourning the death of his wife, tries to remove himself from the violent politics of Dirt even as he is blackmailed into providing security for the diplomatic representative of Loft, a woman three times his age, and the oldest living person he has ever met.

A tale of two cities, designed to be self-contained and complete as individual narratives, the two parts can be read in either order, yet also form a single narrative that has been intricately woven and designed to create a single, novel length story. It is a work that suggests not a single way of reading, but rather two, with conflicting morals that will continue to test the reader's certainty in who, in the cities of Loft and Dirt, is in the right.

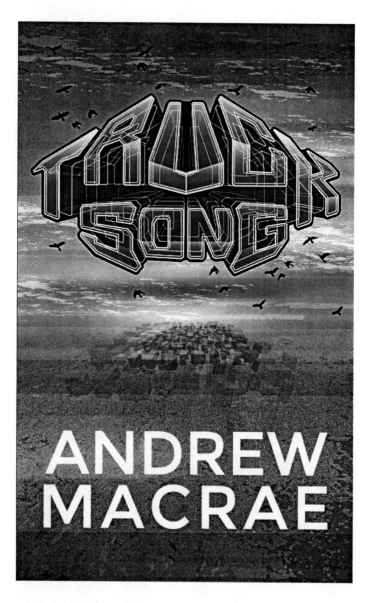

TRUCK SONG

ANDREW MACRAE

Out in November 2013

TRUCK SONG

In a post-apocalyptic Australian landscape dominated by free-wheeling cyborgs, a young man goes in search of his lost lover who has been kidnapped by a rogue AI truck – the Brumby King.

Along the way, he teams with Sinnerman, an independent truck with its own reasons for hating the Brumby King.

Before his final confrontation with the brumbies, he must learn more about the broken-down world and his own place in it, and face his worst fears.

The strange and playful voice of the first-person narrator keeps the story kicking along as he comes to his final realisation that the only meaning to be found in a world in slow decay is that which you make for yourself.

This genre-bending work of literary biopunk mixes the mad fun of Mad Max II with the idiosyncratic testimony of works like Peter Carey's True History of the Kelly Gang or Irvine Welsh's Trainspotting.

About Andrew Macrae:

Andrew Macrae lives behind a secret door on Brunswick Street in Fitzroy, Melbourne. He is a typewriter fetishist, a collector of plastic robots and a finder of lost dogs. He works full-time in his own free-lance writing and editing business called Magic Typewriter. He plays in an instrumental rock band called The Television Sky, wherein he dowses for harmonic distortion and melodic flux with swamp ash and rosewood.

His short fiction has appeared in *Aurealis*, *Orb*, *Agog! Ripping Reads* and *Fantastical Journeys to Brisbane*. He attended the inaugural Clarion South writers workshop in 2004. *Trucksong* is his first novel, and sprang from a childhood spent listening to the mournful sounds of semi-trailers as they crawled up and down the Great Dividing Range.

Find out what he's up to on twitter: www.twitter.com/acidic

See his latest obsessions: acidic.tumblr.com

www.twelfthplanetpress.com

Glitter Rose

Marianne de Pierres

The *Glitter Rose* Collection features five short stories by Marianne de Pierres—four previously published and one new story. Each copy of this limited edition print run is signed and presented in a beautiful hardbound cover, with internal black and white illustrations.

The *Glitter Rose* stories are set against the background of Carmine Island (an island reminiscent of Stradbroke Island, Queensland) where a decade ago spores from deep in the ocean blew in, by a freak of nature, and settled on the island. These spores bring fierce allergies to the inhabitants of the island. And maybe other, more sinister effects. As we follow Tinashi's journey of moving to and settling into island life, we get a clearer picture of just what is happening on Carmine Island.